Something about Lauren bothered Zach, set him on edge.

She was undeniably attractive. But the polished look about her screamed high maintenance. Pretty to look at, cold to hold.

Still, there'd been no mistaking the heat that jolted through him when he'd met her clear blue eyes or breathed in her fresh scent. Her skin had felt like soft, warm satin, and before he'd pulled back from their handshake, he could have sworn she was trembling. That she'd flinched.

He was accustomed to the reaction. Which was why it had been longer than he cared to remember since he'd held a woman. Why he devoted hours to rebuilding the old fighter plane that was as battered and scarred as he was.

He'd finally found a degree of contentment living in this wildly beautiful, isolate place.

And now Lauren Edwards was threatening that fragile peace....

Dear Reader,

International bestselling author Diana Palmer needs no introduction. Widely known for her sensual and emotional storytelling, and with more than forty million copies of her books in print, she is one of the genre's most treasured authors. And this month, Special Edition is proud to bring you the exciting conclusion to her SOLDIERS OF FORTUNE series. *The Last Mercenary* is the thrilling tale of a mercenary hero risking it all for love. Between the covers is the passion and adventure you've come to expect from Diana Palmer!

Speaking of passion and adventure, don't miss *To Catch a Thief* by Sherryl Woods in which trouble—in the form of attorney Rafe O'Donnell—follows Gina Petrillo home for her high school reunion and sparks fly.... Things are hotter than the Hatfields and McCoys in Laurie Paige's *When I Dream of You*—when heat turns to passion between two families that have been feuding for three generations!

Is a heroine's love strong enough to heal a hero scarred inside and out? Find out in *Another Man's Children* by Christine Flynn. And when an interior designer pretends to be a millionaire's lover, will *Her Secret Affair* lead to a public proposal? Don't miss *An Abundance of Babies* by Marie Ferrarella—in which double the babies and double the love could be just what an estranged couple needs to bring them back together.

This is the last month to enter our Silhouette Makes You a Star contest, so be sure to look inside for details. And as always, enjoy these fantastic stories celebrating life, love and family.

Best,
Karen Taylor Richman
Senior Editor

Please address questions and book requests to:
Silhouette Reader Service
U.S.: 3010 Walden Ave., P.O. Box 1325, Buffalo, NY 14269
Canadian: P.O. Box 609, Fort Erie, Ont. L2A 5X3

Another Man's Children

CHRISTINE FLYNN

Silhouette

SPECIAL EDITION™

Published by Silhouette Books

America's Publisher of Contemporary Romance

SILHOUETTE BOOKS

ISBN 0-373-24420-7

ANOTHER MAN'S CHILDREN

Books by Christine Flynn

*The Whitaker Brides

CHRISTINE FLYNN

admits to being interested in just about everything, which is why she considers herself fortunate to have turned her interest in writing into a career. She feels that a writer gets to explore it all and, to her, exploring relationships—especially the intense, bittersweet or even lighthearted relationships between men and women—is fascinating.

SILHOUETTE MAKES YOU A STAR!
Feel like a star with Silhouette.
Look for the exciting details of our new contest inside all of these fabulous Silhouette novels:

Chapter One

Lauren Edwards stood in the living room of her brother's rambling log cabin, feeling completely out of place in her panty hose and business suit, and scanned the list her mother had left her.

She didn't know if she should simply be concerned, or go straight for panic.

For the next week, she would be responsible for her niece and nephew while Sam, her brother, was at work. She adored Jenny and Jason. And she wanted very much to help her brother. She just hadn't been around the toddlers that much. She hadn't been around many children at all, for that matter, which was why she'd asked her mom to leave a checklist.

Dubiously eyeing item number two, "Keep out of reach anything that can be stuffed into a facial orifice," she had to admit she hadn't considered that their daily routine and the list of dos and don'ts would take up three full sheets of a legal-size pad.

Drawing a breath that brought the scent of burning pine from the stone fireplace behind her, she reached for the handle of her travel bag so she could change into something more comfortable. She was sure it was only because she was still in the process of shifting mental gears that the task ahead of her suddenly seemed so daunting. Only hours ago, she'd been in a meeting in Seattle trying to maintain polite professionalism when what she'd really wanted to do was grin like an idiot because she'd finally made the shortlist for a store of her own.

It was hardly a sure thing, and managing a Brenman's department store wasn't going to save a rain forest or cure the common cold, but she'd worked desperately for this promotion. For the past two years, she'd sacrificed evenings, weekends and her social life to prove that she could handle the responsibility—which was why now had not been a good time to tell Andrew Nye, her boss, that she needed to take time off. Andy, who happened to be in line for promotion to the new store Brenman's was opening himself, lived, ate and breathed retailing. Anyone under him who expected to get anywhere in the company had to regard it as their sole reason for existence, too.

That was undoubtedly the other reason she was feeling less than certain at the moment. Abandoning ship an hour after being told she was in the running hardly made her look like a team player to those monitoring her performance. She could only hope that Andy would be up front with the rest of upper management and make it clear that she'd made arrangements last week to be gone, should anyone ask for her. A person couldn't schedule family emergencies the way she could a vacation. And her family was in the middle of a crisis that had struck like the proverbial bolt from the blue.

Sam, her older, and only, sibling, had lost his wife in a car accident two weeks ago. It still seemed impossible to comprehend that Tina was gone. But there was no getting past the numbing fact that she was, and that she'd left behind a son, a daughter and a grieving husband. Until yesterday, Lauren and Sam's mom had been taking care of the children, but Beth Edwards had a job of her own she'd had to return to. Since there was no one on Tina's side who could help, it was now Lauren's turn.

That was why she'd spent the last seventy-two hours doing a week's worth of work before promising Andy and her floor managers that she would be available by telephone day or night and driving in the miserable January drizzle to the dock in Anacortes. From there, she and her car had taken the ferry to Harbor Island, Washington, two hours and a world away from nearly everything she knew as civilization, then driven the five miles from the charming seaport village of Harbor Cove to her brother's secluded home on one of the island's isolated inlets.

Her brother had once told her he couldn't imagine ever living anywhere else, which proved just how different they were. They were both city-born and bred. But Sam had apparently inherited the genes of their pioneer ancestors, while her genetic makeup allowed complete adaptation to freeways and cell phones. Different or not, she loved Sam. He'd been her protector when they were growing up, her friend when they'd grown older, and the source of endless encouragement when her own world had fallen apart two years ago. Now, Sam was hurting in ways she could only imagine, and she would do whatever she could to make things easier for him.

Resolved to do her best for his sake, she dropped the list onto the coffee table. Unbuttoning her jacket, she headed for the hall, dragging her wheeled bag behind her. Three steps later, she turned around and picked the pad up again. She was a firm believer in lists and schedules and those sheets were the Holy Grail as far as she was concerned. She needed to keep them intact. That meant keeping them beyond the reach of little hands.

She'd set her instructions on the fireplace mantel beneath the huge wreath of colorful dried pods and flowers and had grabbed her travel bag once more when a heavy knock sounded on the front door.

With a faint frown for the timing, her hand fell from where she'd reached to pull the clip from the tight twist at the back of her head. The only thing her mother had asked of her was that she coax her brother into moving back to Seattle. The only thing her brother had specifically asked her to do was find him a permanent housekeeper and nanny. She thought it might help him if he were closer to family, too, but her coaxing could come later. Since she knew Sam would need more than the week she would be there to tie up his affairs on Harbor, she had placed an ad in the local paper and scheduled interviews days ago.

The first of the two ladies who'd responded wasn't scheduled to arrive for another ten minutes. But Shenandoah Adams was obviously early.

Rebuttoning the jacket of her tailored black suit and smoothing the few strands of wheat-colored hair that had escaped their confines, Lauren hurried to the door before another knock could wake the baby.

The metal latch clinked as she pushed it in, cold air

rushing inside as she pulled open the heavy door. The damp chill raised goose bumps on her skin, sent them racing down her back—and seemed to freeze her welcoming smile in place.

The person blocking her view of majestic fir trees and the sheltered inlet was definitely not the middle-aged, part-time yoga instructor and nanny she was expecting. As her glance moved up a row of buttons on a blue, plaid, flannel shirt, she found herself faced with six feet of obscenely attractive, dark-haired male in denim and a down vest.

His rich sable hair swept back from lean, chiseled features and covered the back of his collar. His cheekbones were high, his mouth firm and he looked more guarded than uncertain when the dark slashes of his eyebrows merged over eyes the same silver gray as the stormy sky.

"You're Sam's sister?"

His voice was low, deep, disturbing. The sound of it rumbled through her like the ominous approach of distant thunder as he swept an assessing glance from the sleek style of her hair to the tailored fit of the suit she never would have been able to afford if she'd had to pay retail.

She hadn't a clue who this man was. But there wasn't a doubt in her mind that he had just mentally stripped her right down to her beige lace bra.

"I am," she returned, unconsciously crossing her arms. Her brother was big and dark-haired and definitely the outdoor type. She was short, fair and definitely...not. Given those comparisons, she could understand why this man, big and looking like an outdoor type himself, might question the relationship.

Yet it wasn't confusion or surprise she sensed in him. It seemed more like displeasure.

"And you're...?" she cautiously prompted.

"Zach McKendrick."

The sound of his name was as hard as he looked in the moments before his eyes narrowed on her protective stance. He seemed to realize he'd put her on the defensive. Suddenly looking as if that hadn't been his intention, he forced the edge from his tone. "Sam said you were trading places with your mom for a while."

"Zach...."

"Sam's business partner."

She knew that. The name anyway.

"Look," he said, his brow tightening again as he glanced at his watch. "I'm in kind of a hurry. Is he here?"

"He went into town about ten minutes ago. To pick up Jason from preschool," she explained, trying to be helpful. Impatience fairly leaked from his pores, but he was her brother's partner, a man she knew to be his friend. "Do you want me to have him call you when he gets back?"

"I can't wait for that. I need a manifest he took." A muscle in his jaw twitched as his glance slid over her shoulder. "It's probably in his den."

There was no denying the tension filling his lean, powerful body as he waited for her to invite him in. It radiated from him in waves, restive, chafing, yet ruthlessly restrained.

Feeling his tension knot her stomach, totally disconcerted by the effect, she stepped back, as much to escape the unnerving sensation as to grant him entrance.

"Thanks," he muttered and walked right past her.

Her brother's living room was a large open space with overstuffed leather furniture, rustic pine end tables, braided rugs and a wall of male-fantasy-quality electronics that her sister-in-law had softened by blending the elements with knickknacks and books on the floor-to-ceiling shelves. Zach's powerful strides had already carried him past the big-screen TV when she closed the heavy door. By the time she turned around to ask him what a manifest looked like so she could get it for him, he was heading into the hall.

Her first thought was to ask what he thought he was doing. Her second was that this was her brother's house and, since Zach was his partner, she was hardly in a position to stop the man from going wherever he wanted to go. Especially since he seemed to know exactly where he was headed.

"Don't wake the baby!" she hurriedly called to the back of his navy-blue vest.

Without breaking stride, he lifted one hand in acknowledgment and disappeared through the first doorway on his left.

Feeling steamrolled, Lauren stared into the empty space.

If anyone were to ask her what she thought of Zach McKendrick, she would be hard-pressed to come up with anything positive, much less anything complimentary. Considering that Sam and Tina had both spoken of him as if he were the salt of the earth, she couldn't help but wonder what they saw that she was so obviously missing.

Blowing an uneasy breath, she turned from the empty hall. She didn't really know much about the people in her brother's life. Their worlds were both so busy and so different. But she remembered Sam and Tina mentioning Zach during holidays at their parents' home, which were the only times the family had all been together in the last several years. Holidays at Mom and Dad's were mandatory and nothing short of the Second Coming was considered excuse enough to miss them.

The exception was New Year. They didn't usually spend that day together. Yet, they had the last one. And, then, there had been no celebration. They had all spent the dawn of the new year in Tacoma, because that was where Sam, Tina and the kids had been visiting her father when Tina had been killed by a speeding driver the day before New Year's Eve. Because Tacoma had been her hometown, and because her mother was buried there, that was where Sam had insisted the services be held.

Lauren hadn't seen Zach there, though. She remembered that her brother had talked to him several times on the phone, but his friend hadn't attended the funeral. She would have remembered seeing him. No woman with a pulse would forget eyes like that.

The thoughts caught her smoothing the folded afghan draped over the arm of the butterscotch leather sofa. Ceasing her restless motions, she crossed her arms to keep from fidgeting. She didn't want to wonder what had kept Zach away, especially when he could have flown himself in and out of town in a matter of hours. She didn't want to think about how the bottom had been ripped out of Sam's world. She especially didn't want to consider how empty the house must feel to her brother without his wife's vivacious laugh and bright, cheerleader smile. She just wanted to help.

At the moment, however, all she could do was wait for the man she could hear rummaging around her brother's desk.

He was an ex-military test pilot. She had no idea why she remembered that just then, but the detail had impressed the heck out of their father when Sam had told him several years ago that he and Zach were going into business together. According to Sam, who rarely spoke in superlatives, Zach had retired from the military and was now the hands-down best bush pilot in the entire Northwest.

The man can set a float plane down in a puddle, her brother had claimed, *and take off in winds strong enough to knot a plane's wings.*

Since Sam was a bush pilot himself, a job that had prematurely grayed their mother and probably his wife, that was undoubtedly high praise.

She had also heard that he was divorced. That, she'd learned from Tina because her sister-in-law had once mentioned how often Zach showed up for meals at their house. It had been Tina, too, who had mentioned that the man was like a brother to Sam, which, Lauren supposed, accounted for his familiarity with the house and his lack of hesitation entering it.

"It's not in there."

Lauren whirled around from where she stood by the sofa. It didn't seem possible that a man his size could move so quietly, but she hadn't heard a single board squeak when he'd walked back up the hall.

With his hands jammed on his lean hips, his wide brow furrowed, he scanned the toy-cluttered surfaces in the room. "Have you seen it?" he asked, not bothering to look at her before turning away to check the credenza behind him. "What I'm looking for is in a file. Manila. Eight-by-ten. There's a green label on it that says To Be Shipped."

"I haven't seen anything like that. Why is this so important?" she asked, leaning down to check through the stack of newspapers, magazines and children's books on the coffee table. She was more than willing to help. The sooner he found what he was looking for, the sooner he would leave.

"Because we have a pilot who can't take off without

it. We're losing money every hour that plane sits on the ground.''

His hurried search of the credenza proved fruitless. Though he didn't swear, he looked as if he were about to when he turned to the kitchen to check the table and counters in there.

''I can't figure out why he even took it with him,'' he muttered, stepping through the doorway. ''The man isn't paying attention to anything he's doing anymore.''

Lauren's spine snapped straight. He was talking to himself. Not her. But she couldn't believe what she'd just heard. ''I would imagine that if Sam is preoccupied it's because he just lost his wife.''

The sound of movement in the kitchen came to an abrupt halt. In the sudden quiet, she heard nothing but the rattle of a loose vent as the furnace kicked on and the methodical tick of the antique grandfather clock guarding the wall beside the front door. Her heart bumped to that heavy rhythm as Zach's imposing frame filled the kitchen doorway.

He stood like a dark sentinel, unmoving, ready to challenge. ''There is no one more aware of that than I am,'' he informed her tightly. ''And his preoccupation is only getting worse, which isn't helping any of us right now.''

''Isn't it us who should be helping him?''

The quicksilver gray of his eyes turned chill. ''I'm doing what I can,'' he informed her, his tone heavy with restraint. ''I've *covered* for him as much as I can. But I'm not in a position to cut him any more slack.'' His voice dropped like a rock in a well. ''Until he gets himself together, I'm going to have to ground him.''

Lauren stared in disbelief when he left her standing there to resume his search of the kitchen. She knew that the only things holding Sam together right now were his children and his job. Sam loved to fly. He lived for it. It was all he'd wanted to do since he was five years old. She didn't understand his obsession at all, but she didn't have to understand it to know how much of an escape it could offer. No one knew better than she did how pain could be anesthetized by the demands of work. And she was unable to imagine how her brother would cope if his arrogant, insensitive, stone-for-a-heart partner denied him the lifeline his work provided.

The heavy ache in her chest was for her brother as she headed through the kitchen doorway. The pressure behind it was caused purely by the man who'd just managed to push every protective button she possessed.

"I was under the impression you were his friend."

He stood with his back to her at the white-tiled counter bisecting the high-beamed room. Beyond the counter, the small family room was occupied by an old pot-bellied stove, a round oak dining table, a high chair and a playpen. The side with the modern electric range was bright with hanging copper pots, yellow curtains and Jason's artwork papering the fridge.

All she really noticed when Zach turned was that he had the nerve to look insulted.

"I am his friend."

"It doesn't sound like it."

His eyebrow hitched. "Do you want to explain that?"

"If you were a friend," she told him, more than ready to comply, "you'd be more concerned with how difficult things are for Sam right now than with how his preoccupation is affecting business. You'd be trying to make things easier. Not take away all he has left." She understood corporate concerns. She also understood that things happened to people and that temporary adjustments had to be made for their circumstances. Even Andy, who often acted as if compassion were spelled with four letters, grasped that concept. Mostly, she understood that a friend did what he could to help. Not hurt. "You might not care about anything but planes and profits, but Tina was everything to my brother."

Something dangerous washed over Zach's carved features as he took a step closer to where she'd stopped near the middle of the polished pine floor. He took two more, forcing her to either tip her head back to see his face or retreat.

Every instinct in her body screamed for her to back up. Years of having to claw to stay in place allowed her to hold her ground.

"How do you know what I care about?" His voice was deceptively calm, dangerously so. "How could you possibly have any idea how I feel about anything? We've never even talked to each other before."

The line of his jaw was as sharp as a blade, the cut of his mouth blatantly sensual. She was aware of the heat and tension radiating from his body, the fresh air in his clothes, and the scent of something spicy and decidedly male clinging to his skin. Mostly, she was conscious of the bold male confidence that had allowed him to step uninvited into her space.

Everything about him seemed to taunt, unnerve or disturb her, but she was too concerned about his heartless attitude toward her brother to worry about how easily he overrode the air of calm control she managed to present to the rest of the world.

Her voice low in deference to the child sleeping three doors down the hall, she purposefully ignored the triphammer beat of her pulse. "I don't need to have talked to you before to know what…or who…you care about. I believe you just made it obvious."

"The only thing obvious is that one of us has no idea what's going on here."

"And that would be you."

A muscle in his jaw twitched.

In response, Lauren felt her stomach knot. She couldn't believe she was challenging this stranger. He was ex-military, a jet jockey—a *test* pilot, she reminded herself, thinking his old occupation spoke volumes about the sort of man he was. He had actually strapped himself into what amounted to an untried, controlled explosion and blasted himself through the atmosphere at speeds that broke barriers she couldn't begin to fathom. A man like that would have to be utterly confident, disciplined, fearless.

Totally insane, too, in her admittedly unadventurous estimation.

He would also have to believe that he would always come out on top.

That thought threatened to have her add a couple of inches to the charged space separating them. Confrontation wasn't her style at all. If anything, she was known among the people who worked under her for her coolness under fire, her fairness, her tact. But she didn't get a chance to wonder at how swiftly this man had stripped her sense of diplomacy. She didn't have the opportunity to see if he would attempt to defend himself, either—not that she could imagine any possible, plausible reason for him being such a jerk. The soft knock on the front door had her spinning on her heel to answer it.

Zach was right behind her, his footfall unhurried, deliberate. The hair on her neck prickled with the feel of his eyes boring into the back of her head.

She had no idea how badly she was shaking until she

reached for the hammered iron latch—and felt Zach's hand close over her fingers.

The hard wall of his chest brushed her shoulder. With his broad palm covering the back of her hand, his heat searing a path up her arm, there wasn't a doubt in her mind that he could feel her trembling.

"I have my reasons for grounding your brother," he growled, his breath fluttering the fine hair at the top of her head. "And you don't know me. You don't know me at all."

Moving her hand, he reached for the latch himself.

"I'll wait for your brother outside."

She had taken a step back the moment he'd let her go. As she took another, desperate for the distance, her glance darted up and caught on the silvery and striated scar that covered the entire side of his neck.

The disfiguring injury hadn't been noticeable to her at all when he'd faced her. From the side, it was impossible to miss. The pale, slick-looking skin ran from under his jaw to below the buttoned collar of his shirt and behind the length of his thick dark hair.

The thought that only chemicals or fire could cause scarring so severe had her wincing when he pulled open the door. Catching her expression, his own went as cool as the air that rushed inside before he sidestepped the startled woman backing up so he could pass.

The muffled "Hi" he offered the lady sounded impossibly civil.

"Hi, yourself," the waiflike woman replied to his retreating back. Pushing off the hood of her beautifully woven turquoise cape, she watched him take the stairs from the log-railed porch in two strides and jog through the rain to the black truck parked by her pea-green Volkswagen bus.

The nerves in Lauren's stomach were quivering as she forced her attention from the man who still had her caller staring after him.

"Ms. Adams?"

The woman turned with an inquisitive smile. Her long straight hair was parted in the middle, six inches of gray at the roots and dishwater-blond at the ends. A peace symbol, which Lauren assumed to be an antique, hung around her neck.

"It's Shenandoah. Like the river," she explained, her smile fading to skepticism as she eyed Lauren's suit and heels.

The unexpected had just collided with the unforeseen. Taking a stabilizing breath, Lauren smiled politely and asked her to come in.

From behind the wheel of his truck, Zach watched Sam's sister give him a cautious glance before she ushered the aging flower child inside. She looked as wary of him as Tina had of the bear he and Sam had found foraging in her garden last summer. Sam's wife had never much cared for the local wildlife.

It was as obvious as the rain beating on his windshield that Sam's sister felt pretty much the same about him.

They were even. He wasn't crazy about her, either.

Blowing a breath, he dragged his hand over his face and sank back in the seat. He couldn't believe how frustrated he felt. Or how he'd just acted with Sam's little sister. The frustration he could deal with. Lauren Edwards was another matter entirely. With a schedule that was falling further behind by the hour and more worried than he was used to being about the partner he couldn't count on for much of anything right now, he had no patience at all for her judgmental attitude.

Or her presence.

He knew Sam's family wanted him to move back to Seattle. His mother had mentioned it a half a dozen times while she'd been there. Sam had said his mom had even asked if he wanted her to pack some of his things and take them back with her. His sister, Sam had also told him, had offered to find him a place in the city if he didn't feel like looking himself.

Zach knew Sam understood his family's concerns about him. But Sam had also confided that he had no idea what he wanted to do, and that the last thing he did want right now was to have to make a major decision. Any decision for that matter. Just getting out of bed in the morning was hard enough.

Zach was infinitely familiar with the numb, almost paralyzed state the mind slipped into to protect itself from feeling too much. He also knew that his friend would have to deal with his family and the changes that were taking place in his life whether he liked the idea or not.

Sam's sister's insistence to the contrary, he truly was trying to help her brother. In the meantime, he was having to deal with the ripple effects of Tina's death himself. That loss affected nearly everything he'd managed to build over the past five years.

With the grim determination that had always served him well, he reminded himself that change was inevitable—and that the Fates hadn't broken him yet.

It did seem, though, that they wanted to give it another shot. It was entirely possible that his friend could move for the sake of his children. If he did, Zach would lose his business partner.

More disturbing than that, he would lose the closest thing he had here to family.

The thoughts did nothing to ease the tension crawling

through him. He needed to move, to pace, but he had no desire to get out of the truck and get drenched. Instead, he worked at a knot in his shoulder and checked the rearview mirror for signs of Sam.

Seeing nothing but the silver drizzle that turned the forest of spruce, hemlock and pine a hazy shade of blue, he glanced toward the rambling log cabin with its wrap-around porch and winter-bare window boxes.

There was something more bothering him. Something about Sam's little sister that added a different sort of frustration to those he was already dealing with.

She had been judgmental. And she clearly hadn't a clue why her brother's behavior demanded that he be relieved of certain responsibilities. But those weren't the only things about her that set him on edge.

She was undeniably attractive. Beautiful, he conceded, recalling the cameo-like delicacy of her face. There was also a polished look about her that screamed high-maintenance. Pretty to look at. Cold to hold. Still, there'd been no mistaking the heat that had jolted through him when he'd met her clear blue eyes, or when he breathed in the fresh, springlike scent clinging to her sun-shot hair. Her skin had felt like satin to him, soft, warm, and before he'd pulled back his hand, he could have sworn she was trembling.

He'd also caught the way she'd flinched when she'd noticed his neck.

He was accustomed to the reaction by now, though some people were less obvious about it than others. What was visible, though, was nothing compared to what wasn't—which was one of the reasons it had been longer than he cared to remember since he'd held a woman, and why he devoted more hours than he could count to running along the windswept beach below his house, and to rebuilding an old fighter plane that was as battered and scarred as he was.

He dealt with his frustrations as best he could and didn't look for anything more than he already had. He didn't want anything in his life that would change the status quo. He'd finally found a degree of contentment living and working in this wildly beautiful place, and that fragile peace was already feeling threatened enough.

The deep-throated hum of a Chevy Suburban had him jerking around in his seat.

Jamming down all of his frustrations for the sake of his friend, he plastered on as affable a smile as he could manage and climbed out into the rain.

Chapter Two

Zach knew that Sam didn't usually pick up Jason from preschool. At three o'clock in the afternoon, he was usually either on a flight or tackling his end of running the business. Since business was slower in the winter when they didn't have the summer tourists and adventurers to transport, Sam taking off early to get his son hadn't been a problem. Not for Zach. But as he watched his partner climb from his red Suburban and acknowledge him with the lethargic lift of his hand, he couldn't help thinking that everything his friend did now must in some way remind him of the person who was no longer around.

As much as he hated to give Sam's sister credit for anything just then, he had to admit that she was right. Tina had been everything to Sam. She had driven him nuts with her forgetfulness at times and she'd never been crazy about living in "a nature preserve," as she'd called

Harbor, but they had cared enough about each other to overlook whatever differences they'd had.

The fact that Tina had been willing to put up with Zach dragging her husband off for fishing trips and hanging around for her meat loaf and to play with the kids had made Zach think she was pretty special himself. He'd had the feeling he was special to her, too, in a decidedly brother-sister sort of way. He wasn't the sort of man who expressed his feelings well with words. Never had been. Never would be. But he was pretty sure she'd known he would have done anything in the world for her and the brawny pilot who'd just opened the back passenger door of his vehicle and ducked his head inside. Jason was back there, strapped in his car seat and no doubt as impatient as he always was to get out now that the vehicle had stopped.

By the time Zach reached the open door himself, the man in the heavy blue parka was backing up with the three-year-old perched high in his arms to keep the kid's feet out of the mud. A miniature camouflage backpack dangled by a strap from one big fist. In the other, he had a handful of crayon drawings.

Giving his son a little bounce to adjust his weight, Sam glanced toward Zach. "What are you doing here? I thought you were going to work on your plane."

"I'm looking for the manifest file." Reaching forward, Zach shoved the door closed for him, the sound echoing like a gunshot in the cold winter air. The sharp report was immediately followed by the crunch of gravel beneath their feet as they headed for the shelter of the porch. "I need the one for the flight to Orcas this afternoon. The shipment of pottery T. J. Walker is shipping to the gallery," he prompted, eyeing the little boy who'd twisted sideways to see him. ''Chuck's ready to take off, but you've got it.''

From beneath the lopsided hood of his red parka, the impish Jason gave Zach a smile. The blond little boy with the deep dimple in his cheek held up his hand, palm out.

Zach smiled back. The kid had the biggest blue eyes he'd ever seen. Next to the boy's little sister, anyway. And maybe their aunt.

''Hey, buddy,'' he murmured, mentally frowning at his last thought as he greeted the child with their usual high-five.

''Hey, buddy,'' Jason echoed, grinning.

The crunch of gravel gave way to the heavy thud of their boots on steps and porch planks. Beneath the ledge of his dark eyebrows, Sam's normally keen eyes narrowed in confusion as he halted by the door and wiped his feet. ''Why would I have it?''

A two-day growth of beard shadowed Sam's rough-hewn features. His short dark hair looked as if it had been combed by the wind and there was a faintly pink quality to the whites of his eyes that could have passed for the effect of a bad cold or a three-day binge—except Zach knew his friend only indulged in an occasional beer, and that the dull, listless look had been there for days.

Zach figured it was probably from lack of rest.

Or from tears.

The thought made him shift uncomfortably as he jerked his glance to Jason. ''I don't know why you'd have it,'' he replied, giving the kid a playful punch in the shoulder. Now wasn't the time to tell Sam he probably had the document because his thoughts had been a million miles away when he'd picked it up. That particular conversation couldn't be rushed. ''I saw you put it in the day's flight file when we were sorting freight this morning. Chuck saw you take a file from the counter just before you left an hour ago," he expanded, speaking of the other pilot in their hire. "Since that's the only one missing, logic says that's the one you left with."

The confusion remained. "All I took were the invoices I'd told you I'd total."

"They're still there."

Sam opened his mouth as if to say that wasn't possible. Apparently realizing it was, he turned to the door. With Jason wriggling to get down, he let the boy slide to his feet and pushed it open.

Preoccupied as he was, he nearly knocked over the lady Zach had nearly flattened on his way out a while ago.

Lauren had just reached to open the door when it opened on its own. Taking a quick step back so she wouldn't get run over, she sidestepped her brother as he walked in.

"Sorry," he muttered, oblivious to the fact that there was a woman in a turquoise serape on the other side of the tall panel of pine. Concentration creased his rugged, ragged features as he strode past, saying nothing else as he headed for the kitchen.

Jason walked right past her, too, his chin tucked down as he tugged on the zipper of his jacket.

"Is everything all right?" she called after her sibling.

"He's getting the manifest."

At the sound of the deep voice in the doorway, Lauren's heart gave an unhealthy jerk. She'd suspected Zach would be right behind Sam. The thought alone had given her pause. But there was something about the husky sound of his voice and the unblinking way he watched her as he stepped over the threshold that tensed every nerve in her body.

Since she had no intention of letting him know that, she deliberately shifted her focus to the woman emerging from behind the door.

The apology in her expression moved into her voice. "Are you all right?"

The woman, who'd asked to be called Doe, gave her a forgiving smile. "No harm," she replied softly, tugging the strap of her fringed bag over her shoulder. Hair the texture of fine wire shifted as she glanced from the dark and disturbing man blocking her exit to the child who'd stopped in the middle of the spacious room. Jason was still working at his zipper. "It's busy around here, isn't it?"

"Here it is," Sam called, retrieving the file from the top of the refrigerator. "Hi," he said to their visitor, looking slightly puzzled by her presence when he spotted her from the kitchen door.

Doe appeared as sympathetic as she did uncertain as she offered him a smile he barely noticed. "I guess I'll be on my way," she said to Lauren. "Remember to call Maddy O'Toole at the Road's End Café. If you get word out there that you're looking for a sitter, you shouldn't have any trouble at all finding someone. Especially if it's only for a couple months or so."

"Thanks," Lauren murmured, meaning it. "And thanks for your time. I'm sorry it didn't work out."

Though Doe Adams's smile was as gentle as she herself seemed to be, Lauren didn't think the woman who greeted every sunrise in the lotus position looked all that disappointed as she scooted past Zach. If anything, she looked relieved to be escaping the room. Doe was certainly nice enough. Interesting, too, in a decidedly eccentric sort of way. But from the moment she'd walked in, Lauren had had the feeling that she wasn't quite what her brother was looking for. When the woman's first question about the children had been about their birth signs, she was pretty much convinced of it.

With their visitor heading down the steps, Zach moved back into the doorway and took the file Sam handed him. The men were the same height and easily met eye to eye, but her brother was stockier than Zach, more powerfully built. Zach was rangier, leaner. More…predatory.

The word *powerful* described him, too.

Like a panther.

"She looked familiar," Sam said to Lauren as she shivered against the damp chill of the air.

"She said you flew her to the mainland last year. Apparently that was the only time since 1973 that she's been off the island."

"Sounds like a lot of people around here," he murmured. "Is she going to watch the kids?"

Lauren shook her head, less concerned with the apparent idiosyncrasies of the people who'd chosen to live on Harbor than she was with the finely tuned tension snaking between her and the man edging toward the stairs himself. "She only cooks vegetarian and won't work in a house that has animal hides on the furniture."

She glanced toward the leather sofa and armchairs and gave a philosophical shrug. Everyone was entitled to their causes. She would have mentioned that, too, except she didn't want to hold him up from letting Zach go now that the man had what he'd come for.

Zach obviously wasn't interested in being held up, either.

"Listen, Sam." He pulled open his vest, tucking his

precious file between the waterproof fabric and his shirt. "I need to talk to you this afternoon. It's important."

There wasn't a trace of curiosity in her brother's obliging, "Sure. Come back when you're through. I need to talk to you about switching flights tomorrow, anyway. I want to take the first mail run."

"I mean at the office," Zach replied, completely ignoring what Sam wanted to do. "It's business."

"We can't talk business here?"

"Humor me. Okay?"

Looking as if it really didn't matter to him one way or the other, Sam shrugged. "If that's what you want," he murmured. "What time are you leaving?"

"I'll wait until you get there."

Sam gave a mechanical nod. An instant later, having pointedly avoided meeting her eyes, Zach bounded down the steps to his truck and her brother finally closed the door on the cold.

Wearily running his fingers through his hair, he turned to where Lauren knelt to pick up the jacket Jason had left in the middle of the wine-colored rug. Jason himself was at the television set, opening the long drawer under it that housed videotapes. His denim-covered behind rested on the heels of little hiking boots that looked like miniature versions of his dad's and he appeared, for the moment, totally preoccupied.

So did his father.

Lauren had thought a few moments ago that Sam looked a little ragged. Studying him more closely in the light of the bright brass lamps, she decided that he simply looked worn out.

"Do you want me to get you something to eat?" she asked, because food was the only real comfort she could think to offer. "Mom said she left a couple of casseroles in there."

"She did. Lasagnas, I think. But you don't have to worry about me. It's the kids I need help with." He blew a breath, forced a smile. "I really appreciate you coming, Sis."

She knew he did. He'd practically broken her ribs when he'd wrapped her in his greeting hug. Yet, when she'd hugged him back, just as fiercely, he'd immediately eased up and let her go. She'd just wanted to hold him and absorb whatever she could of his pain. But he wasn't the kind of man who could handle sympathy. Rather than make things worse for him by offering it, she would simply offer her support.

That meant doing whatever she could to keep anyone from making his life any harder than it needed to be. And *that* meant dealing with Zach McKendrick.

She knew exactly what he wanted to talk to Sam about. She knew why he didn't want to talk to him at the house, too. He didn't want her around to point out what a louse he was. He'd said he had his reasons for grounding her brother. But she didn't care what those reasons were. She simply couldn't bear the thought of him telling her brother he couldn't do the only thing that provided any real escape for him right now.

"Sam," she began, intent on ignoring the sudden sick sensation in her stomach. "I know your partner asked to see you, but I need to run an errand before you go. Just a quick one," she assured him, darting a glance down the hall. "Jenny's still asleep, so I guess everything should be okay here for a while."

Jason spun around and scrambled to his feet. "Can we watch Rugrats?" Holding up the video he'd selected, he marched past his aunt and handed it to his dad. "It's a new one."

Weighing questions from sister and son, Sam sank into the deep cushions of his favorite chair. Catching his little boy under the arms of his sweatshirt, he hauled him into his lap. "Sure," he said to him. "Do you want to put it in or do you want me to?"

"You do it."

"Why don't I do it?" Lauren smiled as she reached for the brightly colored box. "I'm already up."

Jason didn't look too certain about relinquishing his prize. He didn't really know her. Not the way he knew the grandmother who'd left yesterday and certainly not the way he knew his dad. Lauren knew the child's only real memories of her would have been of three days last Christmas at Grandma and Grandpa's house and the two days she'd been in Tacoma two weeks ago. He'd had no problem at all crawling into her lap for a story or sharing his cookies with her at Christmas. But, during the awful time over New Year's he'd wanted only his dad and the woman who'd left just yesterday.

"Let Aunt Lauren help, Jase. She's going to be here for a while taking care of you and your sister while I'm at work. Okay?"

Beneath the fringe of honey-colored hair, the child's big eyes looked uncertain. The coaxing helped, though. After another moment of hesitation, he handed over the video he'd chosen, then laid his head on his dad's big solid chest.

Had she not been in such a hurry, Lauren would have worried about how Jason would react to being left in her care. With him safe in Sam's arms, her only thought as she slipped the tape into the VCR and got the thing running was that she might not need to be alone with the children at all if she couldn't convince Zach to change his mind.

There was a certain irony in that thought. Especially when she considered how much more comfortable with the kids she would be if Sam were around during the day. Yet, as she shrugged on her long black raincoat without bothering to change into more suitable clothes, and fished her keys from her shoulder bag, she dismissed the thought completely. This wasn't about what she was comfortable with. If it were, she wouldn't be leaving the house.

"Don't be gone long okay?" her brother asked, his eyes, like his son's, glued to the cartoon characters on the large screen. "I need to see what Zach wants."

It was a fair indication of how detached Sam was that he didn't ask where she was going. She'd only arrived ten minutes before he'd left for the preschool. Given that she'd passed the majority of places to shop when she'd driven off the ferry, it was doubtful she needed anything from a store. He knew she didn't know a soul in the area, either. But she was grateful he didn't ask. She could evade, but she'd never been able to outright lie.

"I'll hurry," she promised, keys jangling. He looked as numb as he'd told her he felt. "It won't take you long to get to your office, anyway. Will it?"

"Ten minutes. It's only five miles to the airstrip."

Lauren wasn't exactly sure where she was going. She had only been to Harbor once before. That had been three years ago with her now-ex-husband and that time as this, she'd taken the ferry. They'd been there for two days over a summer festival weekend and she never had made it to her brother's office.

Driving along the narrow, desolate road now, she

rather wished she had asked Sam for a tour of his base of operations. She knew his office was at the airport. She just wasn't exactly sure where the airport was. When a person drove off the ferry, the town was right there. All fourteen blocks of it, including the boardwalk which lead to an aquarium with a huge mural of a killer whale painted on the side. The sign at the end of the pier read, Welcome to Harbor, Pop. 1,200.

Just beyond that greeting a twelve-foot-high post sprouted signs that pointed in eight different directions and included the mileage to the North End, where thousands of hikers and campers headed in the summer, and Hidden Sound, where she understood the kayakers hung out. It also indicated the directions of Seattle, New York and Tibet, useful information to someone she was sure, but there was no indication of where one might find the airport.

The only road she'd ever taken from town was the main one which curved around part of the big, sprawling island. Since she couldn't recall seeing a sign for where she wanted to go along that narrow, tree-lined route, and given that she'd already driven five miles, she stopped at the only sign of life she encountered—a tiny mom-and-pop grocery store with a sign in the window advertising espresso and live bait.

Two minutes later she was backtracking a mile to take the shortcut to the shore road. The short cut, she'd been told, was marked by a white stake nailed with two pie tins that served as reflectors.

She'd noticed several roads disappearing back into the woods. She'd also noticed that the island's citizenry wasn't big on naming them. Tina had once told her that many of the people who lived on Harbor didn't much care whether people could find where they lived. Their friends already knew. No one else needed the information.

Lauren had thought at the time that her sister-in-law had made the local residents sound like hermits. At the very least, the resident artists, entrepreneurs, kiwi farmers and seventies dropouts marched to their own drummers. Her brother was hardly a recluse, but he definitely possessed an entrepreneurial spirit. He was also a quiet man who tended to keep to himself and his family when he wasn't working. Given that he'd always loved the outdoors, she could understand how he'd so easily adapted to this remote and wild place.

She had no problem seeing how Zach fit in there, either.

The man struck her as the classic lone wolf.

The ocean suddenly appeared a hundred yards in front of her, a vast expanse of gray against a paler gray sky. Refusing to dwell on the knot Zach put in her stomach, she followed the curve that made the road parallel the seaweed-strewn boulders and forced her focus back to the reason she was in the middle of nowhere hurrying to see a man who made her think in terms of feral beasts.

She almost missed the turn for the airport. The white sign with the black silhouette of an airplane was about the size of a briefcase, and weather had eroded most of it. There were no markers beyond that. They weren't necessary. With nothing but the ocean on one side and an open field bordered by trees on the other, it was easy enough to see her destination.

A single landing strip slashed through the low-growing weeds and grasses. A pole with a wind sock dancing lightly in the sea breeze stood off to one side.

She'd wondered how she'd find the office when she got there. She needn't have worried. There was only one building on the site. She'd heard her brother mention that the landing strip was public, but the building clearly belonged to him and his partner. The arched white airplane hangar proclaimed E&M Air Carriers in yard-high blue letters on its curved roof. Huge doors were open on one end, exposing a small white plane inside. The only other door was toward the opposite end and had a sign over it, which read Office.

Leaving her car beside the two trucks parked in front of it, she whipped her hood over her head, hurried to the door and stepped inside.

She was pulling her hood down and shaking off the rain when she turned and saw Zach look toward her.

He stood at the side of the counter that bisected the rather cramped little room. A large aerial map covered the wall beside him. Behind the tall counter, which was covered with another map, a gray metal desk overflowed with papers, coffee mugs and what looked to be fishing-fly-tying equipment. The scent of something that smelled like motor oil drifted through the narrow door leading to the hangar, mingling with the smell of fresh coffee from the coffeemaker on the filing cabinet.

Zach slowly straightened.

He didn't have to say a word for her to know he wasn't at all happy to see her. She also had the feeling from the way his mouth thinned that he knew exactly why she was there.

"Is there any possibility you can change your mind about grounding my brother?"

Her voice was polite, her tone reasonable and designed to invite discussion.

His was decidedly not.

"No."

"That's it?"

"As far as I'm concerned it is."

The man looked as solid as a granite pillar standing there, and just about as flexible. His expression was closed, his tone flat with finality. Coupled with the challenge darkening his eyes, his manner had her digging deep for the tact that had so totally failed her earlier.

"I was under the impression," she said, truly trying for civility, "that you and Sam are equal partners in the company. Isn't that true?"

A faint frown flashed through his eyes. "We have equal ownership."

"Then you both have equal say in its operation?"

"Technically."

"Then, technically," she repeated, thinking the man would rather choke than give more than he had to, "what gives you the right to tell him what to do?"

Zach didn't say a thing. He didn't even move. He just stood studying her carefully guarded expression and wondering at how out of place she looked in the utilitarian surroundings. On all of Harbor Island for that matter.

She had *city* written all over her and, while he had nothing in particular against metropolitan women, he had a particular burr on his tailwing for any woman who presumed to know him after three minutes of conversation.

Overlooking the fact that what they'd had hardly qualified as a civilized discussion, he pushed aside the flight schedule he was adjusting and walked into the waiting area with its scuffed linoleum floor and green plastic chairs. Planting himself four feet in front of her, he jammed his hands on the hips of his worn jeans and narrowed his eyes on her upturned face.

"I have the right," he assured her, not bothering to elaborate. As long as she was there, there was something he wanted to know. And he wanted to know it before she said anything else that would make him wish his partner had been an only child. "Do you honestly think I'm more concerned about myself and this business than I am about Sam?"

It was as obvious as the chips of silver in his storm-gray eyes that her accusation had been eating at him ever since he'd left her brother's house. The fact that it bothered him that much would have given her pause, too, had he not just taken a deliberate step closer.

Lifting her glance from his very solid-looking chest, Lauren felt certain that most sensible people would be looking for a little distance right about now. The female part of her, the part that remembered the heat in his touch, told her that was exactly what she should be doing, too.

"What am I supposed to think?" she returned, ignoring sensibility for the sake of her brother. "You know his circumstances, and you still want to take away one of the only things that's keeping him going. You're right," she conceded, without backing down, "I don't really know you. But I know you're a pilot and I'd think that would give you at least some appreciation of what it will mean to Sam to lose his only means of escape right now."

Something dark flashed in his eyes, something dark and haunted and repressed so quickly that only a fine tension remained.

His voice grew deliberately, deceptively quiet.

"I know exactly what flying can mean to a man. And I know what it can mean to face the prospect of not being able to do it. I also know that Sam is as aware as I am of the FAA regulation that prohibits a pilot from flying when he's physically or mentally impaired. And right now," he said tightly, "Sam isn't a competent pilot."

"He's under—"

"He's under stress," he snapped, cutting off her protest. "I know that. And that stress is dangerous because it's interfering with his concentration. The last thing I want is for him to wrap himself around a tree because his thoughts weren't on his pre-flight check and he missed something critical. Or because his mind started to drift and he found himself in a situation he couldn't correct in time. Or, God forbid," he grated, "he had passengers with him when something preventable happened and he took them down with him.

"Yes, it *is* business." His voice was hard, his expression harder still as he pounced on her earlier accusation. "If he kills someone, we lose everything we've built here. But I'd rather do that than have him jeopardize himself. I've already lost one friend. I damn well don't want to lose another."

He hated what she was doing, resented the way she was forcing him to acknowledge the fear he felt for his friend.

He hated the very word. There had been a time when he'd nearly believed that fear didn't even exist for him. He'd learned how to deny it, to bury it under exhilaration and the adrenaline rush of the close call, the near miss. But that had been back when his training had made him believe that admitting to fear robbed a man of his edge, and once he lost his edge he was no longer invincible. Back when utter confidence had often been all that had kept him alive.

He knew fear now, though.

He knew that loss could happen in the blink of an eye.

And he knew that something about the woman so warily watching him now taunted the ruthless control he'd always maintained over himself.

Annoyed with that, too, he lowered his voice as he forced himself to back off, but the tightness remained. "Does that answer your question?"

Lauren had gone utterly still. In the space of seconds, the imposing, quietly irritated man looming in front of her had ripped away the protective anger that had braced her—and seriously shaken her entire perception of him. There was no denying that he was overbearing, arrogant and bolder than any man she knew, but he wasn't heartless.

He wasn't even close.

He was just as worried about Sam as she was. Only he'd had more reason to be concerned because he'd known of circumstances she hadn't even been aware of.

He'd also lost a friend in Tina himself. And she hadn't even considered that.

Trying to regroup, all she managed was a faint, "Yes."

"Good."

"Look. I'm—"

"Do you want to help your brother?"

"Of course I do. But I'm sor—"

"How long are you staying?"

She was trying to apologize, to let him know she regretted her assumptions. Those assumptions might not have been there had he been a little less impossible, but she wouldn't shirk her part of the blame.

With his glance narrowed on her face, it was clear he wasn't interested in making amends. He was, however, confusing her.

"How long am I staying?"

"Here. On Harbor."

There was a measuring look in his eyes, something she didn't trust at all. The muscle in his jaw was jumping.

"I can only take about a week off."

He considered her for another nerve-wracking moment. "That's better than nothing."

"For what?"

"Your brother needs to get away," he told her, expressing no interest at all in what she could only take a week off from. "He said he'd give anything to get away from all the memories of Tina for a while. But there's no one to stay with the kids. If you really want to help, tell him you'll watch them for him so he can go over to my cabin. It's over on Gainey," he said, speaking of one of the other seven hundred islands in the area. "I'll fly him there myself."

The discomfort she felt suddenly shifted course. "Why would he need to go to another island?"

"Because it's isolated there."

"This place isn't?" Incredulous, even more confused, she swept her hand toward the door. "His house is the only one on that inlet. The only house for miles," she felt compelled to point out, since the location was now taking on an entirely new significance. "I'd think that would be about as remote as it gets."

"Trust me." His tone went as flat as the map on the wall. "There's a difference between being a few miles from town and being in a place you can't leave."

"But being isolated couldn't possibly be good for him right now. He needs his friends. He needs family."

"Why?"

Why? she echoed, but only to herself. As tempting as it was, she wouldn't fall for the challenge carved in his face. He'd just proved he wasn't anywhere near as insensitive as he'd first seemed. She did, however, have major philosophical problems with his perceptions of her brother's needs.

"Because he needs people around him," she replied, not sure why he couldn't see it himself. "To help keep him occupied. To help him deal with his grief. Being alone would be so much worse."

"Or maybe," Zach suggested, doing a commendable imitation of her patently patient tone, "it would be easier. Maybe what your brother needs is the opportunity not to be stoic for all those other people and to deal with whatever he's feeling head-on."

"He doesn't need to be stoic around me."

"Of course he does. You're his little sister."

"What's that got to do with anything?"

The look he gave her held amazing tolerance. "A man doesn't want to show weakness around a female member of his family. And he sure as hell doesn't want to show it in front of another male. The life Sam had is gone and he needs to come to grips with that before he can move past it. The only way that can happen for some people is to leave them alone so they can deal with whatever they're feeling without worrying about how it's affecting everyone else. That includes you. Your parents. Me. Everyone."

There was something about the way he included himself in that list that caught her attention. It was almost as if he were making a conscious effort to keep from adding to her brother's concerns. But that thought was lost in the face of his absolute certainty. It was heavy in his voice, mirrored in his eyes.

Conviction like that wasn't born of assumption. The only place something that deeply felt could come from was personal experience.

"Everyone has to deal with what they're handed in their own way," he muttered, suddenly looking uncomfortable with the way she was watching him. "The choice isn't yours or mine, anyway. It's Sam's. And whether he chooses to stay or go, he's not flying for a while."

He sounded as if he expected her to disagree. Given that they hadn't agreed on anything either had said so far, the expectation was reasonable. But she wouldn't debate his decision about Sam flying. Zach had made his point. She just wasn't at all convinced that what her brother needed right now was solitude.

"Does he know he isn't a competent pilot?"

"I doubt it."

"Is he going to argue with you about it?"

"I imagine he will. He's been taking extra flights so he can be away from here. He's not going to like the idea of being stuck where he doesn't want to be."

The faint buzz of fluorescent lights underscored the soft whir of a space heater in the far corner. Over those quiet sounds came the sharp, electronic ring of the telephone and the thud of Zach's boots on the scarred linoleum floor when, without a word, he moved to the counter to answer it.

The deep, authoritative tones of his voice carried toward her as her glance skimmed his profile and the wide scar covering the side of his strong neck.

She'd told him she didn't know him. And she didn't. The things she knew about him were that he was divorced and that he was no longer in the military. If she had to guess, she would put him near her brother's age. Thirty-seven or so. Only eight years older than she was herself. But those things were superficial. It was what he'd said about how some people needed solitude to deal with whatever it was they had to confront, and how they needed space so they didn't have to be stoic for everyone else, that hinted at what might have shaped him.

He had spoken with the voice of experience. And

though she could only wonder at what that experience had been, she had the uneasy feeling that he had suffered himself, and that he'd done it alone.

"I have to go." Zach made the flat announcement as he dropped the receiver back in its cradle. Taking the note he'd just written, he moved to the map on the wall. After using a ruler and string to calibrate the distance between two points, he scribbled the result on his note. "Tell Sam I have to go to Vancouver for a pickup, so I can't talk to him now. I'll stop by the house about eight. You have until then to convince him to leave the kids with you. If you can do that, I won't have to talk to him about being grounded."

Chapter Three

Lauren stood at Jenny's bedroom door watching her brother as he leaned over the side of the white crib. He looked big and male and decidedly out of place among the pale pastels of Bo-Peep and her sheep on the walls, and the frilly touches of pink eyelet on the curtains and comforter. But there was no doubt in her mind that he belonged right where he was, and that, at that moment, he found as much comfort as he gave.

His flaxen-haired little girl was finally falling asleep. Jenny's silky eyelashes formed crescents against her plump pink cheeks. Her breath came softly as Sam slowly rubbed his thumb above the bridge of her little button nose. Soothed by her father's touch, the child lay curled on her side, her arms around the puffy purple bunny her grandma had given her for her first birthday last week. According to Sam, Jenny dragged it everywhere with her and parted with it only when it came time for her bath.

Tonight, she hadn't wanted to let it go even then, which was why Lauren had escorted it to the laundry room in the basement for a quick trip through the dryer, then wrapped it in a towel to tuck into the crib when the child had started crying for it before it was quite dry. In between, she'd wiped the water from the bathroom floor and helped Jason into his pajamas while Sam dried Jenny and got her ready for bed. Jason hadn't seemed to mind her help, especially after she'd shown an interest in the dinosaurs on his pj's. But Jenny had wanted only her dad.

At that moment, as he stood quietly studying the beautiful child his wife had given him, it seemed Sam only wanted to be with his daughter, too.

Feeling as if she were intruding, Lauren backed away from the door, moving quietly so as not to disturb her brother or Jenny or the little boy already fast asleep in his room next door. She felt helpless to ease her brother's sadness, and it was perfectly logical that children would prefer a parent over someone they barely knew, but those troubled thoughts only added to the uncertainty she felt about what Zach wanted her to do.

She moved down the hall, picking up toys along the way and dropped them in the toy box on the far side of the living room. A fire crackled brightly in the fireplace. The television was on, its volume muted. She couldn't tell if it was still raining. It was too dark outside to see, and the log walls of the house were too thick to allow much sound to pass through. But she was listening for outside sounds anyway. Specifically, the sounds of Zach's truck.

The afghan Jason had wrapped himself in to watch television lay puddled in front of the set. Picking it up, she considered that even if she did agree with Zach about what was best for her brother, which she did not, she had other reservations about his recommendation that she stay with the children. Despite the man's assertion that this place wasn't as isolated as his cabin on the other island, it was still miles from town and it was still surrounded by forest and all the back-to-nature things her brother loved and she'd never seen outside a zoo. Her sister-in-law had even refused to let the kids have a pet for fear that one of those beasts would have it for lunch.

It wasn't that she was afraid. It was more that she was dealing with unknowns, and she'd dealt with enough of those to last her a lifetime. She liked knowing what to expect. She liked knowing what was expected of her. She found security in habit and organization and there was little here but the unfamiliar. When she added the concern of being in such a secluded place without Sam around at night to the concern of taking care of the children completely on her own, she felt none of the confidence she'd acquired at her job. She felt downright apprehensive. Especially when she considered that any child-care skills she possessed were based purely on untested instinct and her mom's checklist.

She was folding the afghan over the back of the sofa with the same care with which she would have arranged a sales display, when she heard the muffled thud of her brother's stockinged feet on the pine floor of the hall. She didn't have to see him to envision the weary slump of his broad shoulders or the fatigue shadowing his deep blue eyes. She could hear his exhaustion in the shuffle of his footfall. Every time she'd looked at him that evening, she'd seen a man who was running on empty.

Masking her trepidation, she offered him a smile. In the past two years, she'd tackled a lot of things she knew nothing about when they'd first been thrown at her and she'd somehow managed to survive. She just hoped that whatever her brother chose to do, his children would be able to survive her.

"How about something to eat now?" she asked, watching Sam pick up the remote control unit for the television from the coffee table and head for his favorite overstuffed leather chair. "You said you weren't hungry when the kids ate, but you should be by now."

"I had some of Jason's noodles."

He'd had two bites. Both taken to encourage the child to eat. "That's hardly enough for a man your size. You need more fuel."

"You sound just like Mom." He gave her a smile, faint but forgiving and dropped into his chair. "I'll make a sandwich later. Okay?"

She started to tell him she would be happy to do it for him herself. He really did need some nourishment. But she had the feeling he was no more interested in food than he was in the deodorant commercial he was staring at on the screen, and that the only reason he'd mentioned the sandwich was to make her feel better.

He needs to get away so he doesn't have to worry about how he's affecting everyone else.

Zach's words echoed in her head, the conclusion nudging hard at her own convictions.

She nudged right back, certain that this evening would have been so much more difficult for him if he hadn't had his children to hug and to think about.

Then, she remembered that getting away hadn't necessarily been Zach's idea. Sam had apparently told him that was what he wanted to do.

Her brother had yet to turn up the volume on the television. Now that the children weren't crawling on and off his lap and demanding his attention, he didn't seem able to sit still himself. Tossing the remote control onto the lamp table beside him, he rose and shoved his fingers through his short dark hair.

"Your partner should be here pretty soon," she said, watching him walk to the bookcase and take out a book, only to put it back again. "He said eight."

It was nearly half past now.

"He could have gotten fogged in." Walking to the fireplace, he pushed around the flaming logs in the hearth, sending sparks up the chimney, and set the poker back in its holder. "The ceiling was pretty low this afternoon."

"Wouldn't he call?"

"If he can, he will."

Now would be a good time to mention the cabin, she thought, as he walked to the coffee table. Now, while he looked as if he were ready to pace out of his skin and there was nothing else distracting him. There had been no opportunity to bring up the subject before with all the activity with the kids.

Part of her still balked at the idea of Sam being all alone. Another part knew that if he didn't go, Zach would tell him he couldn't fly.

"How did he get the scar on his neck?" she asked, working her way up to mentioning the cabin.

His attention elsewhere, Sam's brow furrowed. "Zach?"

She hummed a note of affirmation. "It looks like a burn."

"It was. He crashed a jet when an experimental guidance system failed." Looking as preoccupied as he sounded, he picked up a coloring book and distractedly flipped through the pages. He didn't seem to pay any particular attention to the scribblings. He didn't even seem to be seeing the pages at all, until he came upon a beautifully colored castle.

From the painful way he winced, Lauren had the feeling the picture was one Tina had colored for the kids.

"How long ago?" she asked, as much for the distraction it would offer Sam as her own desire to know.

The furrows in his brow deepened. Whether in thought or in pain, she couldn't tell. "About seven years by now, I'd guess."

"Do you know how long he's been divorced?"

"I have no idea." He closed the book carefully and set it down. "He was divorced when I met him. That was five years ago."

It was a true reflection of her brother's mental state that he showed no interest at all in her interest in his partner. He'd been in that distracted fog ever since she'd arrived—which explained why he hadn't bothered with introductions when Zach had followed him in for the manifest. When she'd told him earlier that evening that Zach had gone to Vancouver, he hadn't even asked how she'd come by that information.

It was entirely possible that he did need time to himself, she conceded, but she'd no sooner opened her mouth to ask if that was what he wanted, than a heavy, decisive knock on the door stole her brother's attention—and made her need to talk to him that much more urgent.

"Wait!" she called, taking a step after him as he started for the door. "I need to ask you something before you talk to your partner. It'll just take a minute."

"Now?"

"Now," she quietly insisted. "Please?"

She must have looked fairly desperate. "I guess," he murmured, giving her an odd little glance. "Just let me let him in first."

She had no choice but to stand back and allow Sam to open the door. Already uneasy, an odd sense of disquiet moved through her the moment Zach stepped inside and his hooded eyes locked on hers.

Droplets of rain clung to his overlong dark hair. The down vest he had worn earlier had been replaced with a brown leather bomber jacket that made his shoulders look a mile wide. He brought with him the scent of fresh sea air and pine, and, as she pulled in a deep breath, she doubted she'd ever again think of the forces of nature without recalling his dominating presence.

Without a word to her, his unreadable glance took an impersonal sweep of the casual burgundy jeans and sweater she'd changed into and promptly settled on her brother.

"Hey, buddy," he muttered, closing the door with his elbow since his hands were full.

Sam turned back into the room. "How was the flight?"

"Weather's minimum. Barely made it in."

"Air?"

"Bumpy over a thousand."

"Chuck make it back?"

"He logged in about an hour ago. The GPS in the 185 is working fine now." Zach lifted a brown paper bag. In his other hand, he carried a six-pack of beer. "Let me get rid of these," he said, and headed for the kitchen with the familiarity of a man who felt no need to question his welcome.

Much of their verbal shorthand had been lost on Lauren. The only flying she ever did was in commercial jets and her technical knowledge was limited to the operation of seat backs, tray tables and the overhead oxygen mask. But she had no interest in their shop talk. Conscious of

Zach ignoring her as he walked past, her only concern was her brother.

"What did you need, Sis?"

From where she and Sam stood in the middle of the living room, she heard the refrigerator open and bottles rattle as the six-pack was shoved inside.

"I just wondered if you wanted to get away for a while," she said, keeping her voice low. "I'll be here with the kids, so if you want to go some—"

He was shaking his head, cutting her off before she could even finish. The sound of the silverware drawer opening filtered in from the kitchen. "I can't ask you to do that."

"You're not asking. I'm volunteering."

"That's nice, Sis. It really is. But I can't leave Zach with all the work."

"You can talk to him about it," she suggested, needing for him to at least consider the idea before Zach pulled the rug from under him. "I'm sure he wouldn't mind taking care of things for you. He's your friend," she pointed out, in case he was wondering how she could possibly know that.

"I don't think so."

"You don't think he's your friend, or you don't think you should go?"

"Look," he replied, patiently. "Now isn't the time. We'll talk about this later."

"Go ahead and talk about it now," came the deep voice from the kitchen. "It sounds like a good idea."

Zach appeared in the doorway with a large bowl of vanilla ice cream in one hand and a beer in the other. Looking as if he were only now hearing the notion himself, he walked toward them both. "You said the other day that you'd like to get away for a while," he reminded his friend. "Now you have the opportunity."

He handed the beer to his partner, then looked toward Lauren.

"Do you want anything?"

His manner seemed as comfortable with her as it was with her brother. On the surface, anyway. If not for Sam, Lauren was sure he would have preferred to ignore her. It was that kind of tension she could feel slithering beneath the facade. But this wasn't about them. This was about Sam, and she would have to be as dense as the forest beyond them not to realize that Zach was doing what he could to make things easy for her brother. He clearly preferred that Sam choose to take a break on his own, rather than insisting on it himself.

"No. Thank you," she replied, as committed as he was to doing her part.

"I'll pass on the beer myself," Sam told him. The bottom of the brown bottle hit the coffee table with a quiet click. "I'm flying in the morning."

"You'll be over the eight-hour rule before you fly again. Go ahead if you want it. Chuck or I will take the morning mail run."

"The eight-hour rule?" she asked, as much to stall the course of the conversation as to understand what they were talking about.

"FAA regs," Sam muttered. "Eight hours, bottle to throttle. A pilot can't consume alcohol within eight hours of a flight. And I told you I want the early run," he reminded the big man dwarfing his sister. "I'll take whatever's on the log for the afternoon, too."

"They're already covered." Clearly intending to avoid that particular topic for the moment, Zach stabbed his spoon into the heaped blue bowl. "Let's get back to what your sister was saying,'' he suggested casually. ''Getting away is a good idea, Sam. You remember the fishing streams over on Gainey, don't you?''

For a moment, Lauren didn't think Sam was going to let the change of subject go. He could be as stubborn as sin itself at times and there was a decidedly mulish look to his brow now. She also had the feeling that Zach was even more obstinate—if not downright bullheaded.

Sam was apparently feeling too apathetic to press his point. Either that, or the men's relationship was such that they took turns getting their way. Her brother picked up the beer and, after taking a swallow, sank into his chair. Zach claimed the overstuffed chair on the opposite side of the sofa and propped his booted feet up on the ottoman.

''Sure I do,'' Sam murmured. ''The best salmon I ever caught was in the pool by that waterfall. You can't beat spring run up there.''

''Or the winter steelhead,'' Zach reminded him just before a spoonful of ice cream disappeared. He looked perfectly comfortable, perfectly…at home.

Her brother's focus settled on the neck of his beer. ''Those are the best streams I've ever fished.''

''Better than Alaska?''

''Darn near.'' In the flickering light of the fire, Sam backed his quiet agreement by slowly nodding his head. ''You know, I can't even remember the last time I was there.'' Trying, looking as if the memory just wouldn't form, he shook his head again. ''When was that, anyway?''

''Before Jase was born, I guess. You know,'' Zach said mildly, taking another poke at his ice cream, ''the steelhead fishing should be pretty good right about now.

There's that stream right behind my cabin. And you can't beat the solitude there.''

For a moment, Sam remained silent. He simply contemplated the neck of the bottle in his hand.

''Yeah,'' was all he finally said. ''Yeah,'' he repeated, but this time there was longing in the word.

Lauren could hear it herself. She could even see it in the thoughtful way her brother continued to stare at his bottle. Over a fishing stream, she thought, wondering what it was about such a thing that could leave a guy looking so wistful.

She was still wondering when Sam tipped back his beer for another swallow and she felt Zach's steady gaze on her.

She hadn't budged from where she stood by the coffee table. As interested as she was in the outcome of the conversation, it hadn't occurred to her to move, or to be offended by the fact that she wasn't being included in it.

Zach clearly intended for her to include herself now. He arched one dark eyebrow at her, his expression plainly saying that she could jump in here anytime now and re-inforce her offer to take care of the home front.

Slipping around the table, she lowered herself to the sofa cushion nearest her brother. ''It sounds like a place you'd like to see again, Sam.'' She had a saying taped inside her Day Planner. When in Doubt, Bluff. Calling on the adage now, she spoke with calm conviction. ''Jason and Jenny will be fine here with me if you want to go. I'll be here for a week anyway.'' She nudged his arm, gave him a smile. ''You might as well take advantage of me. It's been years since you've had the opportunity.''

She was talking about all the times he bribed her into cleaning his room when they'd lived at home. But remembrances of their childhood were lost on him just then.

"The cabin is yours if you want to use it," Zach told him.

"I don't know…"

"You might as well get away for a while, Sam." Finality slipped into Zach's tone. "There isn't going to be that much for you to do here."

Sam's glance bounced from his friend to his sister and back again. "What are you talking about? There's plenty to do. We've got all that work on the float plane—"

"I'll do it myself."

"You'll…?"

"Your concentration is shot, Sam."

For a moment Zach simply held his glance. The way Sam was waffling wasn't leaving him any choice but to bring out bigger guns. But he didn't need to press his point. Sam was getting the message.

"This is about my taking that manifest today, isn't it? Anyone can pick up the wrong file—"

"It's not just the manifest," his partner calmly replied. "That didn't cause anything but a delay. This is about you forgetting to tell the mechanic about the problem with the alternator in FE 22," he said, identifying one of their planes by the numbers on its tail. "And the wrong weights on the freight a couple of days ago." Zach paused, clearly troubled by the errors and oversights. "You know the regs as well as I do, Sam."

"It's about you needing time for yourself, too," Lauren reminded him. She wanted to keep the focus on his emotional needs. That seemed wiser, kinder than enumerating the things he was doing wrong. "I can see how hard it is for you to be in this house right now. And I know you have decisions to make about how long you'll stay here. I don't understand why you'd want to be *quite* so far away from everything, but if going to that cabin is what you need, then you should go.''

The glance Zach cut her was as sharp as glass. Yet, as he dropped his feet to the floor and leaned forward, his expression bore nothing but concern.

''It's more important that you just come to grips with what's happened,'' he said to Sam. ''Once you do that, you'll be able to concentrate on whatever else it is you need to do.''

It sounded to Lauren as if Zach didn't think Sam should consider anything at all about his future while he was gone. She wasn't going to call him on his advice, though. The man seemed to understand her brother in ways she couldn't begin to comprehend. Part of her was touched by his empathy. Another part was more curious than was probably wise about where that understanding had come from.

Sam hadn't moved. He was still sitting slumped in his chair, staring at the beer bottle. Only now he was picking at its label. ''I'd like to go,'' he finally, reluctantly, admitted. ''I'm just not sure about leaving the kids.''

Lauren reached over, touched his arm. ''I'm here for them.''

''I'm not sure about leaving you here, either.''

He looked up then, his despondent gaze settling on Lauren. A moment later, it shifted to his partner. ''She doesn't know anyone on the island…and it's a long way from town.'' A strip of label curled as he pulled it away. His voice dropped. ''Tina really hated that at first.''

For a moment, he said nothing else. He just continued to contemplate his handiwork as his thoughts drifted back to his wife.

Lauren felt her throat tighten at the pain he so valiantly tried to hide.

Zach, looking uncomfortably male, focused on his melting ice cream.

Conscious of them both, Sam cleared his throat.

"I really would like to go," he repeated, his voice quiet but steady as he looked to his friend. "But the only way I can do that is if you'll check in on Lauren to make sure everything is okay. I don't want to have to worry about her and the kids."

Zach didn't even hesitate. "You've got it."

"Are you sure you're okay with this, Sis?"

She didn't possess Zach's lack of compunction. Thrown by her brother's request of the man openly watching her, a couple of seconds passed before she managed a commendably unruffled reply. "Of course. But the kids and I will be all right," she assured him, certain that if she repeated it often enough it would be so. "Your friend doesn't need to bother with us."

Sam didn't respond to her claim. Zach didn't, either, though as the men worked out a departure time for the next day and she asked Sam what food she should pack for him, it occurred to her that she shouldn't have expected a reply. Sam was too preoccupied. And Zach, she realized, now that she was thinking about it, had undoubtedly agreed only so her brother would go. As little as he wanted to do with her, she was dead certain he had no intention of checking up on her.

Sam left at two o'clock the next afternoon for the airport with his duffel bag, his steelhead rod and the week's worth of groceries Lauren bought for him in town that morning. By three o'clock, Jenny was awake from her nap and fussing for a snack. Since graham crackers were on the "approved" list her mom had left, Lauren settled the toddler in her high chair with a small stack of the brown squares and a sipper cup of milk, finally coaxed a smile out of her by letting her have a spoon to bang with on her tray and turned her attention to Jason, who was crying for his dad.

The only way she could find to distract him was by having him help her make chocolate chip cookies and letting him load up his dump truck to drive the dough to the oven to bake.

That project took as long to clean up as it did to prepare. It also had the advantages of distracting her from the worry she felt about her brother heading into seclusion, and of occupying the kids until supper time. Though neither child was interested in eating what remained of the casserole her mom had left for them, she finally got Jason to eat chicken soup. Jenny's appetite was as tiny as the child herself. Not sure what she was doing wrong since the little girl seemed more interested in chewing on her spoon than on what was in it, Lauren eventually coaxed a few bites into her and by the time she got them bathed, read Jason a story while rocking Jenny, and tucked them in for the night, she was ready to fall into bed herself.

She couldn't indulge in that escape, however. She still had to do dishes and throw a load of towels into the washer, since she'd just used the last two clean ones. If she didn't, she'd have nothing to dry herself off with after her shower in the morning.

There was also something wrong with the furnace.

For the past hour, the air in the house had grown steadily cooler. At first she'd thought it was because, busy as she'd been, she'd forgotten to add another log to the fire and the fire had gone out. So, between Jason's story and tucking Jenny into her crib, she'd turned up the thermostat in the hallway.

That had been at least twenty minutes ago and the chill had yet to disappear.

Standing in the hall with her arms crossed over the cabled sweater she'd pulled over her jeans, she frowned at the thermostat's thermometer. It was actually four degrees colder than when she'd turned the heat up.

The thermometer read fifty-nine degrees. Since it was all of forty degrees outside, she wasn't interested in seeing just how cold the house could get before they all got pneumonia.

The washer and dryer were in the basement. Taking the load of towels down with her, she tossed them into the washer along with the soap and had the machine running when she turned to warily eye the black behemoth of a furnace in the middle of large, cement walled space.

She hated basements. They were cold and damp and shadowy and the corners were inevitably filled with boxes and old furniture that took on sinister shapes when illuminated by a single bare bulb.

Reminding herself that she was an adult, she ignored the set of narrow night-blackened windows high on the wall above the agitating washing machine. The furnace was still running. She could hear the fan or whatever it was that pushed the air to the upper floors. But the air it was pushing was cool.

So was the heavy black metal of the huge contraption when she reached her hand, palm out, toward it.

"Great," she muttered, then felt her heart knock against her ribs at what sounded like a faint groan above her.

It's just the house settling, she chastised herself, torn between figuring out what the problem was with the heat, wishing her brother were there and indulging her chronically overactive imagination. She was trying hard not to think about what might be in those woods. She was also trying to avoid the thought that, while she was an adult, she was the only adult around for a lot more miles than a scream could carry.

An instruction manual dangled by a chain from one of the pipes that poked like the arms of a saguaro cactus from the furnace. Spotting it, she pulled it from the plastic envelope protecting it and flipped through pages of schematics and diagrams that were as clear to her as Sanskrit.

A creak sounded again, louder this time. Closer.

She could have sworn it came from behind her.

The manual hit the cement floor when she jerked around, her hand pressed to her hammering heart.

There was no one in the space other than her and now, no sounds beyond the rhythmic splash and chug of the washing machine and the low drone of the furnace. But even as her heart rate slowed, she acknowledged the fact that she hadn't a clue what she was looking for, so poking around down there was pointless.

She was at the bottom of the flight of narrow wooden steps in a matter of seconds.

She'd made it halfway up them when she made the decision that all laundry would be done during daylight hours.

She'd reached the top and had just stepped into the welcoming light of the kitchen when someone big and dark stepped in front of her and she slammed into the wall of his chest.

Chapter Four

Lauren froze in the basement doorway. She was already spooked. Granted, she'd done that particular number on herself, but she wasn't into rationalizing as she jerked back from the unyielding wall of hard muscle, flannel and leather and sucked in a lungful of air. Panic shot pure terror through her veins. A scream rose in her throat—only to lodge there when the scent of spice and sea air registered the instant she glimpsed the scar below the lean, hard jaw and realized whose grip it was biting into her arms.

With every nerve in her body primed to fight or flee, fear and relief fused into a single adrenaline surge.

Ripping one arm free, she hauled back and slugged Zach hard in the shoulder. "What do you think you're doing?"

"Hey!"

"You scared me half to death!"

"Be careful!" he shot back, grabbing her wrist when she hauled back to slug him again. His other hand shackled her upper arm, his fingers gripping hard through her sweater. "And calm down. I knocked, but no one answered."

"Calm down? You walk in here uninvited, and you expect me to calm down?"

"I told you, I knocked," he growled, pulling her against him when she jerked back to keep her from pitching backward. "I thought there was a problem."

He couldn't believe how badly he'd startled her. The color had drained from her porcelain skin, leaving her face as white as a snowbank. The awful fear had left her eyes, replaced by truly impressive fury as they narrowed on his, but he was far more concerned with keeping her from breaking her neck than the fact that she wanted to wring his. With her struggling to free herself, she was half a step from backing down the long flight of stairs behind her.

Needing her to listen, he lowered his voice, forcing demand from his tone.

"I'm sorry I frightened you. I am," he insisted, gentling his voice even more to quell the doubt in her eyes. "But if you don't take it easy and stop pulling away, you're going to wind up in the basement. The first thing you'll do if I let you go is back up, and you don't want to do that. There's nothing behind you but air."

At his warning, she whipped her head around to glance over her shoulder. Realizing that he was all that kept her from breaking something essential, the tension shifted in her body, struggle dying as instinct drew her closer.

She was already pulled hard against his body. Apparently just now realizing how very close they were, her glance jerked up.

There were chips of turquoise in the blue of her eyes. He noticed them an instant before he heard the soft catch of her breath.

Beneath his hands, he could feel the delicate bones of her shoulder blades, the long curve of her spine. He was aware of the fullness of her breasts against his chest, and the quick heat where her flat stomach pressed the front of his jeans. He was also only inches from her lush and undeniably inviting mouth.

Grabbing her had been necessary. He had no excuse for holding her any longer. Having her in his arms was a mistake. He already knew the softness of her skin and her fresh, seductive scent. Now, he also knew how perfectly her body fit his.

Something about that combination felt as dangerous as flying mach one without an oxygen mask. Unable to imagine why the Fates were using this particular woman to torture him, he eased the tension in his arms. "Are you all right now?"

Lauren gave him a small almost imperceptible nod. "Yes."

"Are you sure?"

Though she managed another nod, this one marginally more convincing, she really wasn't sure at all. Her heart was pounding furiously against her ribs. She was no longer frightened. At least, not with the sort of shock that had raced through her when she hit the top of the stairs. The quality of that alarm had definitely changed. Zach's body felt as hard as marble against hers. Strong and solid. Powerful. Undeniably male. It had been over two years since she'd been in a man's arms for anything other than a platonic hug. Though all Zach was doing was keeping her from backing down the stairs, the way he was holding her didn't feel platonic at all.

The heat pooling low in her stomach didn't feel all that innocent, either.

She wasn't sure which confused her more. The gentleness she'd heard in his voice, his presence, or the way her nerves were humming when his hands slid from her body.

Trying to regroup, she decided it was all three.

"I...I'm sorry I hit you."

"Forget it."

His glance swept her face, his expression as guarded as she felt in the moments before he left her by the old potbellied stove near the table and picked up Jason's truck from the middle of the kitchen floor.

Ten feet of space gaped like a demilitarized zone between them when he set the truck on the tiled counter dividing the room, glanced toward the dishes in the sink, then leaned against the counter himself.

Lauren stayed right where she was. "How did you get in? I know I locked the doors."

"I used my key."

"You have a key to this house?"

"Sam gave it to me a long time ago," he replied, crossing his arms over his broad and solid chest. "Tina was always calling for him at work because she'd locked her keys in the house or in the car. Since Sam wasn't always available, he gave me a set in case I was around so I could help her out."

Lauren hadn't had any idea that Tina was so scatterbrained. But she was more concerned at the moment with what was going on in Zach's mind as he quietly scanned her face. There was a look of weary determination about him, as if he were resolved to some purpose he definitely wasn't crazy about.

"I wasn't sure what the problem was in here," he

continued evenly. "I waited a couple of minutes on the front porch for you to answer, then came around back when you didn't. When I couldn't get an answer there, I came in to make sure everything was okay."

"I was doing laundry." He had to be as conscious as she was of the distance they were keeping from each other. After all, he'd put it there. "It's hard to hear in the basement."

In the otherwise quiet house, it was easy to hear the muffled chug of the washing machine drifting through the basement's open door and the faint drone of the furnace fan still uselessly blowing air. Appearing conscious of the sounds himself, Zach seemed to understand why she hadn't heard him. But he said nothing to acknowledge that a rescue hadn't been necessary.

He'd already apologized for scaring her. She could hardly expect him to do it again. Especially since he'd only done what he'd felt was right.

"Did Sam get to your cabin all right?" she asked, thinking it best to change the subject completely.

"Yeah. He did. That's one of the reasons I came by."

"You could have just called."

The determination shadowing his carved features slipped more firmly into place. "I was coming over anyway."

"To check up on me," she concluded.

"That's what your brother asked me to do."

"Zach," she began, quietly determined herself, "I appreciate you taking the time to come over, but you and I both know you only agreed to do it so Sam would go. Now that he has, you don't have to worry about us. I have everything under control," she assured him. "You don't need to bother again."

She was trying to let him off the hook. Zach understood that. He even wished he could take the exit she was so graciously offering him. From the caution in her manner, it was apparent that she didn't want him around any more than he wanted to be there, but there was no way he could disregard his obligation to his friend.

"I told you before that you don't know me."

"And I tried to apologize for jumping to conclu—"

"If you did," he said, still refusing her that bit of absolution, "you'd know that when I give my word, I never go back on it. And if you have everything here under control," he contended with a pointed glance at the way she was hugging herself, "why is it so cold in here?"

The challenge in his eyes didn't surprise her. He seemed to thrive on provocation. Where she was concerned, anyway.

"It's cold," she explained in her best I've-got-this-covered tone, "because the furnace isn't working. I'm going to call someone first thing in the morning to come fix it."

"So why don't you have a fire in the fireplace?"

"Because it went out. I got busy," she defended when his eyebrows merged.

He didn't say another word. He just stared at her long enough to make the nerves in her stomach jump, then strode to the basement doorway and headed down the stairs.

She didn't at all appreciate the way he'd ignored her claim that she could handle the matter herself. She wasn't too crazy, either, about the patently tolerant glance he slid toward her when he reappeared two minutes later and flipped off the light switch at the top of the steps.

The hinge gave an arthritic squeak as he closed the door.

"You don't need to call a repairman," he announced flatly. "You need to call the fuel company. You're out of oil."

The thought that she was out of fuel had never even occurred to her. She had electric heat in her little apartment. The baseboard kind that needed nothing but regular payments to the power company to make it work.

"Oh," was all she said, then felt her heart stall when she saw him watching her mouth.

Apparently realizing what he was doing, his glance jerked up, his gray eyes glinting like diamonds as they locked on hers. For a few frantic heartbeats, the awareness snaking between them felt as sharp and unexpected to her as it had in those scattered moments he'd held her in his arms. Then, his jaw tightened, his features hardening as he stepped in front of her.

By the time she realized she was holding her breath, he'd walked past her and was frowning at the round black stove.

"You're going to have to use this for heat. It's more efficient than the fireplace." The edge in his voice sounded like irritation. With her or with himself, she couldn't tell. "Do you know how to build a fire?"

Edgy herself, she gamely eyed the squat iron stove. The fact that he'd come barging in because he'd figured there was a problem he needed to check out had already told her he didn't have much confidence in her abilities. That conclusion was confirmed by the skepticism slashing his carved features as he ran a measuring look from her restrained hair to the gold studs in her ears and over her stylish cropped sweater.

Had she been alone in the house, she would have told him she was quite adept at handling matches and kindling. Everyone had their own set of survival skills and she'd discovered that sheer stubbornness was one of hers. But she needed to have a warm place for the children in the morning and the needs of the little ones came ahead of her own.

"I understand the theory. I just haven't had much practice."

"*Much* practice?"

"Any. I've never had a fireplace," she conceded, refusing to consider the lack of that particular skill significant. She had more shortcomings than she could count—a fact that her ex-husband had quite generously pointed out to her the day he'd announced that their marriage was over. But she wasn't going to add this to her list of failings, even if Zach did make her feel like it was. "I wasn't a Girl Scout, either."

Zach didn't say a word. The defensiveness he heard in her voice wasn't there only because of him. There was a knee-jerk quality to it, something that made him wonder what sort of a bruise he'd bumped.

He didn't want to wonder about her though. And he definitely didn't want the heat he'd felt when he'd touched her. As he headed for the back door, shrugging out of his jacket and dropping it over the back of a dining chair on his way, he just wanted to do what he had to do and get out of there.

Newspapers were stacked on the mudroom floor under pegs that held jackets and coats. Grabbing a few sheets, he headed back past the high chair and round oak table and crouched in front of the stove. Paper crackled as he wadded newsprint into a loose ball.

From the corner of his eye, he saw Lauren kneel slightly behind him. "I want to see what you're doing," she said ever so reasonably. "So I'll know how."

"Fine," he muttered, wishing he didn't have to breathe

when her light scent drifted toward him. The small iron door on the curve of the stove's belly opened with a faint squeak. "Hand me the kindling. It's the little stuff," he explained when she frowned at the antique coal scuttle sitting on the stove's brick pad.

There were two sizes of split wood in it. Small and smaller. Since there wasn't much wood of either size, Lauren edged the scuttle over to where he could reach it.

Beneath the heavy blue chambray covering his broad shoulders, hard muscle shifted and bunched as he moved from scuttle to portal. The dark denim of his jeans stretched over his powerful thighs. She knew the feel of those muscles. She knew the compelling strength of his hands.

"What brought you to Harbor?" she asked, as much to distract herself as to learn something about the enigmatic man her brother trusted so implicitly. "It's not like it's on the way to anywhere else."

A small pile of pencil-size sticks landed on top of the paper. "I used to boat over to Harbor Cove every few months to get supplies when I was living at the cabin."

"You lived there?"

"Yeah," he murmured, reaching for more wood.

"And you moved here because...?" she prompted when he offered nothing else.

"I'd heard that the pilot who owned the local charter service wanted to retire, and I was looking for something to do."

"What were you doing on the other island?"

He hesitated. "Nothing that made me want to get up in the morning," he finally replied. "Buying a charter service sounded interesting."

He was evading. Badly, too, she thought, but it seemed wiser to stick with the direction he steered the conversation. She couldn't begin to understand the need he'd apparently once felt for such isolation, or what would have driven him to seek it. She just knew that, for the moment, they weren't at each other's throats, and she wanted very much to keep it that way.

"That was the service Sam worked for," she concluded.

He told her it was as he stuffed smaller sticks into the opening. "The guy was going to sell off his planes and close the business. That would have left Sam without a job and me without anyone who knew anything about charters, so Sam and I decided over a beer to buy the operation ourselves. That's when I moved here."

"I can't believe how simple you make the decision sound."

"It *was* simple."

Stupid simple, he thought. He'd never done anything that had felt so meant-to-be. He'd never questioned it later, either. When he and Sam had bought the little charter airline, it had consisted of two planes, one of them a relic from the Alaska bush that had been held up by faith alone, and most of their revenue had come from hauling hunters and fishermen into the wilderness. In five years, between his willingness to gamble and Sam's sound business sense, they'd replaced the derelict plane, bought another, added another pilot to their payroll and acquired contracts to deliver mail and provisions into the more remote places in and beyond the San Juans.

They'd both been pleased with their little operation, content with the niche they'd found and as certain as anyone could be that they would continue as they had as long as they worked hard and ran a safe show.

He just wasn't feeling anywhere near as certain about

the business now. Not when he was faced with the very real prospect of losing his partner.

"You and Sam didn't even know each other and you decided to go into business together?"

An old familiar tension moved through his shoulders as he tossed two bigger chunks of wood atop the pile. He knew with unquestioned certainty that nothing would ever be exactly the same as it had been—and that feeling was far too familiar, too.

"I'd always gone with my gut when it came to flying," he finally replied, "and I'd managed to survive to that point. I just decided that was how I was going to live the rest of my life, too."

From beside him, she studied his profile, her silence pensive, thoughtful.

"Did you come to that conclusion at your cabin?"

Zach had just started to stand when her quiet question froze him in place. He hadn't said a thing of any consequence to her about his life. Certainly, he'd given away nothing of the two years he'd spend patching it back together. He never spoke of it to anyone.

His deliberate silence on the subject only made her perception that much more disturbing.

"I came to a lot of conclusions there," he admitted, and pushed himself upright.

She rose with him, as graceful as a dancer, but she made no further attempt at conversation. Caution shadowed her face. That caution was in her posture, too, as she took a rather obvious step back.

She stood with her arms crossed, her fingers curved around her slender biceps. It was possible that she could have been hugging herself because the room was so chilly. Considering the shielding quality to her stance, he found it more likely that all the complicated, incomprehensible things that made her female were simply putting a barrier between her and him.

He'd heard the catch of her breath and seen awareness darken her eyes when she'd been in his arms. It did something to a man to know a woman wasn't immune to his touch. Ignited desires. Made him want.

Defenses kicked into place as the tension knotting his shoulders moved into his voice.

"You're going to try to talk your brother into leaving Harbor, aren't you."

His tone was utterly flat, removing any pretext of query. The knowledge had preyed on his mind since before he'd laid eyes on her. With thoughts of her supple body preying on it, too, now seemed as good a time as any to set his priorities straight.

"That's what Mom would like him to do," she confirmed. "Dad would, too. They both know how hard it will be raising the kids alone, and it would be better for Jason and Jenny if they were raised around family."

She sounded totally oblivious to the impact such a move would have.

"They'd have their father."

"Who has to work most of the time," Lauren reminded him, wondering at the accusation in his tone. "From what I understand, Tina was always with them during the day. When Sam asked me to find a housekeeper for him, he said there are times when he can't get back at night because of the weather, so they'd be with a stranger all day and all night, too. That's why he wants someone who can live in, until he decides what he's going to do."

"It's not down that often."

She shook her head, as bewildered by his lingo as by

the air of censure that had slipped over him. "I'm sorry. I don't understand…"

"The weather. *Down* means you can't fly in it. We get fogged in up here sometimes. Or seasonal storms can keep planes grounded. But it's not like it's every day." He mirrored her stance, only on him, crossed arms looked more combative than self-protective. "What else do your parents think?"

Until moments ago, the antagonism she'd noticed about him before had been conspicuously absent. Now, it colored his tone with frustration, shaded his features with a hardness that made them look carved of stone.

She had no idea what she'd done to resurrect that irritation. She knew only that she couldn't counter what she couldn't understand. "You should talk to Sam about this. Not me."

"Sam isn't here. Even if he were, you're the one with the information I need."

"Information?"

"I need to know what you're all trying to get him to do."

His eyes settled hard on her face, his impossibly sensual mouth set in a determined line. There was something more than concern for his friend pushing him. Something more essential. It was that kind of resolve she sensed in him. Yet, she also sensed hesitation, and uncertainty. It was almost as if he were bracing himself for whatever it was he was about to hear.

The thought that he could feel uncertain about anything would have struck her as impossible—until she realized that her brother's decisions would affect Zach, too.

The imposing man silently waiting for her reply had already lost one friend when Tina had died. If Sam decided to do what his family was advocating, he would not only lose his business partner, he would lose another friend as well.

She braced herself right along with him. "They've suggested that he sell his share of the business. To you, I imagine," she said, though she doubted they had considered the financial and operational logistics that would necessarily be involved. She had no idea if Zach could afford to take it on alone. "Then, he could go to work for one of the major airlines based out of Seattle. He wouldn't have to work as many hours as he does owning his own company.

"Half of his own company," she amended for Zach's benefit. "Dad has already checked with a couple of carriers and they both want to talk to Sam as soon as he can get them a résumé. As for the kids, with them living in Seattle, they can stay with Mom and Dad if he has to be gone overnight."

Zach said nothing. He just watched her, quietly absorbing her words while the set of his mouth grew more grim.

"Since Tina's family is even farther away and can't help at all," she continued, feeling it only fair that he should also know those circumstances, if he didn't already, "Mom and Dad's solution does make a certain amount of sense."

Not a word she had said made what he was dealing with any easier. "Is that what you think he should do? Sell and move?"

The beams in the roof creaked, the house settling in for the night as Lauren studied the strong, sculpted angles of his face. There was character in the deep lines around his intriguing eyes, sternness around his beautiful mouth, a determination to persevere in the furrows of his brow. Under it all lay a strong sense of compassion for a friend—and an unspoken desire to not lose more than he already had.

"It seemed like the most practical solution," she admitted, hedging. "I know Mom thinks it is." Simple and practical didn't necessarily seem right, though. Not now. Not when she considered what her brother had built here. How he'd always loved the place. What his friend would lose. "The option Mom and Dad are offering him is certainly viable—"

"It's only one option."

"I didn't say it was the only one," she pointed out patiently. "I imagine he can stay here and make things work reasonably well if I can find him someone who will provide the stability Jason and Jenny need. Like you said, Sam is their father. He's their closest family and the most important person in their life right now."

The shuttered look in his eyes turned cautious. "So what are you going to do?"

"Only what Sam wants me to do. You mentioned yesterday that a person has to deal with what they're handed in their own way," she reminded him. "The choice is my brother's. Not mine." Or my parents, she thought, though she doubted their mother would let go of the idea all that easily. "I'm just here to help while I can."

The last thing Zach expected was for her to echo his own philosophy. But, then, he had to admit he hadn't expected her to play along so well last night when they'd worked on Sam to get him to go—or what he'd found when he'd gone down to check the oil gauge on the furnace a while ago.

The furnace manual had been on the floor, halfway between the furnace and the steps.

He didn't want to be intrigued by the idea that she had actually been trying to figure out how to fix the contraption herself. He didn't want to respect the fact that she'd swallowed her pride and admitted she needed help to ensure she had a fire going for the children in the morning. More than anything else, he didn't want to stand there wondering why he couldn't shake the thought of how incredible she'd felt in his arms.

He snagged his jacket from the back of the chair. After shrugging it on, he pulled a box of matches from one of its pockets and set it atop the stove.

He'd done what he could to make sure Sam's kids had heat in the morning. It was definitely time to go.

"All you need to do to start this is open the damper," he said, showing her which way to turn the silver knob on the side of the black chimney that disappeared through the ceiling, "and light the paper. You'll need to add one of those quartered logs over there every hour or so to keep it going."

Dubiously eyeing the foot-high stack of wood by the wall, she gave him a nod and backed up so he could pass.

"You might want to call the fuel company first thing in the morning, too. If Harbor is already on their schedule," he said, on his way to the front door, "you might not have to wait for oil. If it's not, it could be a few days before they can get over here."

He reached for the latch on the door. "Call me if you need anything else," he finally said, with a glance toward her. "I'm in and out of the office all day, but leave a message and I'll get back to you."

She told him she would, but only because it was the polite thing to say. She really didn't want to call on him for anything if she could possibly avoid it.

From the level look he gave her just before he headed into the damp and misty night, she didn't doubt that he knew that, too.

Chapter Five

Lauren typically awoke at 6:00 a.m. and came to full consciousness in the shower. By the time she'd dealt with the blow-dryer and makeup and dressed in whichever outfit she'd carefully laid out and accessorized the night before, the last vestiges of sleep were gone and she'd mentally reviewed her schedule for the day. She'd also tried to anticipate possible glitches and decided which item on her agenda could be sacrificed if the need for extra time arose.

She needed to feel organized. She needed to feel prepared. Being intimately familiar with her job, she usually had a good feel for potential problems with personnel, vendors and customers and faced each morning knowing pretty much what to expect and what people would need of her.

When she awoke at 7:00 a.m. on the narrow hide-a-bed in Tina's sewing room to a cold house and a three-year-old soberly telling her he'd had an accident in his pajamas, she felt none of the assurance of a familiar routine.

Not awake enough to panic, she immediately reminded herself that she had her mother's schedule to follow. As long as she stuck to it, she'd be fine. She would simply do what she always did and readjust where necessary.

She'd just decided that the first item she would sacrifice would be her shower, since there were no dry towels, anyway, when Jenny awoke and started fussing for a clean diaper and breakfast. Assuring Jason with a hug that there was no harm done, she pulled on her old gray sweats and tackled item number one on the list—giving Jenny a bottle to drink. Since stripping Jason's wet bed wasn't on the schedule, she squeezed that task in between lighting the fire in the stove, changing him and Jenny into dry clothes in the kitchen once the room warmed up and feeding them oatmeal and juice for breakfast.

As occupied as she was, and as tired, since she'd spent half the night listening for the children in case they awoke, she shouldn't have been distracted by stray thoughts. At the very least, her thoughts shouldn't have kept straying to an ex-jet jockey who seemed to regard her with more distrust than he'd probably ever felt toward the F-15s or 30s or whatever-they-weres he'd flown.

Thoughts of Zach were there anyway. Just as they had been when she'd lain listening for the kids in the long hours before dawn.

He was a fascinating man. Rugged, but oddly refined. That was the military officer in him, she supposed. A man who could protect and destroy, but who possessed the qualities of a gentleman. Not that he'd behaved like a gentleman with her. But the honesty was there. The integrity.

The loyalty.

She was thankful that her brother had such a trusted friend. And she was enormously grateful to him for laying the fire that had the kitchen toasty warm in no time. But she had no reason to deal with him until he returned with her brother next week, and no intention of asking for his help. Over the past couple of years, she'd developed a rather desperate need to stand on her own.

She knew exactly why that was, too. She'd been that way ever since her ex-husband had walked out the door. She figured that was also why she'd become so compulsive about staying in control of her day, but that was what happened to a woman when she'd been blindsided. She'd been aware of problems between her and Ed, but she hadn't realized how dead their marriage was until the week after he'd passed the bar exam and she'd discovered that she was the only wife who hadn't attended a dinner given by the firm that had just hired him. His excuse for not mentioning it had been that he'd felt she would be uncomfortable. After all, she had nothing in common with the people he worked with.

It was actually he, she had painfully discovered that night, who wouldn't have been comfortable with her at his side. She hadn't grown the way he had. She'd failed to become the sort of wife an up-and-coming attorney needed. As it turned out, all he *had* needed from her for the previous couple of years, had been the paycheck she'd provided, and even though she had pointed out that she hadn't had the opportunity to 'grow the way he had' because she'd spent her time putting him through school, she chose not to dwell on the finer points of that particular conversation.

Picking up another towel from the stack she'd dumped on the kitchen table, she darted a quick glance to where

Jason was playing underneath it. Jenny stood inside her playpen in the corner, her little fingers gripping the edge for support while she chewed on the blue padding covering it. Lauren preferred not to think at all about that disastrous time in her life. It wasn't even often anymore that she did. She preferred to remember only that she'd survived being used.

She had survived it on her own, too. She'd finished her last year of college by going to night school after working all day and most weekends. She'd bought a decent car and was now saving money to buy her own condo. She hadn't quite salvaged her trashed self-esteem, but getting the promotion she'd slaved for would go a long way to curing that particular casualty. Even if she didn't get a store of her own, no one could take away the fact that she had worked her way up to assistant manager of the store where she'd started as a stock girl.

Her thoughts smacked of a pep talk. The kind she tended to give herself before she had to fire someone, or tell Andy that half of the store's departments were out sick. She was trying to remind herself that she was capable, that she could handle whatever arose.

Unfortunately, faking ability didn't work quite so well in totally unfamiliar territory.

She'd already blown her mother's carefully choreographed schedule.

Jason was late for preschool. The morning class at the Harbor Community Center began at nine and was out at noon. The afternoon session ran from noon to three. Jason had always stayed for both sessions because Tina had been one of the teachers there and, according to a note on the list Lauren's mom had left, he could attend whichever session was convenient. Unfortunately, the afternoon session wasn't looking any more promising.

The key to her brother's Suburban was missing. She couldn't find it anywhere. She needed the larger vehicle because she couldn't get the children's car seats into her little coupe and, aside from needing to take Jason to preschool, she needed to go to the store or they would be out of milk by morning.

Though she hated to bother her mom at the business school where she worked as a secretary, she called her to see if she knew where a spare set of keys might be— only to learn that her mother had used Tina's keys while she was there and had inadvertently taken them home with her. She had no idea where Lauren might find another set.

It was with a certain sense of apprehension that Lauren realized she knew exactly where she could find what she needed. Since her mom was now worried about how she was going to get milk, Lauren quickly eased her mind by telling her she was pretty sure Sam's partner could help and hung up after gamely assuring her that everything was going "just great."

She really didn't want to call Zach. And not just because she needed to prove that she could handle matters for her brother alone. For the past two years, she'd devoted nearly all of her energy to her job and kept her relationships with men strictly business. Not once in that time had any man made her notice him as anything more than an acquaintance or business associate.

Zach did more than make her notice. Never before had she met a man who altered her breathing simply by watching her, or who so thoroughly unsettled and intrigued her. Beneath his commanding, demanding exterior she'd glimpsed understanding, and a sort of gentleness she never would have expected. There was also a part of himself that he staunchly protected.

Or, maybe, she thought, remembering his allusions to how a man needed to confront his demons alone, he'd simply shut that part of himself down.

With a half-folded towel pressed to her stomach to keep the folds in place, she ducked her head so she could see under the table. "Are you sure you don't know any place your daddy would keep extra car keys?" she asked the little boy driving his big yellow dump truck between the chair legs.

Keeping his hand on the cab of his rig, Jason looked up, his little features screwed up in contemplation.

Rather soberly, he finally said, "I have a key."

"You do?"

His golden cornsilk hair brushed his eyebrows as he nodded.

Crouching down in front of him, she gently nudged back those impossibly soft strands. "May I see it?"

His big eyes met hers as his mouth twisted. She had no idea what went on in the three-year-old's mind as he weighed, measured and concluded, but she had the feeling the process was incomprehensibly male in the moments before he abandoned his truck and did a double-time crawl from under the chair.

An instant later, like a sprinter leaving the starting block, he was on his feet and racing through the kitchen and down the hall.

Jenny, who'd yet to take her first step alone, chose that moment to lose interest in the padding. Lauren didn't know if it was because her brother had left the room or because she was simply getting tired, but the child sat down on her cushioned bottom with a thump and her big blue eyes filled with tears.

By the time Jenny started to whimper, Lauren had her in her arms and was quietly assuring her that everything was fine. She had the feeling her tiny niece didn't believe her though. The whimper turned to a pathetic sob as the flaxen-haired child buried her rosy-cheeked little face against Lauren's shoulder and rubbed her runny nose on her aunt's favorite worn-out sweatshirt.

"Maybe it's nap time," Lauren concluded, cuddling her closer. "Let's check the schedule. Okay?"

"Here."

Jason's red flannel shirt was completely untucked from his jeans as held up an intricately turned, four-inch piece of metal.

Lauren felt the hope fade from her smile. What he held was definitely a key, but it was the old-fashioned kind that had fit a door lock built at the turn of the past century.

Crouching down with the unhappy baby biting down on her shoulder and going "uhn, uhn" in her ear, Lauren held out her hand. "Thank you, sweetie," she said, taking it because she didn't want to hurt his feelings by rejecting his offer. She didn't want him running back to his room with it, either. It didn't take a degree in child development to know the thing could put out an eye. "I don't think this one's going to work. But I'll put it up here for now." Shifting the fussing Jenny in her arms as she rose, she set it on the counter. "Okay?"

"'Kay," he agreed, sobering again. "Can I have a cookie?"

"How about yogurt instead?"

"I don't like yogurt."

"Grandma says you do."

"I want Grandma."

Me, too, Lauren thought, distractedly rubbing the baby's back as she headed for the refrigerator and glanced toward the pile of towels she'd been trying for the past hour to fold.

It was now after eleven o'clock, nearly time to fix the children's lunch and she still hadn't combed her hair. All she'd had time to do was pull it into a ponytail with a scrunchie to keep it out of her eyes and to brush her teeth.

Reminding herself to run a washcloth over her own face the next time she washed the kids', she took the milk from the fridge while holding Jenny on her hip, set it on the counter and reached back in for the yogurt and a jar of peaches. When she turned back, Jason was at the counter, his arms stretched above his head and his fingers curved around the edges of the jug of milk.

He'd pulled the container halfway over the edge when she gasped, "Jase. No!"

Blithely ignoring her, he informed her that he wanted milk and backed up. The plastic jug promptly slipped right through his hands, the disklike lid popped off and over half of the half-gallon puddled by his sneakers before she could snag the handle and rescue what was left.

Jason's eyes were as big as the wheels on his truck. "Do I need a time out?"

She bit back a sigh. "I think we just need towels."

Ever so helpfully, the little boy turned to the pile on the table behind him. "I'll get it."

"I've got it," she assured him, snagging the clean bath towel before he could drag it down to the floor. "I mean paper ones."

The child was off like a shot, ingenuously working his way past the child lock on the cabinet below the sink to pull off the entire roll of paper towels from the holder inside the door. Leaning over Lauren's shoulder with part of her aunt's sweatshirt in her mouth, Jenny grasped for the jug herself.

Lauren closed her eyes, made herself draw a breath. Instead of calming her, the second of silence allowed her to hear the crackle of the fire burning in the woodstove—which reminded her that she needed to add more wood before the fire went out.

Preschool wasn't going to happen today. The need to get to the store, however, had just become more pressing. There was now barely enough milk to get the kids through lunch and give Jenny a bottle for her nap.

She cast a dispirited glance toward the telephone. It didn't matter that she'd rather not have to deal with Zach. He appeared to be her only option.

"You have a couple of messages there."

Zach's head snapped up as he walked into the office and tossed his flight log on the counter. Chuck Boyle, the young pilot who had come to work for them last year fresh from a three-year stint in the Alaskan bush, had flown in just ahead of him and was diligently filling out his paperwork at the cluttered metal desk. Chuck had been married less than three months and was as anxious as always to be done with the dreaded part of his job so he could be with his bride.

Zach could sympathize. He hated paperwork, too. He just couldn't remember the last time he'd been in any rush to get home.

"I took 'em off the answering machine," Chuck continued, pointing in the general direction of the pink message slips pinned to the corkboard as he frowned at his forms. He'd twisted his Seattle Mariners ball cap around so the brim was in the back. A tuft of sandy-brown hair poked out the front. "One of 'em's from Air Tech in Bellingham. The parts you ordered for the tank are in."

The tank was Zach's nickname for the old plane he

was restoring out in the hangar. Most of the thing lay in pieces, little more than a shell surrounded by parts of the engine he'd broken down.

"Great," he murmured, a smile forming as he reached for the flight ledger to see when one of them could pick up the order. As restless as he'd felt the last couple of nights, it would be good to get back to working on the old wreck again.

"The other's from Sam's sister."

Zach's smile stalled like an engine fresh out of fuel. "Did she say what she wanted?"

"Nope." The rangy pilot in the flannel shirt scratched his ear with the end of his pen. "She just asked you to call her when you got in." A contemplative frown creased his youthful features as he finally glanced up. "Sam's really kind of lucky, you know? Not counting Tina," he scrambled to explain, flushing a little at the thought. "Man, that's got to be the toughest thing there is to handle. He's lucky with his family, though. I can't imagine any relative of mine dropping everything to help out the way his have done. Especially when they'd have to leave their jobs."

Zach's furrowed expression mirrored his employee's. Lauren wouldn't have called unless she had to. "Sam's mom works at a business college. It wasn't in session most of the time she was here."

"Yeah, but his sister is some management type. Can't remember where she works, but Maddy over at the Road's End told Brandee she had a hard time getting away. Seems she had to work nights getting ahead enough to come here."

Brandee was Chuck's wife. Maddy O'Toole was the biggest gossip on Harbor.

"How would Maddy know something like that?"

"Sam's mom told her."

Zach didn't doubt that for a moment. Maddy had a huge heart, a willing ear and made the best pies on the island. Between the three she prompted more confessions than the local priest.

He talked to her on occasion himself. She was fun, friendly and he felt nearly as comfortable at her café as he had at Sam and Tina's table, but he had never spoken to her about anything of personal import. Not that she hadn't dug. Since the first time he'd sat at her counter, she'd hinted and pried and flirted to get him to talk about how he'd wound up on Harbor. He'd pretty much told her the same things he'd told Sam's sister, which hadn't been much at all. But he did like her pies.

He'd avoided the café for the past couple of weeks, though. He'd heard that talk there lately had centered on speculation about Sam and the future of E&M, and he didn't care to have whoever was there turning that speculation on him.

The soft whir of the space heater merged with the click of calculator keys. Chuck had turned back to his task. Wanting to find out what Lauren wanted, Zach tossed the pink slip with her name on it into the trash and picked up the telephone. He didn't know if he felt justified or guilty when it came to the Edwards family. He knew he resented the ideas they had presented to Sam, but, to be honest, he had to admit that the man's parents were good people. From what little he knew of her, his sister seemed to be good people, too.

There was no denying how much Lauren cared about her brother. After all, she hadn't hesitated to jump to his defense when she'd thought he would be hurting Sam by grounding him. And when she'd come after him at the office, she'd possessed the protectiveness of a mother bear defending her cub. But he hadn't considered that she would, indeed, have put her life on hold to be there for her brother.

Until Chuck had reminded him that she had a job—at a department store, if he correctly remembered what Sam or Tina had once mentioned—he'd given no thought to what that life even was.

Not wanting to be curious about it now, he dialed the number he knew as well as his own.

Lauren didn't answer until the fifth ring.

Dusk had given way to darkness when Zach bounded up the steps of the familiar porch with its redwood bench and winter-bare planters and knocked on the front door.

He tried hard not to stare when Sam's sister answered it.

Her usually restrained wheat-colored hair had been pulled into a slightly tangled ponytail that listed to the left at the top of her head. Her face had been scrubbed free of makeup, leaving her looking more like a sixteen-year-old than a woman pushing thirty and the baggy gray sweats she wore nearly swallowed her whole. She had a fussing baby propped on one hip, a fistful of paper towels in her hand and the spark in her lovely blue eyes was conspicuously absent.

Behind her, through the kitchen doorway, he could see Jason sitting in full pout on the breakfast counter.

"I appreciate you coming by," she said, apparently expecting him to hand over the keys and leave, since she made no move to let him in.

The keys remained right where they were, in the pocket of his khaki cargo pants. "What's the matter with Jase?"

"He's unhappy with me."

"Why?"

"He jumped on his juice box."

Zach's eyebrow arched. "And he's unhappy with you?"

Either she didn't want to let out the house's scant heat, or she'd realized he wasn't going anywhere without checking out what was going on. Looking resigned, she stepped back with the baby so he could come in.

Jenny had her bunny by a puffy foot and was fretfully chewing on one long ear. Looking as if the motions had become automatic, Lauren slowly swayed from side to side while she rubbed the child's narrow little back.

"I need him immobile until I can get the mess wiped up. He was walking in it."

Jason knew Zach far better than he did her. Lauren knew that. And it became clear in a hurry that he was looking for the familiar. Before Zach could close the door, the somber-looking little boy was off the counter, charging through the doorway and clinging like a little barnacle to the big man's leg.

"Hey, buddy," Zach murmured, resting his hand on the child's soft hair. "What's the problem here?"

His little face crumpled. "I want my mommy."

It wasn't the first time that afternoon that Lauren had heard that plaintive plea. Hearing it again, a fresh wave of distress washed over her, bringing her to her knees in front of the little boy she had no idea how to console.

"Oh, sweetie," she murmured as Jenny's fussing turned to tears. "I know you do. And I'm not trying to be mean by having you sit on the counter," she explained, because she was sure the restraint was only making him feel worse. She also wanted desperately to change the subject. "Do you want to sit at the table instead?"

"Mommy," he repeated, unable to be swayed. Weeping, his little voice became choked. "I want Mommy home."

Jenny, tears rolling down her cheeks, echoed one of the few words she could say that had real meaning to her. "Mama," she softly sobbed, and began repeating the single word in a sorrowful little refrain.

Lauren swallowed. Hard. With her nephew's face buried against khaki and Zach's hand covering the top of his head, she gently stroked his trembling little back and cuddled the whimpering baby closer.

"Has it been like this all day?"

At Zach's question, Lauren tipped back her head, glancing up to where he was frowning down at her and the child clinging to him. For a moment, she could have sworn he looked as helpless as she felt.

She had no idea what he saw in her expression. But her silence apparently answered his question.

"Come on," he murmured.

Sliding his big hand under her elbow, his touch all business, he helped her to her feet, then bent to scoop up Jason. He'd barely even straightened before the heartsick child wrapped his little arms around his neck and buried his head in the crook of his strong neck.

"It's going to be okay, buddy," Zach murmured, his voice sounding impossibly gentle. "It's going to be okay."

There was conviction in his assuring tone, and the promise that everything would, indeed, eventually be all right. It was only when he glanced toward her again that Lauren realized he sounded far more convinced than he looked.

"He was all right until I started to put him down for

his nap,'' she told him. ''That was when he started asking for his mom.''

Disheartened, she rocked Jenny to soothe her and reached to rub Jason's back again. Her only thought was to ease the children—until she breathed in Zach's familiar scent and realized how close they were standing.

When her hand slid away, his obligingly replaced it.

''He never did sleep,'' she said.

For a moment, the only sounds were the children's sobs and the muffled drone of the television. Zach said nothing. He had no idea what to say to ease the naked concern so evident in her eyes, or to take away the pain of an innocent child. With Lauren trying to comfort the little girl in the pink rompers, he figured all he could do was try to distract Jason.

Setting the little boy on his feet, he crouched down in front of him and pulled a pristine white handkerchief from his back pocket. He wiped the child's tears, then his nose, and went back for a couple of tears that tried to sneak past him.

''You doing okay there, sport?'' he asked, tipping the child's head to see his eyes.

Jason's response was a shuddering breath and the blink of his long wet eyelashes.

''Tell you what,'' Zach murmured, taking one more swipe. Deciding a hug was in order, he gave him that, too, then dabbed at his cheeks one more time for good measure. ''Go get your jacket. You can come with me. Do you want to do that?''

Jason remained mute, but he gave a solemn nod, dutifully turned on the heels of his little boots and headed through the kitchen to the mudroom.

''Where are you taking him?''

''To the store. You said you needed to go. I'll need

your list," he continued, turning to face her, "but before we get to that, there's something I want to know." His brow slammed low. "Why did you lie to me?"

Lauren gave a disbelieving blink. "Lie to you?" Through the kitchen, she could hear Jason dragging the wooden step stool under the coat pegs. She could only hope he didn't drag his coat through the juice. "What are you talking about?"

"On the phone. When I called you back, I asked if everything was all right. You said everything was 'just fine.'"

"It was. Relatively speaking."

"Relative to what?"

"To what it had been like before."

He opened his mouth, and promptly shut it again. He wasn't sure he wanted to know what all she'd been dealing with since he'd left her last night. He wasn't sure what Jenny's problem was, either, because she usually never failed to give him a little smile. Much preferring to deal with the boy than either of the two females, he motioned to Jason when the child walked back in dragging his red parka.

"What do you need from the store?" he asked Lauren, crouching down in front of Jason again.

"You don't need to go for me. If you'll just leave me the keys, I can take care of it."

He had one of Jason's sturdy little arms tucked into one small sleeve when he looked over to where she still rocked the crying baby. "I'll leave you the keys," he assured her over the discomfiting noise. "But I'm going to the store."

"That's really not necessary."

The metal rasp of a zipper joined Jason's quiet sniff.

"Yes," Zach calmly replied, "it is."

"Zach—"

"Why are you being so stubborn about this?"

"I'm not being stubborn. It's just that I can do it myself."

He wasn't saying that she couldn't. He would have told her that, too, had he not been struck just then by how vulnerable she looked holding Jenny with her eyes full of what he could swear was worry.

The impatience left his tone. "Can you honestly tell me you'd rather cart these kids off to the store the way they are right now, than have me go for you?"

Jenny started rubbing her jaw with the bunny's ear and making little snuffling noises. Refusing to admit that she felt like crying herself because she couldn't figure out what was wrong with the child, Lauren tried valiantly to resurrect her resolve. But the thought of the energy it would take to get the kids bundled up and into car seats and to the store and back into the house again with all that dark surrounding them was almost more than she could bear at the moment.

Almost.

What actually had her backing down was the realization that she would insult Zach if she refused his help. She'd already done that when she'd accused him of thinking only of himself and the business. Considering that she really didn't want to offend her brother's friend, she felt it wisest to concede.

"There's a list on the table."

He rose, knees cracking.

"I need paper towels, too," she told him, following him into the warmth of the kitchen to add the item to the list. "We've had a little problem with spills today."

Zach eyed the golden-brown juice puddle and the

splatters in front of the sink. "I see," he muttered. "Did you do that, Jase?"

The little boy shadowed his every step. Stopping by the table when Zach stopped, he tipped his head back and nodded.

"Why?"

Jason's shoulders lifted nearly to his ears with his shrug.

"Just wanted to see what would happen, huh?"

Zach offered the conclusion as he picked up the four-item list lying atop a long yellow notepad. With the pencil that had been lying next to a couple of toy soldiers, he wrote "p. towels" on Lauren's short list, stuffed the paper into the pocket of his leather jacket and frowned at what was clearly a schedule.

The writing on the pad was different from that on the grocery list, less precise, less…tidy, he supposed.

He turned to see Lauren at the counter. The woman desperately trying to ease the usually angelic child bore little resemblance to the person he'd encountered two days ago. But it was more than the lack of makeup and tailored clothes that caused him to realize how painfully neat and in control she had appeared before, and how defenseless she looked now.

He didn't want her defenseless. She was safer when her guard was up.

"What's with the checklist?" he asked as she offered Jenny a cracker from an open package on the counter.

The baby vigorously shook her head and turned away.

Discouraged that her offering hadn't helped, Lauren pushed a stray stand of hair from her face. "I asked Mom to leave it for me. I've never watched kids by myself before and I didn't want to miss something I was supposed to be doing."

Not that she was following the schedule at all by now, she thought. The hour of creative play suggested for late afternoon had been devoted to rubbing Jenny's forehead to get her to nap after she'd settled Jason in front of the TV. The caution her mother had written about not letting him spend more than an hour a day watching television had been ignored completely. To keep his mind occupied with something other than the fact that his mom was no longer there, she'd let him spend most of the afternoon parked in front of it.

If the child turned into a creatively challenged couch potato it would be all her fault.

"What?" she asked when she noticed Zach frowning at her.

"You've never been alone with kids before? Any kids?"

The incredulity in his tone was unmistakable. So was the uneasy concern. That same concern etched his face as his glance bounced from the little boy patiently waiting for him to the child gumming the purple rabbit.

Lauren already felt awful about her inability to make the children happy. The last thing she needed was to let him make her feel inadequate.

"You don't have to make it sound so odd."

"I wasn't even thinking about that," he informed her, still scowling. "But now that you mention it, it is unusual. Isn't it? For a woman I mean?"

"For a woman?"

"Well, yeah," he defended. "You're all right with kids, aren't you? I know some women are into their careers and aren't that crazy about children, but your instincts are okay, aren't they?"

Baffled, she blinked over a headful of pale curls. "My instincts?"

"The ones women have. About kids."

Lauren's head started to hurt. For a moment, she just stared at her brother's friend while her thoughts rolled between the needs of the children, the tension tightening the back of her skull and the improbable course the conversation had just taken. But just as she started to inform him on principle that not all women are naturally maternal, it occurred to her that he wasn't being a chauvinist. He was just worried about his friend's offspring.

"My instincts are fine," she assured him, praying she was right. "I like children. If it'll help your peace of mind, I'd even thought I would have my own by now, but my life hasn't exactly turned out the way I'd planned. If it had, I'd have more experience with this and I wouldn't be winging it here."

That lack of first-hand knowledge had her torn between wanting to drop the subject completely and the need to take advantage of whatever resource she had available. Her mom hadn't been home when she'd tried to call a while ago. Thinking only of the child she held, she pointedly asked, "How much experience have you had?"

"I don't think I'd need a list," he muttered, refusing to be curious about why her plans hadn't worked.

"Well, I do. So please leave it alone and tell me what you think is wrong with her."

The concern in her eyes overshadowed the frustration she so obviously felt with him. Seeing that concern, his own made a quick shift. He'd figured the baby was fussing because her routine was shot. It hadn't occurred to him that there might actually be something wrong with the child.

"What do you think is the matter?"

"I don't know. She's been like this most of the day."

"Has she gotten sick?"

Lauren shook her head. "She just keeps rubbing her jaw and fussing and chewing on everything. And the only things she'll eat are yogurt and Jell-O."

Coming toward her, he held out his hands. "Let me see her."

Jenny, not feeling good enough to be social, promptly turned from him and buried her face against the woman who'd offered her comfort all day.

Zach didn't attempt to pull the child away. Ignoring the slight, he simply settled his hand at the side of her little neck.

He actually looked as if he knew what he was doing when he felt along both undersides of her little jaw. "She doesn't feel warm. And nothing feels swollen. Is she pulling at her ear, like she might have an earache? Jason gets a lot of those."

The loose strands of hair framing Lauren's face swayed as she shook her head. "I haven't seen her do that. She just gums everything and rubs at her cheek."

"Which side?"

"Left."

"Hang on."

He was onto something. Lauren was sure of it when he stepped around the juice drying on the floor and washed his hands. Moments later, he'd tossed aside the towel he dried them with and was back.

"Jenny?" Lifting his big hand toward the child's face, he ran a gentle finger along her round little jaw. "Look at me for a minute. Okay?"

With some reluctance, the child turned, the tip of the bunny's ear wedged back in the corner of her rosebud mouth.

"Can you open your mouth for me?"

Blinking her big blue eyes, she opened her mouth and the wet appendage fell out.

The fair-haired little girl was apparently familiar with what he was doing when he rubbed his index finger along the back of her gum. She didn't move. If anything, she looked like his gentle massaging motion felt wonderful.

"What is it?" Lauren asked, quietly amazed by the child's stillness.

"I think she's teething. There's definitely a little lump there."

"A lump?"

"The tooth under the gum. It's no wonder she's miserable. That has to hurt like he—...heck," he amended in deference to the little boy now sticking his own finger into his mouth to see what he could feel along his own gums.

"Is there anything I can do other than rub it?"

"I've seen Tina give her a plastic ring thing to chew on. I remember her doing that with Jason, too. She'd put it in the freezer first. I guess cold helps. And pressure. That's probably why kids bite down on whatever is handiest."

Lauren remembered seeing a plastic ring with floating fish inside it in the baby's playpen. But the liquid inside was...liquid...and she had no idea how long it would take to freeze. "What else can I do for her?"

"I don't know. I'll stop by the drug store and ask if they have something that will help. In the meantime, rubbing it seems to work."

"How much pressure are you using?"

Reclaiming his finger, he wiped it off on his jeans and lifted his hand to her face.

"About like this," he said, and touched the outside of her jaw.

His fingers curved under the delicate line of her jaw-bone, his thumb inadvertently brushing the corner of her mouth. He wasn't sure who hesitated first, but he felt himself go still the moment her breath caught.

Her skin felt like warm satin to his touch, her bones impossibly delicate.

With his eyes on the caution in hers, he consciously moved his thumb from the curve of her lower lip and increased the pressure of his index finger enough to rub a slow circle near her chin.

"That's all I was doing," he murmured.

He could have sworn her head moved into his touch. The motion was almost imperceptible, but he felt it, just as he felt her breath shudder out, warm and soft on the back of his hand.

"Got it," she said, her voice little more than a whisper.

Still watching her, he curved his fingers into his palm and stepped back.

When his glance dropped to the soft part of her mouth, his gut tightening at the thought of how she would taste, he cleared his throat and scooped up Jason.

"We won't be long," he said, and left her staring at his back.

Chapter Six

She'd had worse days. Lauren was sure of it. On a scale of one to ten, with ten being sheer disaster, this particular day probably only rated a seven.

Overlooking the fact that a seven on the Richter scale could level a major city, she headed for the freezer to dig out an ice cube for Jenny. Thinking about the baby made far more sense to her than dwelling on all that had gone wrong.

It was also infinitely preferable to considering how all Zach had to do was touch her to make her tremble inside—and how all she had to do was breathe in the heady combination of sea air and warm male clinging to him to remember the protective way he'd held her at the top of the basement stairs.

She hated to admit how badly she'd wanted to feel his arms around her again before he'd walked out the door.

Fortunately, the opportunity to worry about that disconcerting desire was brief.

Zach and Jason had been gone all of two minutes when the secretary she shared with Andy, Ruth Moyer, called her, frantic because the computers were down, and she couldn't access the bi-monthly staffing schedule Lauren had compiled before she left. The schedules had to go to the department heads first thing in the morning.

Because she had no access to a fax, the best Lauren could do was call Ruth back after she'd situated Jenny in her playpen and read the schedules of all the employees from the hard copy she pulled from her briefcase. Forty-five minutes later, she was still pacing a rut in the kitchen floor and reading to the beleaguered-sounding woman when she heard the front door open.

Zach's voice carried toward her, firm and deep as he instructed Jason to slow down. Seconds later, accompanied by a window-rattling slam when the door closed, her nephew came skidding through the kitchen doorway with two white sacks that smelled suspiciously of hamburgers and fries.

She had no idea why she had assumed Zach would knock, but she didn't bother concerning herself with the fact that he hadn't. Giving the grinning child a smile as she hurriedly asked the secretary to hang on, she tucked the phone under her chin, took the sacks so Jason could take off his coat and simply accepted the fact that the rules of behavior weren't clear where her brother's friend was concerned.

He was more family than guest in this house. She was actually the stranger there.

It was with that awkward thought that she stood back when Zach walked in, dumped a grocery bag on the counter and glanced from the spill she'd yet to clean up to the phone she cradled and her open briefcase. The only thing different from when he'd left was the fact that Jenny wasn't fussing. The little girl sat sprawl-legged among the colorful array of stuffed animals in her play-pen, silently gumming the ice cube Lauren had wrapped in a white washcloth and secured with a rubber band.

"Business?" he asked, watching her clear the toy soldiers from Jason's place at the table.

She flattened the phone against her sweatshirt so the caller couldn't hear. "Unfortunately."

"How much longer will you be?"

"Ten more minutes," she said quickly. "I'm almost finished."

"Leave that." The overhead lights caught strands of silver in his dark head as he nodded toward the table. With the faint rasp of metal, he slid down the zipper on his jacket. "I'll get him fed."

A flicker of disbelief at the unexpected favor flashed over her face as Zach shoved the milk into the fridge and motioned the little boy away from the tempting sacks. He was actually relieving her of duty. But her wonder at his willingness to do that lasted only long enough for her to pull the printouts from under her arm, tell Ruth she was back and head into the living room while reading the accessories department's schedule before starting lingerie's.

The children were his concern. He wasn't helping her so much as he was helping them.

With other demands dividing her attention at the moment, she didn't consider her conclusion beyond that. She simply let herself appreciate what he was doing, no matter who he was doing it for. For the first time all day, she didn't feel as if she were on a leaky life raft that was about to spring another hole. And the children finally, she thought thankfully, seemed content.

She was pretty sure Jenny was feeling that way because the ice made her gums feel better. But when she heard Zach call Jason to come help him clean up the apple juice from the floor and the little boy literally ran to the task, there was no doubt in her mind that the big guy was the reason the little one seemed so much less agitated. Zach eventually even managed to do what she hadn't been able to do and got the child to eat all of his meal.

She hadn't realized how worried she'd been about the children not eating well until she walked back into the kitchen minutes later, glanced across the breakfast counter at the table and smiled at the flat, empty wrapper Jason had used for a plate.

Zach sat beside the child patiently showing him how to draw airplanes on the paper with a French fry and ketchup. Hearing her walk in, he glanced at her over his shoulder and rose with the scrape of chair legs on pine flooring.

At his response to her presence, her smile faltered. It was almost as if he wasn't comfortable making himself at home with her there.

"I didn't expect you to bring dinner," she told him.

"I didn't think you'd mind."

"Zach got milk shakes," Jason informed her, holding up his paper cup with both hands.

"I see that." Giving the child's chocolate mustache a weary smile, she turned a wary one in Zach's direction. "Thank you. And I definitely don't mind," she told him, rather wishing he hadn't felt so compelled to move. When he stood, he took up more room, made her more aware of his long, leanly muscled body. "I'm sure he wouldn't have been that enthusiastic about anything I cooked for him tonight."

A smile tugged at the corner of Zach's mouth. It was clearly meant for Jason. His little buddy had just added a French fry tail to the drawing on his plate.

"Forget it," he said to her, dismissing what he'd done. Paper crackled as he wadded the wrapper from the burger he'd devoured and stuffed it into one of the empty sacks. "He likes fries. And chocolate milk shakes are his favorite. After the day he'd had I didn't think it would hurt to indulge him a little."

He didn't need to explain. He especially didn't need to explain why he'd felt compelled to do something special for the child who seemed to regard him with the same adoration he did his own father. She knew why he did it, though. It was as obvious to her as the affection between man and child that he wanted her to know what she had already acknowledged—that he hadn't done what he had for her. He'd done it for Jason.

And for Jenny. The little girl still sat in her playpen, chewing on her ice cube, a telltale streak of chocolate smeared on one cheek.

The thought of Zach crouched by the playpen, feeding her milk shake from a spoon, held far more appeal than was wise.

Lauren's briefcase remained open on the table. Dropping the printouts onto the files inside, she closed it with a quiet snap and set it on the refrigerator.

"I'm sure it won't hurt him," she agreed, and turned to add another log to the stove.

"I just did that."

"Oh. Well," she murmured. "Thanks for that, too. And for the floor." Threading her fingers through her disheveled hair, she nodded to the clean spot in front of the sink. Whether he wanted to admit it or not, he had done that for her benefit. The kids couldn't have cared less if the juice had been cleaned up or left to dry to a mess as sticky as flypaper. "I would have had it cleaned up, but the phone rang right after you left. There was something I needed to take care of for the store."

"Yeah," he muttered. "I sort of figured that out." He'd also been aware that the work matter she'd needed to tend had come on top of the problems she was having with the kids. That was why he hadn't taken his own burger and headed home when he'd returned.

Opening the cabinet door under the sink, he stuffed the sack into the trash. "I'd heard you got caught up before you left."

The sound she made was half laugh, half sigh. "There's no such thing as being caught up in retail. Where did you hear that?"

"Local grapevine." Not wanting to be curious about what the problem had been, his brow pinched. "I thought you said you had a week off."

"I told you I can only be gone a week," she clarified, aware that he looked more confused than accusing. "I'm still working. I'm just doing it by phone." A little more of her energy faded. "This really isn't a good time for me to be gone."

"At least they got that part right."

"Excuse me?"

"Nothing," Zach muttered, not wanting to be curious about the timing problem, either. He'd been reminding himself ever since he'd walked away with the softness of her skin on his fingers and the feel of her body burned in his brain, that his only concern was the kids. That, and making sure Lauren had what she needed to take care of them and herself. That was the promise he'd made to her brother.

"Is the problem cleared up now?"

"That one is," she said, regarding him a little uncertainly. "I'm sure they'll be more."

"Tonight?"

"Only if I'm being punished for sins from a past life."

Her mumbled response was accompanied by the scrape of chair legs as Jason stood up on his seat. "More ketchup, Zach."

"I don't think so," he muttered to the towheaded youngster climbing toward the bottle in the middle of the table.

From the playpen in the corner came an unhappy whimper. Lauren's attention immediately shifted to the baby, the instincts Zach had questioned carrying her to the child and softening her voice as she picked up the little girl and promised her a clean diaper and dinner, since she was too little for hamburgers just yet.

"Did you get something for her tooth?"

"In the sack." With his arm around Jason's waist, Zach swung him to the floor and eyed the boy's messy hands. "The drug store was closed, but I ran into the woman who owns the herb shop and video store. She said the stuff she gave me is what Tina used before. By the way," he said, ushering Jason out of the kitchen, "there's a burger there for you, too."

Lauren didn't get a chance to thank him. When she straightened with Jenny in her arms, Zach was already heading down the hall to the bathroom with her nephew. She didn't question the odd combination of businesses he'd mentioned, either. Tonight, there were too many other things on her mind for the peculiarity to do more than register. Zach's behavior was one of them.

She never would have guessed that he would be so good with children. And she definitely would never have pegged him as the type to willingly pitch in and help with their care. But that was what he had done.

It was also what he continued to do by keeping Jason occupied while she fed Jenny and got her ready for bed. By the time she had fixed the baby's bottle, he had helped Jason through the ritual of brushing his teeth and changing into pajamas and was reading him a story in his room. She could hear the low, soothing tones of his voice as she cuddled the tired baby in her arms in the pink-and-white nursery and rocked her to the gentle creak of the rocking chair.

Jenny was asleep in minutes.

Since he hadn't had a nap that day, Jason hadn't lasted much longer than his baby sister.

"He's out. We didn't even make it to the end of the story."

Lauren glanced up from where she was sweeping French fries from under the table.

Zach remained in the doorway, his shoulders seeming to fill the space as he watched her prop the broom against the wall. He made no effort to enter the kitchen and she could hear the jingle of his keys when he pushed his hand into the front pocket of his pants. Now that there was no longer reason for him to stay, she could only assume he was preparing to leave.

As she had all evening, Lauren moved from one task to the next without letting herself think about much more than simply what needed to be done.

He would need the jacket he'd left draped over one of the stools on the dining side of the counter. Knowing that, she picked it up and brushed a cracker crumb from one leather sleeve.

"He had to be exhausted," she replied, walking toward him. "It was a really hard day for him. With his mom gone. And with his dad not being here, I mean."

His smoke-gray gaze held hers when she stopped in front of him, his deep voice quiet and a little chiding. "I know what you meant, Lauren. I could see that it was rough."

For both of you, he could have said, but it seemed safer to keep his focus on the children. If he let himself consider how weary she looked, he would be tempted to smooth her tousled hair from her face, take her by the shoulders and steer her to the nearest bed. But touching her didn't seem like a good idea when he'd spent the better part of the evening avoiding just that.

The woman looked as if she had just come in from a storm, and the kindest thing he could say about the faded and worn sweats that camouflaged her every curve was that they held up well against a drooling baby. Yet, even as bedraggled as she looked, the thought of getting her near a bed conjured images of his hands tangling in all that silky-looking hair, her lovely mouth softening beneath his and her long limbs wrapped around his body.

Forcing his glance from her mouth, he noticed that she'd crossed her arms over his jacket. The protective stance seemed to be becoming a habit around him.

"The day was rough," she agreed, "but you being here made it so much easier for him tonight." She offered a faint smile, looking as if she really wanted him to know that. "Thank you for staying."

"I was glad to do it. Jase is my buddy."

"I noticed," Lauren murmured, watching his hands as he withdrew his keys and picked out a silver one. He had wonderful hands. Strong. Capable. Yet, they were gentle enough to soothe a child—and to arouse a woman.

Hugging her arms more tightly, she lifted her eyes to his. "May I ask you something?"

Beneath the heavy knit of his sweater, his broad shoulders lifted in a shrug. "Sure."

"Do you have children of your own?"

"Why do you ask?"

"Because you're so good with them." Having had a family could easily explain his comfort with her niece and nephew. Having lost that family could also explain the wall he had erected between parts of his life and the rest of the world. "Children, I mean."

"If I am, it's because I like kids," he admitted with an ease she wouldn't have expected, "and Sam's are the best. Jenny's still kind of little, but Jase is great.

"And no," he told her because she still looked curious, "I don't have any of my own." He'd planned to have them. Just as she had. It just hadn't worked out for him, either. "My brother has a couple of girls, but he's on the east coast and I never see them. These two are more like family than they are."

"I'd heard that. That you were like family to Sam and Tina," she explained. "And like an uncle to the children."

She'd heard it. She just hadn't had any idea how truly well he must have fitted into their lives. He had moved through Jason's bedtime routine well enough to betray how often he must have heard or observed the ritual. Having witnessed his efficiency, she wouldn't be surprised at all to learn that he'd helped Sam with those same routines on evenings Tina had attended community or church meetings.

His keys clicked together when he curled them into his palm. "You've probably figured out by now that I feel that way about them, too." A faint edge marred his tone, adding an odd note of defense to the statement before he stepped closer. "May I?" he asked, holding out his other hand.

"May you...?"

"Have my jacket? You're choking it."

Lauren's glance jerked to the stranglehold she had on the rich coffee-colored leather. The man was becoming more of a mystery to her by the moment. So were her responses to him when she felt his fingers close around her wrist and he lifted her hand to free his coat.

Beneath his fingers, her pulse leapt.

"Of course," she murmured, letting go.

"Thanks."

He'd felt the betraying leap himself. She was sure of it from the caution that slipped into his eyes in the moments before he turned, shrugging on his jacket, and headed for the front door.

She followed, needing to lock the door behind him.

"I'll see you tomorrow," was all he said before he opened the door himself and walked out while she was still trying to think of why it was that that wouldn't be necessary.

After the day she'd had, the reasons wouldn't form. She would have been lost that evening without him.

Latching the door and leaning against it, finally giving her body permission to admit fatigue, she knew she'd be a fool to deny that, too. Had the evening gone like the day, it would have been monstrous to handle alone. But her thoughts were crowded, as much with what he'd revealed about himself as with her gratitude for what he'd done.

She'd really had no idea of all he stood to lose if her brother left Harbor. He'd even admitted that he was closer to her brother's family than he was to his own.

As she headed through the house, checking locks and turning out lights, she couldn't help but wonder what had brought him to live so far from the people who should have cared about him most.

She fell asleep that night with the same thought nagging at her—and awoke wishing she had his special touch with Jason.

It was a good news, bad news sort of morning. Being an optimist, Lauren chose to focus on the good news part. For once, the sky wasn't dripping. Even better, the herbal concoction Zach had bought from the lady at the herb and video store soothed Jenny's sore little gums enough that the child was actually giggling as Lauren tried to figure out the straps on her car seat. The fact that the little girl was bouncing and waving her bunny wasn't helping her efforts, but the child was happy and Lauren was learning in a hurry how to work around a moving obstacle.

Her sense of accomplishment was totally out of proportion to the task, but she couldn't believe how good she felt when she finally snapped the strap's lock into place.

Jenny congratulated her with a drooling grin.

Lauren was actually on schedule. That was only because she'd made herself get up an hour early so she could shower before the kids woke, but removing an hour's sleep from the agenda seemed a small price to pay for the sense of control that had been missing yesterday.

The not-so-good news was Jason. He'd had another accident in bed and the first person he'd asked for that morning had been his dad. At least with his father, she could assure him that nothing bad had happened to him and that his dad was coming back soon. But she wasn't sure the child was convinced by her claims. His mom had left and never returned, and Lauren had the feeling Jason was afraid the situation would be the same with Sam.

At that very moment, he stood on the redwood bench on the porch in his thick red parka, craning his neck to see down the graveled drive that led into the spacious, open yard. He'd told her he was going to watch for his dad.

"Come on, sweetie," she called to him. "We have to go now."

Backing from the rear seat of the family-friendly Suburban, she lifted her hand to hold back the hair the wind tugged from her clip. In the distance, she could hear the crash of the sea against the enormous boulders of the inlet. Behind her, the dark emerald of pine trees was muted by the wispy, low-lying fog that kept the inlet from view.

"We don't want to be late for preschool, Jason."

"No-o," he called back, the two-tone way he sang the word more pleading than defiant. "I'm waiting for Daddy."

"Honey, your dad isn't coming home today. Remember what I showed you on the calendar? We cross off every day and when we make five more Xs he'll be here."

He wasn't listening. Not to her anyway. Utterly determined to do what he'd said, he climbed onto the narrow arm of the long bench, balancing himself like a tightrope walker as he looked back toward the road.

"Jason, be careful! Jason!" she repeated as he rose on tiptoe to see farther. "Get down!"

"It's Zach!" Arms outspread, a smile on his face, he leapt off the arm and landed on all fours an inch from the railing. A gasp later, he was on his feet and racing across the porch and down the steps as the drone of a powerful engine robbed the peace from the brisk, breezy air.

Lauren had barely taken a half a dozen steps toward the porch to haul Jason down herself when he'd launched himself from the bench and scrambled to his feet. Not totally sure who was jerking around with her heart rate the most—her nephew or his hero—she turned from where she'd come to a halt on the lawn and watched him run full steam ahead toward the truck materializing like a great black beast out of the thready mist.

With the breeze swirling the low patches of fog over the ground, her surroundings seemed almost surreal. That feeling was compounded when Zach stopped to let Jason in the passenger door of his truck, then killed his engine and got out with the muffled slam of his door. He headed straight for her, his long, powerful strides shrinking the distance and his focus steady on her face.

He hadn't bothered with a jacket. But the heavy fleece shirt he wore made his shoulders look impossibly wide when he set his hands on the hips of his jeans.

"I think I know how we can do this," he began without preamble. "I have to go by here every morning on my way to the airfield, so I might as well take Jase into school. I won't be able to pick him up, but that'll save you one trip into town a day. Did you call the oil company?"

The breeze fluttered a lock of hair by her cheek. Snagging it back, she eyed him in confusion. "Yes, I did," she replied, not at all sure what the "this" was that had him looking so utterly certain. "But you don't have to take Jason to school. That's where we're headed now."

"Were you going into town for anything else?"

"Not just yet," she had to admit.

"Then it doesn't make any sense for you to make the drive when I'm going in anyway. When are they coming?"

"The oil people?"

"Yeah," he muttered, as if he couldn't imagine what else she thought they were talking about. "The oil people."

Keeping up with him was like keeping up with Jason. Still confused by his purpose, she focused on his concern about the lack of heat. "Not for a few days," she replied, thinking that the first lesson one needed to learn in order to live on Harbor was to plan ahead. "We're on the schedule for the end of the week."

His mouth thinned as his glance cut to the lean-to at the end of the house. Beneath the low, wide shelter, cords of firewood lay neatly stacked. She'd moved several of those logs to the porch.

Noticing that, his focus shifted back to her. "Then I'll take care of getting the wood in, too. You can take care of everything else with the kids and house."

The note of conclusion in his voice made it apparent that he'd given the matter his due consideration, and that he deemed his solution appropriate. The only problem was that she didn't regard the problem as his to solve.

"Look. Zach," she murmured, not wanting to appear ungrateful, but not caring much for his tendency to steamroll, either, "I appreciated your help last night. I really did. But I have everything under control now. There's no need for me to impose on you that much."

Having shared her own conclusion, and wanting to stay in control by not getting behind, she turned her attention to her duties and the little girl straining against the straps holding her into her car seat. Jenny's tiny fingers grasped toward the bunny she'd dropped.

Lauren had barely stepped toward the car to retrieve it when she felt Zach's fingers circle her arm. Even through the layers of her turtleneck, her sweater and the beige anorak jacket she wore with her jeans, she could feel the insistence in his light grip.

"You won't be imposing," he informed her quietly. "And don't tell me you can do it yourself," he insisted when her mouth opened in protest, "I know you can. But it will be a lot easier on both of us if we work together on this. You have an obligation to your brother. So do I. And I'm as intent as you are on seeing it through."

With a nod toward his truck, he drew her attention to the little boy sitting quietly in the passenger seat. "It'll be easier on the kids, too."

His mention of the children effectively cancelled Lauren's objections. Zach could practically see her mentally putting the brakes on her arguments as hesitation entered the clear blue of her eyes.

He had no idea why she resisted accepting help, but he knew she wouldn't ask for it for herself. He'd noticed that about her before. Just as he'd noticed how she swallowed her pride to accept help when it was necessary for someone else. He liked that about her, that selflessness. He had to admit, too, that he was drawn by her indomitable spirit. She didn't seem to balk at anything she had to do, whether she knew how to do it or not.

Beneath his hand, he became aware of a faint tension shifting through her slender muscles. Or maybe, he considered, the tension he felt was in him. Realizing that he'd yet to let go, and that she'd made no attempt to move, he loosened his hold.

Her breath eased out as his hand slid away.

Lauren hadn't even been aware she'd been holding it.

"I won't argue with you about you taking Jason to school," she conceded, forcing herself to concentrate on compromise. "It would be good for him to know he'll see you every morning." She paused, glancing toward the blond head barely visible over the truck's dash. "He can use the reassurance of being with someone familiar. I think he's afraid his dad isn't coming home."

"Why would he think that?"

Because his mom didn't, she started to say, but that silent understanding passed between them the instant his eyes met hers.

"I'll talk to him," he murmured.

"Thanks. I've run out of ways to convince him," she confided. "But I really can handle everything else," she hurried to assure him. "The logs aren't that heavy."

For a moment she thought Zach was actually going to concede. The logs didn't weigh all that much. Certainly no more than the weights she'd lifted at the gym, on the three occasions in the last six months that she'd been there, anyway. She didn't doubt his determination to meet his obligation to Sam, with or without her cooperation, but even he had to admit she could handle that particular task on her own.

He had an odd look on his face, however, as he rubbed the bridge of his nose. "It's not just a matter of them being heavy, Lauren. The logs you have by the front door are from the wrong stack. You need the split logs by the back door. Not the whole ones."

"I want the big ones because they'll burn longer and I won't have to stoke the stove so often."

"The big ones won't burn through. They just sit there and smoke and smolder and go out."

Lauren felt her certainty falter. The idea had seemed

so efficient when she'd first thought of it. "There's not much split stuff back there."

"Then somebody's going to have to split it."

"As...with an ax?"

She'd seen him smile before. At her brother. At Jenny. With Jason. He had a gorgeous smile, actually. The quiet kind that deepened the little lines at the corners of his eyes, kicked up one corner of his mouth and threatened to be positively devastating if he ever put his heart into it.

He'd never bestowed that smile on her. He didn't now, either. She could swear he deliberately suppressed it as its light glinted in his eyes.

"That would be one way of doing it. A chain saw works, too. Wood burns better if the sides are rougher, though." His glance narrowed, the glint still evident. "I don't suppose you've ever used a chain saw, have you?"

The look she gave him was as bland as the oatmeal she'd fed the kids for breakfast. After their little discussion by the potbellied stove the night before last, he probably knew she'd never even touched one.

He said nothing else, though, as he waited for her to decide what she wanted to do.

Even if there had been room in her schedule for chopping wood, her desire to tackle such a task was definitely lacking. She could do it if she had to. Would if she had to. But he was proposing a perfectly logical alternative, and if she had learned anything at all in the years she'd spent moving her way through the ranks at Brenman's, it was that tasks were always better accomplished when assigned to people with the necessary talent or expertise.

"What would work better for you?" she quietly asked. "Chopping it in the morning or after work?"

The corner of Zach's mouth twitched. As stubborn as

she tended to be, he knew she could have gone either
way. But the fact that she accepted his help with something that would only help her actually made him feel
kind of good. "That depends," he told her, and lifted his
hand to her face.

With the tips of his fingers, he pushed back the strands
of silk the wind pulled across her cheek. Her skin felt
cool to his touch, and smooth, like the skin of a peach.
Her hair felt soft, too, incredibly so, when he tucked it
behind her ear.

It was only when that softness registered that he realized what he was doing and slowly pulled his hand away.

"How are you for firewood now?" Taking a step back,
he pushed his hand into his pocket. "Is there enough split
to last until tomorrow?"

He'd been caught as off guard by what he'd done as
she had. Lauren felt certain of that in the awkward moments before she cleared her throat and told him she was
sure there was.

"I'll come earlier tomorrow and split more then. I'm
running a little late now. And no," he said, before she
could even open her mouth, "I'm not that late. You don't
need to take Jason."

She felt oddly disconcerted as she watched him lean
into the back seat of the big red vehicle, hand Jenny her
bunny and unfasten the car seat beside her for her older
brother to use in his truck. Lauren just wasn't sure which
disturbed her more—that he had an uncanny knack for
reading her mind, or the strength of the pull she felt toward
a man who seemed to have adopted her brother's family
rather than find a wife and have children of his own.

She was still wrestling that strange confusion three
hours later when she walked into the Road's End Café

with Jenny slung on her hip and met the woman Doe Adams had insisted knew everything worth knowing about the citizens of Harbor Island.

Chapter Seven

The Road's End Café sat, appropriately, at the end of Main Road, which ended a hundred feet from the ferry dock and would have been Main Street anywhere else. But this was Harbor, and Lauren had come to learn in a hurry that people had their own way of doing things here.

The café itself was an eclectic, brick-walled place filled with paintings by local artists and primordial-looking ferns hanging from the high rafters. An espresso machine that scented the air with hazelnut cream and French roast hovered behind a glass bakery counter laden with a multitude of delectable sins. A trio of old pier posts topped with a plaster pelican guarded the front door and the paned windows were graced with curtains made of Irish lace.

To Lauren it was as if the establishment's owner couldn't decide on a theme or design so she'd chucked convention and simply used whatever appealed to her.

As a person whose desire for order compelled her to co-ordinate everything from outfits to kitchen towels, Lauren rather envied her that freedom.

The chin-length red bob of the chatty owner, Maddy O'Toole, had been streaked with gold to hide the gray, a ready smile softened her sharp features and her green eyes betrayed a keen and sincere interest in every person she met.

Lauren had no more than walked in and introduced herself than the woman ushered her to one of the green upholstered booths, confiding on the way that she was glad they had a chance to meet. After all, she'd heard so much about her.

"I know Joanne Melford was talking about calling you for an interview," the friendly third-generation islander confided as she set a foamy vanilla latte in front of Lauren. "She retired from working the toll booth at the ferry dock last year and is feeling at loose ends, so I know she has the time. And Winona Sykes, she's the wife of our mayor," she helpfully explained, "said she'd already offered to watch your brother's kids, but she's got three little ones of her own and would have to do it at her house. Are you sure Sam won't consider bringing them into town?" she asked, handing Lauren a packet of crackers from the pocket of her kelly-green apron.

"Only if he has to," Lauren replied, peeling off the wrapper and passing a cracker to Jenny, who was gnawing on her bunny in the booster chair across from her. She had taken Doe Adams's advice and called Maddy two days ago to ask if she would post an ad on her bulletin board. Since the woman Lauren had scheduled to interview that afternoon had canceled, and since she had twenty minutes before she needed to pick up Jason, now had seemed as good a time as any to see if there had been any responses to it.

"He wants to lessen the adjustments the children have to make," she explained to the woman smiling at the baby. "It will be easier to do that if they stay in a familiar place. He's going to need help with housework and cooking, too," she told her, repeating what she'd relayed on the phone as she slipped off her jacket. "I understand that the weather gets unpredictable here and he doesn't always know if he'll make it back in the evening. That's why he needs a live-in."

"He's decided to stay then?"

Lauren hesitated. She was between the breakfast and lunch rush. Not, she suspected, that there was ever much of a rush for anything in Harbor Cove, especially in winter when the tourists left the islanders alone with their blustery weather. But she was pretty sure the three other customers in the cozy little space were listening to every word they said. The bearded old fisherman alone in the booth across from her had been staring at the same spot on his newspaper since she'd come in, and the two women sitting near the bakery case eyeing the cocoa fudge cake had now gone silent.

Suddenly aware that every word she said could feed the local grapevine, she set her jacket on the seat beside her and reached for her latte. "I'm not sure what decisions he's made," she said carefully. "I'm just watching Jenny and Jason for him until I can find them a babysitter."

Maddy looked thoughtful. "Your mom said there's a good chance he'll go back to Seattle."

Lauren couldn't help her faint frown. Her mother, it seemed, was getting a little ahead of herself. "You met my mom?"

"More than met her," the forty-something woman assured with a smile. "She'd drop off Jason at preschool every morning while she was here and come in with this sweet little thing." Reaching over, she absently smoothed Jenny's cornsilk curls. "She'd have coffee and a bagel and we'd visit."

Her voice dropped, confiding, sympathetic. "I know she's worried sick about Sam and his babies. No one can blame her for that. But like I told her, he has good friends here. And he's got his work. And there's bound to be someone willing to work for him at his house. I bet Doe would even do it if he'd get rid of the rawhide," she claimed. "But I can see where your mom would be wanting the little ones closer to her."

She sighed, sounding very much like a woman wanting grandchildren of her own, then stuffed her hand in her apron pocket. The emerald studs in her ears shimmered as she shook her head. "As much as we'd hate to see Sam go, Zach McKendrick has to be sick at the idea. Not that he'd ever say so," she murmured. "All he's said to anyone about any of this is that Sam will do whatever he needs to do, and there's no sense speculating about what that something will be."

She clearly found that bit of logic totally unenlightening.

Lauren thought it sounded just like Zach.

"We're all sure the business will be fine," Maddy continued, looking as if Zach's restrained attitude could be a source of frustration on any number of levels. "All you have to do is see that house of his to know he has money, and I'm sure he can find another pilot if need be. But that man is nuts about Sam's kids. Anyone who's ever seen him with that little boy knows it. Joanne even ran into him with Jason over at the preschool a couple of hours ago,'' she pointed out, shaking her head, her bangs swaying. By the time they stopped, the arches of her carefully penciled eyebrows had almost merged. "He told her he was dropping him off for you."

As curious as the chatty woman was, it seemed she didn't feel she could just come right out and ask Lauren why he'd done that. After all, she was there specifically to take care of the children. So why would her brother's friend be doing part of her job for her?

"He's just helping us out," Lauren replied, seeing no reason to define who "us" was. There was no need for the town to know that her brother wasn't around just then. It was no one's business how totally lost Sam felt, or how his grieving had affected his work. Zach was obviously protecting him on that score, and she would, too. "He's been a good friend to Sam."

The curiosity that had entered Maddy's keen eyes moments ago moved to full-blown speculation as Lauren finally lifted her mug.

"I'm sure he has," Maddy quietly agreed. "Zach's a good friend to a lot of people. He's who we call when we need help with everything from search and rescue to moving something heavy. And some of those old-timers back in the woods could get sick and die in their cabins if he didn't hike in there and check on them once in a while."

Her head tipped thoughtfully, her hair gleaming like the copper pots suspended from the brick walls. "I've never known him to walk away from any situation he thought he could make easier for someone else. You don't even have to ask and he's there."

Like this morning, Lauren thought, wondering at the fondness in the vivacious woman's tone. He'd charged in like a rescuing knight to announce his solution to her situation. Only now she knew there had apparently been nothing at all extraordinary about him wanting to help her.

"What do you think of him?" Maddy asked.

The question caught Lauren off guard. She wasn't totally sure what she thought of him anymore. But there was no mistaking Maddy's admiration of the man. Ever since Zach's name had been mentioned her manner had become more intense, more interested.

It was entirely possible, Lauren realized, that Maddy O'Toole had a thing for him.

She also realized that whatever opinion she shared was about to become public.

"I think my brother is lucky to have him for a friend," she replied, giving away nothing of the indefinable little pang she felt. As attractive as Zach was, as disturbingly…male, of course he would have a woman somewhere.

The owner of the café glanced toward the older man in the opposite booth. Having heard nothing that interested him, he'd finally turned a page of the newspaper and was working on his ham and eggs. The women near the pastry case, however, were clearly straining to hear.

Looking as if she simply couldn't help herself, Maddy slipped into the booth beside Jenny and leaned toward Lauren. "I mean as a man," she practically whispered. "Do you know much about him?"

"I only met him a few days ago."

"Your brother hasn't ever said anything about him, though? Like what happened with his wife? Or what his life was like before he came here? We know he got that scar when he crashed a jet. It was apparently some military hush-hush thing because he won't ever talk about it. But he rarely says anything about himself," she stressed, clearly baffled by that fact. "He won't even date anyone around here, so it's not like he has any annoyed exes willing to spill what they know."

"Maybe he has a girlfriend in one of the places he flies to," Lauren suggested, a little baffled herself by what she was learning.

"That's what Crystal thinks."

"Crystal?"

"She owns the herb and video shop. Sydney Sheridan thinks so, too. She has the pottery shop across from the post office," Maddy said by way of identification. "Sydney insists that a man that hot has to be getting it somewhere."

Sydney sounded very astute.

Preferring to block the provocative images of Zach that formed in her mind, Lauren picked up her latte. "Probably," she murmured, taking a sip of foam.

"Oh, well." Maddy blew a breath that caused her bangs to flutter. "I've always thought he'd be perfect for T.J., Crystal's daughter," she explained with alacrity. "So does Crystal. He likes her a lot, too. He even told me he thinks she's one of the nicest women he's ever met and that's why he doesn't want to lose her as a friend. He says that's what'll happen if he goes out with her, too, because Harbor is too small a place for ex-lovers. It's like he just *knows* a relationship will be over before he even gives it a chance to start."

For a moment, Lauren simply stared at the woman's totally perplexed expression. She had to admit that it did sound as if Zach had no faith in the permanence of relationships. Or, maybe, he simply lacked interest in a permanent one himself. Despite his involvement in the community and his friendship with her brother's family, there was something very remote about him. Something very solitary.

Even as she acknowledged the incongruity, becoming more aware of the isolation she sensed in him, she couldn't help the smile tugging at her mouth.

Maddy wasn't interested in Zach for herself, Lauren realized. The woman was just a dyed-in-the-wool matchmaker.

"He dated Moonbeam from the Natural Earth Spa," one of the women by the case supplied.

"They weren't dating," the other chimed in. "He was just helping her get her roof back on after that storm. I think we've decided on that cake, Maddy. We're going to split a piece."

Maddy apparently hadn't realized that her voice had returned to more audible tones, but any consternation she felt about having been overheard was forgotten as she told Lauren she'd be right back, slid from the booth and headed behind the counter, stopping to refill the elderly gentleman's coffee mug on the way.

Lauren would have loved to stay and hear whatever else the women would have cared to share, but she needed to pick up Jason. Even if she had decided to be a little late, by the time she cleaned the soggy cracker crumbs from Jenny's grinning little face and bundled her into her puffy pink parka, the clang of the big brass bell at the pier announced the arrival of the noon ferry. The ferry usually brought a few hungry passengers, and the lunch crowd was already drifting in.

From the side window of his plane, Zach caught a glimpse of the ferry as he left the airstrip behind and banked west. He'd wanted to leave hours ago, but he'd had to wait for the low-lying fog to clear before he could take off. He was flying VFR today—Visual Flight Rules—since many of his primitive destinations didn't have approach controllers and the sophisticated electronics that made instrument flying possible. Some of the places where he landed didn't have much more than hard-packed earth for a runway, and barely enough length to set a plane on at that.

Below him, he could still see thready patches of the mist that had delayed him hovering over Harbor and the ocean, but he had a clear view of his first destination, a tiny dot of an island three islands due north. He was behind schedule, but he could make up the time with his deliveries of mail and provisions if those patches of fog didn't merge into a gray blanket that would make it impossible to see to land. If Lauren was on her schedule, she would be picking Jason up right about now.

With a frown, his glance swung to his altimeter, and he began to level off. Thinking about Lauren wasn't anything he wanted to do right now. Just the thought of her made him edgy and restless, and he was already feeling restless enough to pace out of his skin. What he should be considering was what he would do if Sam decided to leave. But neither the option of selling one of the planes or hiring another pilot made him feel any calmer. And thoughts of Lauren intruded anyway.

He hadn't realized how badly he'd wanted to touch her until he'd found himself doing just that. The fact that she had so easily accepted the contact had only made it that much harder not to do it again.

From the corner of his eye, he glimpsed another small plane paralleling his course a half a mile away. Keeping an eye on the traffic, which could be considerable in a place where people relied on wings for transportation the way most people did wheels, he reminded himself that he was doing the right thing by checking up on her in the mornings. By not stopping at night, there was less chance of being alone with her, and more chance of keeping everything focused right where it should be. On her brother and the kids.

That was the conclusion he'd drawn after he'd left her last night. It was sensible. Practical. It was also the easiest way he could think of to keep his word to his friend.

He'd repeated that same logic to himself all the way home last evening. Even then, he'd very nearly gone back to see if she was all right. But with the kids in bed, and as tired as she'd looked, he'd known there hadn't been a thing he could have done for her. He'd also known that what he'd really wanted was to pull her into his arms.

It was one thing to care about her situation. It was another entirely to let her get under his skin. So he would do what he had to do and avoid her when he could— which was why he arrived at the crack of dawn the next morning to chop wood and carry in a load before taking Jason to preschool. Since Lauren was running late with the kids' breakfast, there was no time for any conversation that didn't deal with getting Jason out the door. That was fine with Zach. In his mind his plans were right on track.

Unfortunately, those particular plans only worked for one day. They were derailed completely the next by the weather.

Zach had his keys and his coffee in his hand at eight in the morning when Henry Putnam's nurse caught him walking out the door. Henry was one of the two doctors in the island's small clinic. The white-haired old islander could handle anything from flu to fractures and the occasional birth, but without a hospital on the island and with one of his elderly patients having chest pains, he needed emergency transport to the hospital in Bellingham, twenty miles away.

Zach had pulled out two seats from one of E&M's six-passenger Cessnas to lock the stretcher into place and was in the air with the doctor, his patient and his patient's distraught wife half an hour after the nurse called. The only call he made himself was to Chuck. He radioed from the air to tell him what was going on and asked him to call Lauren so she could take Jason to school. He also asked him to tell her he'd stop by sometime that evening, then moved on to switching runs with Chuck since he was already on his way to Bellingham. He would pick up the plane part that had come in the day before yesterday and do the courier deliveries on Chuck's schedule. Chuck could do the mail runs.

Focused on work, the patient in back and the low visibility, Zach's actions were automatic, his thoughts controlled. There were times when he sorely missed the pure adrenaline rush of putting a jet through its paces, of making split-second decisions at speeds that punched holes in the sound barrier. He missed the responsiveness and feel of a machine so finely tuned that just thinking a command could almost make it so. But he was flying, and that was all that really mattered to him.

He never gave much thought anymore to the time when the doctors and therapists had all said he'd never have a throttle in his hand again. He'd even forgotten the fear he'd felt the first time he'd sat in the left seat four years after that pronouncement.

Almost forgotten it, anyway. He had a different perspective on flying now.

His fingers flexed on the T-shaped control, his mind instinctively absorbing the information on the instruments in front of him, the feel of the plane under him, the voice coming through his headset from the tower in Bellingham okaying his approach.

He had a different perspective on a lot of things.

"How's the wood holding up?"

"There's enough to get the fires going in the morning. I don't think you need to bring any in tonight."

"I'd rather do it now, in case something comes up again and I can't make it back in the morning." Looking as intent as he sounded, Zach headed for the kitchen doorway. His dark hair covered the collar of his brown leather jacket. Faded jeans hugged his lean hips and long legs. "You're going through it faster using both the fireplace and the stove anyway."

Lauren stood in front of the gray stone fireplace in the living room holding Jenny bundled in a thick blue towel. Jason sat huddled on the sofa, wrapped in a towel of his own. Cuddling the baby closer, she watched Zach disappear and heard the door of the mudroom open.

He had arrived thirty seconds ago, ruffled the towel draped over Jason's head, made his pronouncement and swept through the room, seeming to take all the oxygen with him on his way.

After Maddy's comments about him, Lauren was fairly certain she wasn't the only person he left blinking in his wake. If he decided something needed to be done or he saw a problem to fix, he simply moved in, took care of it and moved on with the cool efficiency of an attack force. She'd seen him do it with her brother. He'd done it with her.

She couldn't help but wish she could turn him loose on her suddenly impossible boss.

Drawing a breath that brought the scents of soap and

baby shampoo, she returned her attention to the kids. She had the whole evening to worry about what was going on at the store. Right now, she needed to think about the children.

To mask her agitation, she smiled at the little boy leaning over the sofa arm to see where his buddy had gone. "Come over by the fire and let's get you dressed before you freeze."

"I want Zach to do it."

"I'm sure you do," she agreed. Jason had been asking for Zach all day. And all day, she'd kept assuring him that he would arrive. She hadn't minded at all. It was better than him crying for his mom and dad. "But he's busy."

"What's he doin'?"

"Bringing in wood."

"Like Daddy?"

Sinking to her knees in front of the crackling blaze, she sat Jenny down by the two pair of pajamas she had dropped on the rug. "Like Daddy," she echoed, swearing she could feel Zach's glance on her back as she dried off Jenny's little arms and chest and pulled her yellow pajama top over her head. With an expertise she'd lacked only days ago, she had the diaper and bottoms on the wriggling child moments later and was towel-drying Jenny's hair.

Jason had decided he would be warmer by the fire after all and sat down by his sister. "Can I watch Hot Wheels?"

"Sure," she murmured, marveling at the child's mental leaps of subject—and quietly relieved that he hadn't pursued the subject of his father. Pointing out the Xs on the calendar only worked once in a while. "We'll start it after we get your pj's on. You can watch it while I get your sister into bed.''

"No-o," he moaned in that two-tone, singsong way that managed to give the word two syllables. "I want daddy to watch it with me.''

"Sweetie, you know your daddy isn't here right now.''

"Then, Zach.''

"Zach's busy.''

"Uh-uh.''

"Yes-uh," she mimicked back. Smiling, she touched her finger to his little nose—and looked up to see the man presently under discussion standing in the doorway.

He had a load of split logs in his arms. Looking very rugged, and maybe a little impatient with his brow draw down, Zach's glance moved slowly from the children to her.

She had been vaguely aware of him opening and closing the back door. Mostly because a cold draft drifted across the floor each time he'd done it. Preoccupied with the children, she hadn't realized he'd also intended to bring in a load of wood for the living room.

"Are we in your way?" she asked, thinking they probably were. She had the kids sitting on the rug directly in front of the warming fire, a few feet back from the wide, foot-high stone hearth.

For a moment, Zach said nothing. On his way through the kitchen, he'd noticed that Lauren had cleared the table and put the dinner dishes in the sink, but that the counter was spread with papers from her open briefcase. The telephone lay atop a yellow legal pad covered with notes.

It was obvious that she was still trying to keep up with her job while managing the kids and an unfamiliar house. She seemed to have a better handle on the latter tasks, too. But that wasn't what impressed him as he watched the firelight throw shades of gold into her wheat-colored hair.

The sweater she wore with her jeans was a shade of blue that made her eyes look as dark as sapphires. Her hair was pulled up in its usual clip and a few rebellious strands of it tumbled loosely around her face. The heat of the fire flushed her cheeks.

She looked beautiful in the golden light, seductive in a way that coiled pure molten heat low in his gut. Yet, what rooted him in the doorway was the gentleness in her voice as she'd talked with Jason, and the ease in her manner with both of the children. That ease definitely hadn't been there just a few short days ago.

She had been right. There was nothing at all wrong with her nurturing instincts. But there was something inherently dangerous about a woman who could make a man ache to seduce her even as he realized what a great mom she'd make.

"You're fine," he finally muttered, jerking his glance to the hearth. "Keep the kids where they are. Is there anything else you need for me to do before I go?"

"Actually, there is," she told him, pulling Jason's towel back over his head to dry his hair. "Are you in a hurry?"

Logs clattered against stone as he stacked them in the built-in bin. "There's nowhere I have to be just now, if that's what you mean. What do you need?"

She had Jason's cooperation, but the baby had crawled to the hearth to pull herself up. Too preoccupied to notice how Zach qualified his response, she snagged the wobbling little girl around the middle, headed the baby toward the coffee table at a crawl and looked to where Zach glanced over his shoulder.

"Help with this guy," she said, pulling Jason around

to snug his back to her front while she dried off his sturdy little legs. "He needs someone other than me to watch a video with him."

"Zach can dry me."

"Drying you is my job," she said to the child, drying between little toes.

"No. Him."

With a slow blink, she met Zach's eyes.

"He really could use your company," she murmured, her eyes soft and caring as she smoothed back the little boy's damp hair. "As long as we've agreed to split some of the responsibilities, it would make my life a whole lot easier if you'd plant yourself in front of the television with him while I get Jenny into bed."

Suddenly agreeable, Jason looked wide-eyed at his friend. "Can I sit on your lap?"

At the quiet request, Zach turned and sat on the hearth. With his booted feet planted two feet apart, he rested his elbows on his denim-covered thighs and considered the child tucked against Lauren.

Jason had never made such a request of him before. He usually only sat on his dad's lap to watch television. Over the past couple of years, Jason would sit beside Zach. He would lie at his feet. He would even prop himself against him as if he were the back of a chair. But he'd never, not once, asked Zach to hold him.

The child was asking to be held now, though. From the way Lauren held his glance over the boy's head, her eyes sympathetic, it was obvious she understood that, too.

Zach's determination to take care of whatever needed to be done and leave was suddenly history. Between the guileless expression in her delicate features and Jason's big, blue-eyed plea, there wasn't a force on earth that could have made him say anything other than, "Sure."

A smile exposed Jason's dimple. Tipping his head back to his aunt, he let her see it, too, then helpfully pulled on his pajama bottoms.

"It'll be a minute, though," he warned the little boy. "I need to bring in wood for the stove first."

"Is that your job?"

"Yeah. That's my job."

"'Kay," the child replied, the easy acceptance making it sound as if, at that moment, all was as right as it could be in his little world.

It felt good to Zach to know that he had provided that moment's ease. Feeling the warmth in Lauren's grateful smile, he had to admit how good it felt, too, to know that she needed him to help her. He just didn't allow himself to consider the phenomenon too closely as he finished his tasks, then made Jason squeal when he hauled him to the sofa after the little boy had put in the proper video.

"Don't get him wound up!"

"Yes, ma'am," he called back and turned a conspiratorial grin to the little boy lying against his chest. Though Jason smiled back, it seemed to Zach that everything about the youngster was subdued. Even his little screech had sounded half-hearted.

His smile faded as he held the sweet-smelling child a little tighter.

He really could use your company, Lauren had said. And that was what took precedence right now. It didn't matter that he would eventually find himself alone with the woman he could hear murmuring softly to the baby in the next room. Lauren seemed to have accepted his presence, just as he had accepted the fact that hers was necessary, too. So he would do what he'd done the other night and stay until the little boy fell asleep. Then, when there was no longer reason for him to stick around, he would leave.

The only problem he encountered with that decision was that the longer he stayed, the more aware he became of Lauren moving through the rooms picking up toys, doing dishes and checking to make sure the windows were locked when there was no reason she would have unlocked them to begin with. And the closer it came to the time for him to leave, the more aware he became of her growing agitation.

He'd first noticed her disquiet shortly after she came from the baby's room.

By the time he'd tucked a sleeping Jason into bed and was heading for the kitchen, he was beginning to wonder if she was doing okay in the house at night by herself.

Knowing he probably should have already asked if she was, feeling a little guilty that he hadn't, he stopped inside the kitchen doorway. She was at the counter, restively tapping a pen against the ceramic tiled surface and frowning at the notes she'd pulled from under the phone.

"Lauren," he began, his expression as preoccupied as hers, "how are you doing being alone here with the kids?"

Whatever she was so focused on had her full attention. Her head came up, incomprehension written clearly in her elegant features.

"I can see that you're doing better with them," he explained. "I'm talking about being so far from town."

"Oh," she murmured, the agitation he'd noticed before still evident in the distracted way she continued to tap her pen. "I try not to think about it. At night, anyway," she qualified. "During the day, I've been too busy to give it much thought." Her glance slid past his arm, her thoughts seeming torn as the tapping stopped. "I should check Jason."

"He's fine."

"He didn't wake up when you put him to bed?"

Something was bothering her. He could tell by the twin worry lines spiking between the wings of her eyebrows. The problem just didn't appear to be what he'd thought it was. She really didn't seem to be concerned with being alone in such a remote place. Not the way Sam's wife had been.

Grateful for the reprieve, not crazy about what he would have felt compelled to offer if she had had a problem with it, he pushed his hands into his pockets and leaned against the door frame.

"He didn't even open his eyes," he told her, then nodded toward the papers on the counter. He'd told her brother he would look out for her. Because of that, he wanted to know what was wrong. "Another crisis at work?"

The sound she made was half laugh, half groan as she shifted gears once more. "Not really. There are certain times of the year in retail when you can expect nothing will go right. If a person accepts that as the norm, then everything is easier to deal with."

"You sound as if you actually expect things to go wrong."

"I do."

"Always?"

"More often than not."

She watched Zach's dark eyebrows merge at her unequivocal response. His frown seemed more thoughtful than disapproving as he watched her, though, the contemplative expression more appealing than intimidating. But, then, the way he'd looked cradling her sleeping nephew against his broad chest had made him seem terribly appealing, too.

Pulling her glance from his, she ignored the hint of longing he'd caused her to feel when she'd caught glimpses of him with Jason. The feeling wasn't anything she wanted to explore. Especially with him so near. What she'd felt tugged at buried dreams, and needs long denied. Needs that grew stronger every time she thought about being held in his arms herself.

"I never would have thought you a pessimist," he told her.

"I don't think I am." Trading her disturbed thoughts for what had been troubling her when he'd walked in, she toyed with the edge of her pad. "It's just that, between staffing, merchandising and loss prevention, there's never a day without problems.

"Then there's coordinating with advertising, customer service and dealing with vendors," she muttered, because those could be the real headaches. "If you expect things to go wrong, then you're not thrown when they do."

"And if by some miracle they don't, it's a bonus," he concluded. "You don't have to convince me," he said, his tone matter-of-fact, "I had the same attitude about a job once." His glance swung to the pad she fidgeted with. "So what went wrong today?"

The job he'd once had was flying jets with systems that had yet to be proved. Of course he would know what she was talking about, she thought. Every time he crawled into a cockpit, he had to expect that something could go wrong. Drastically so.

She couldn't begin to relate to why he'd chosen such a profession, but she didn't doubt for an instant that he understood crisis management.

"The flu has us short-staffed so we had to bring in

temps. Inventory is two days behind for the same reason, and Andy is yelling at me because the home office is going to yell at him. The inventory clearance sale isn't moving merchandise off the floor fast enough in the Tacoma store so we're getting half of their markdowns, which means we can't move new merchandise from the stockrooms onto the floor.'' She took a deep breath, released it. None of that was extraordinary. It was simply business as usual and part of the industry the public never saw. But there had been one little glitch in the day that did have her concerned. ''And I missed a meeting.''

Considering what she'd just told him, she could think of a dozen questions he might have asked.

All he said was, ''Andy?''

''He's my boss.''

''Does he always jump on you when there's a problem?''

Lauren hugged the long pad to her middle and crossed her arms over it. ''Not usually.''

''So why now? Because of the inventory?''

''It's not the inventory that's bothering him. That was just the catalyst. He's jumping on me because I should be there and I'm not,'' she admitted, since the real reason Andy was being crankier than usual was because she was gone.

It didn't matter that Ruth had called her about the staffing problem and that Lauren had authorized the number of temps to hire before he'd even known how shorthanded they were. It didn't matter that there was really nothing she could do at the store at the moment that she wasn't handling right from where she was. Andy was feeling pressures of his own and he clearly regretted that he'd allowed her to go. He'd even told her he'd changed his mind and wanted her back tomorrow. Her insides had knotted in panic, but she'd maintained her composure and calmly said she'd be there, but that she'd have to bring her brother's kids in with her. Ten seconds of silence later, he'd changed his mind again and said she could have the rest of the week after all.

She was trying hard not to let his unreasonableness get to her.

"He knows what's going on here, doesn't he? What you're doing for your brother?"

"Of course," she murmured, thinking of how completely she identified with what Zach was going through himself. She was totally torn between her responsibility to Sam and what she might be doing to her job. Zach felt that same unswerving loyalty to her brother and the state of his business seemed no more certain than hers. "It's just not his crisis."

"And the meeting," Zach said, managing to zero in on the only other matter of true concern to her. "Was it important?"

"On a scale of one to ten," she murmured, "it was about a nine. The company is opening a new store in Bellingham, and I'm on the list for manager. Andy's on the list, too. So is the assistant manager of the Mountlake Terrace store. If she gets it, I keep the position I have in Seattle. If Andy gets it, I could get the store where I work now."

"What was the meeting for?"

"The president and the chief operations officer came in to talk about transitioning if one of us leaves."

Zach slowly straightened, the lines fanning from the corners of his eyes deepening as he considered the worry she wasn't even trying to hide. "Do you trust him. This...Andy?"

One slender shoulder rose with an uncertain shrug.

"Andy was my mentor. He gave me more responsibility than I probably had a right to handle at first. I'd worked for a long time as a clerk, but when I let him know I wanted to get into management, he pushed me and taught me and took pride in every promotion I received.

"I don't want to think he'd deliberately sabotage me," she finally admitted, "but I learned a long time ago that most people tend to serve their own interests first. I know he wants the new store. He also knows I'd be happy with either one. I just hope that whatever he says about me being more suited to the Seattle store doesn't leave me out of the running completely."

Old timber creaked as the house settled in for the night. Beyond the log walls the wind picked up, tossing rain against the curtained window. The fact that it had started raining again barely registered with her. Her focus was on the man mentally weighing everything she'd just told him.

"I take it that being store manager is something you really want?"

The disquiet faded from her eyes. Unquestioned certainty replacing it. "I've worked sixty hours a week for the past two years to move up in this company. The only time I wasn't working that much was when I finished school, and then I only worked fifty. Yes," she said with quiet conviction. "I want it."

"Does he have the power at this point to take it away from you?"

"At this point?"

"He's obviously not the only person who knows you're qualified, Lauren. By the time a selection process gets this far, the people who make the final decision are pretty well acquainted with everyone's motivations. Right?"

He spoke as if he believed the logic would certainly have occurred to her, and he was only reinforcing it. It wasn't as if the decision were up to Andy. He might influence it, but not without others being aware of his own motives. That particular bit of rationale, however, had escaped her completely.

She could have kissed Zach for pointing it out to her now.

Since he was keeping such deliberate distance between them, she settled for a smile. "Right," she murmured. "And thank you."

"I didn't do anything."

Her smile softened. "Yes," she countered quietly, "you did." He'd just kept her from stewing all night about Andy. All she had to worry about now was how understanding the president and the COO really were about her absence.

"Can I get you something. Coffee?" she asked, a little uncertain about the protocol now that there was no real reason for him to stick around.

"No, thanks," he murmured. His boots made soft thuds on the floor as he crossed to the mudroom and reached around the doorway for his jacket. "It's been a long day."

Catching her scent as he passed her, trying to ignore its effect on his body, Zach couldn't help thinking it could be an even longer night.

He had wanted to believe that the protectiveness he felt toward her existed only because she was part of his friend's family, part of an obligation he'd agreed to tend. But what he was feeling couldn't be attributed to her relationship to Sam. Or to any promise he'd made her brother. The thought that her boss could undermine what she'd worked so hard for jerked hard at feelings that weren't all that neat and tidy to explain.

As much as the thought disturbed him, it would have bothered him more if she had been sticking around for long. As adamant as she was about wanting the promotion, he didn't doubt for a minute that she would be gone as soon as Sam returned.

There was a reprieve in that knowledge. Something that made her very…safe.

"Do you have everything you need here?" he asked, pulling on his jacket as he headed for the front door. "Milk? That teething stuff?"

"Got it. And Jenny's doing much better, by the way."

"I noticed."

"Zach?"

He stopped with his hand on the knob, the sound of beating rain filtering through the heavy wood.

Her eyes were as clear as a summer sky when they met his.

"Do you think Sam's okay?"

He'd been wondering that himself. "Yeah," he murmured, because she was already worried about so many other things. "I'm sure he's doing…as well as we'd expect," he concluded, unable to look into those incredible eyes and lie.

She seemed to accept that he'd given her the best he could in the moments before she tipped her head, her expression turning thoughtful.

The skin of her neck looked so soft it fairly begged to be touched.

"May I ask a favor of you?"

"Sure," he said, stuffing his hands into his pockets. "What do you need?"

"For you to come back tomorrow night. For Jason."

Chapter Eight

"I know he said he'd be here, honey, but it's really foggy outside. Maybe he just couldn't get back from wherever it is he went today."

Lauren sat on the edge of Jason's bed, waiting for him to crawl back between the race-car-print sheets. Jenny was already asleep. She had been for nearly an hour. But Jason refused to settle down. He kept crawling out of bed and climbing on the blue desk chair he'd pulled under his window, holding vigil for the man she'd told him that morning would be there. Zach had even said he'd try to be in time for dinner.

She wished now that she'd never mentioned that he was coming. The child was far too young to look so worried, and she was going to wring Zach's neck if he wasn't already lying somewhere in a ditch. Even if he couldn't call her himself, he could radio the guy named

Chuck who'd relayed the message from him yesterday and let her know why he was so late.

They had expected him two hours ago.

"Why don't I read you another story?" she suggested, hating the thought of what must be going through her nephew's mind. She held up a book. "We haven't read Dr. Seuss yet."

Soberly, he looked back at her and let the red curtain fall back into place. Without a word, he crawled down from the chair, padded across the room in his footed pajamas and crawled up onto the bed beside her.

Cuddling him close, melting a little inside at the way he nestled into her, she tucked the thick red comforter around him and started to read.

Despite her own concern for Zach, she couldn't help but marvel at how quickly her heart had been lost to these children. She'd loved them before, but she hadn't felt the bond that had been forged in the past few days. It had been a baptism by fire, for certain. For all of them. But they were surviving her, looking to her for their needs, and she couldn't believe how protective she'd come to feel toward her brother's little boy and his precious baby girl.

She couldn't believe, either, how hard it was becoming to deny her longing for a child of her own.

She should have been a mother by now. It had certainly been part of the life she'd envisioned for herself. But, back then, back before she'd realized how easily life's course could be altered, she and Ed had put it off because the timing hadn't been right. There had been school to get through, student loans to pay. His career to establish. Her education to finish. It had never occurred to her during those frugal years of working toward the day when they would start their family, that the man she'd married had no intention of seeing those plans through, and that her future would hold little prospect for nurturing anything other than her job.

Jason's index finger gingerly touched the furrows between her eyebrows. "Are you mad?"

"Oh, no, sweetie," she murmured, making herself smile to prove it. Curling his little fingers in hers, she dropped a kiss to the top of his head and looked back to their story. "Where was I?"

"Right here." Freeing his hand he pointed to the cat in the lopsided hat. A half a page later, his attention totally sidetracked, he jerked his head toward the window.

The deep-throated rumble of the vehicle pulling into the drive had him diving for the chair in three seconds flat.

Because she didn't want him leaping off that chair to race for the door, possibly breaking something in the process, she scooped him into her arms with the announcement that he could let Zach in and hauled him into the living room with her.

She barely caught a glimpse of the fatigue shadowing Zach's carved features when she pushed open the storm door, before Jason fairly leapt into his arms.

"Hey, buddy, let me get out of my coat." Fatigue faded with his deep, pleasant chuckle. "I'm dripping on the floor."

"What happened?"

Lauren hadn't intended to sound so demanding. She especially hadn't planned to look as concerned as she must have, considering the puzzled glance he gave her. Letting Jason slide to the floor after he closed out the cold, he brushed droplets of rain from his dark hair and popped the snaps on his black parka in one quick motion.

Water dripped on the entry rug as she took the garment so he could pick up Jason again.

"Chuck had a problem with his plane. I had to fly a new tire out to him."

"A tire?"

"He had a flat."

"On a plane?"

A shrug entered his voice as he lifted the child clinging to his leg into his arms. "It happens."

She supposed it did, along with all sorts of little mechanical difficulties she'd never considered. She also now understood why he hadn't had Chuck call, since Chuck was who he'd been rescuing. "Don't you guys carry spares?"

"Don't need them often enough to justify taking up the weight and the space. Sorry I'm late," he finally said, rubbing Jason's skinny little back. "There was just no way I could get here sooner. I thought you might be in bed by now," he said to the child hugging his neck. "How come you aren't, squirt?"

Being only three and a half, Jason didn't know how to respond. Because Zach didn't seem to appreciate how concerned his little friend had been, Lauren responded for him.

"Because he was worried about you," she quietly told him. "He's been watching for you from his window."

The ease melted from Zach's expression as he glanced back to her. Comprehension dawned in a heartbeat. "Oh, man," he muttered, "I didn't even think about that. You don't think he thought…?"

"We didn't talk about it."

"But it was pretty obvious?"

"Very."

He winced.

Lauren just shook her head as if she didn't know what to do for the boy, either.

The child was beginning to develop a real fear of the people he cared about disappearing from his life. For all Lauren knew, the fear might have been perfectly normal for his age. After all, she'd learned just that morning from Maddy when she'd stopped again for coffee and conversation, that one-year-olds often develop anxiety with strangers and tend to cling more to their parents, a stage Jenny, blessedly, had yet to enter. But Jason had more reason than most children to become anxious, and it was clear from the way Zach's eyes held hers, that he felt as bad as he did helpless about what the child was going through.

"It'll be better when Sam gets back."

"I hope," she murmured and tipped her head toward the mudroom. "I'll hang up your coat."

Jason still wasn't asleep when Lauren poked her head into his room twenty minutes later. He wasn't going to last much longer, though. He lay tucked under his blankets and comforter, his hair pale against the brightly printed pillowcase and his eyelids growing heavier with each blink. Zach sat where she had been just a short while ago, his dark sable hair flowing down his neck, faded denims stretched over his powerful thighs and a heavy gray sweater turning his eyes the color of smoke.

Seeing her, he turned the book he was reading to the little boy facedown and kept those smoky eyes on hers.

She stepped into the room, drawn in as much by the force of his presence as the reason she'd come to begin with. There was a reckless streak buried beneath all that ruthless control. There had to be, she thought, for him to have done what he had for a living. There was undoubtedly a strong streak of adventure in him, too, considering what he did for a living now. But he also possessed gentleness and patience and the ability to care openly for a child.

That the combination appealed to her should have disturbed her far more than it did.

"Don't let me interrupt you." Lauren kept her voice low, nearly to a whisper. "I just wanted to see how he was doing."

Hearing her anyway, Jason pried open his eyes. Sounding as sleepy as he looked, he struggled to one elbow. "Can I have a drink of water?"

"Of course you can," she murmured, and was back moments later with a yellow plastic tumbler.

Conscious of Zach's eyes following her, more conscious of his big body taking up space on the narrow mattress, she moved to the side of the bed. "Here you go," she quietly said, and held out the cup.

Still propped on his elbow, Jason drank down the small amount of water she'd put in it and wiped his mouth with his pajama sleeve.

Zach's bent knee was inches from hers. Carefully avoiding it as she leaned forward, she took back the tumbler and smoothed Jason's baby-fine hair. "Good night, sweetie," she murmured, and kissed his soft little cheek.

With his arms wrapped around her neck, Jason kissed her back.

"Zach, too."

"Hmm?" she hummed, not understanding.

"Kiss Zach 'night, too."

Her pulse skipped. She had no idea what to say to the innocent directive. She wasn't even sure what had brought it on, unless the child was simply equating kisses with his night-time routine. She didn't consider the request beyond that, though. If humoring him would make him feel more secure somehow, she would do what he asked.

Before it could become a big deal, she turned to the man silently waiting to see what she would do, curved her hand at the side of his neck to bring him closer and gave him a quick kiss on his cheek.

He needed a shave. The thought registered vaguely as she breathed in the enervating scents of sea air and warm male. She was immediately aware of the feel of hard muscle beneath her palm, the heat of his skin and a flutter of response low in her stomach. What unnerved her more was the realization that she'd grabbed the burned side of his neck.

She hadn't even considered which side of his neck she'd reached for—or that his injured skin might be tender. Even as she jerked her hand back, pulling back herself in the hope that she hadn't hurt him, her glance darted to the silvery and striated flesh.

Frowning at what she'd done, her eyes met his. An instant later, she felt her heart sink to her toes.

Seconds ago, his expression had held little beyond a hint of mild curiosity. In the space of seconds, his entire body had stiffened, his eyes had shuttered and he'd deliberately turned his attention from her to the little boy who was already snuggling back down beneath his covers.

"I'll stay until he's asleep," Zach said, his voice as cold as an arctic night. "You don't need to close the door."

He wanted her gone. His dismissal of her couldn't have been more explicit if he'd held the door for her himself. Yet, as she backed up, she wasn't entirely sure which transgression had caused the bewildering shift in his manner; touching the scar or kissing him.

She still wasn't sure when she heard the squeak of a floorboard a few unbearably long minutes later and she turned to see him in the hallway.

Having pretty much paced a rut in the rug waiting for him, she waited now for him to enter the brightly lit living room.

"I'm just going to get my coat," he told her and headed for the mudroom.

Unwilling to let him walk out before she understood why he was doing it, she started after him. "Wait, Zach. Please?"

The overhead lights were off in the kitchen, but the stove light was on. Though the area was dim, it was easy enough for Zach to see her when her plea caught him by the breakfast bar. Drawing a breath that brought the faint scent of chocolate chip cookies, he reluctantly made himself turn around and face her where she'd stopped six feet away.

He knew exactly what he was going to hear. He knew exactly how she would look as she glanced everywhere but at him while she stumbled all over herself trying to come up with some excuse for her reaction. He'd seen aversion to his scars before, borne the curiosity, the questions and the delicate shudders of ill-concealed distaste when a woman realized just how extensive those scars were. He'd consciously avoided putting himself in a position where he'd have to face the worst of those reactions, but the instant she'd jerked back at the feel of his skin, he felt the sting all over again.

A log broke apart in the potbellied stove, the sound muffled, the greedy flames hidden. It had taken him over a year to be near fire without breaking out in a cold sweat.

Lauren took a tentative step closer. "Zach, I'm sorry," she said, her eyes guarded but unbelievably steady on his. "I only kissed you because I thought it might help Jason. Make things seem more normal for him," she explained, her tone caring and confused. "And I didn't think about your skin before I grabbed you. That it might be sensitive, I mean. I hope I didn't hurt your neck. If I did," she hurried on, instinctively reaching toward him, protectively pulling back, "I'm sorry. I really am."

In the pale light, the delicate curves and angles of her features were pinched and anxious. Her blue eyes were utterly guileless as she searched his face. To Zach, she looked just like she sounded, as if causing him discomfort was as painful to her as she imagined it must be to him. Only he hadn't expected what he saw in her face, what he heard in her voice, and he could practically feel his defenses jamming as she waited for him to forgive her.

She'd actually been thinking of him when she'd pulled back. She'd been afraid that she had hurt him.

He couldn't remember the last time anyone had caught him so unprepared.

"You didn't hurt me," he finally said, years of well-honed defenses scrambling to seal the breach she'd just made in his wall. "All I felt was the pressure of your hand." And its warmth, he thought. But not its softness. The nerves there were too badly damaged to feel anything subtle.

"Then why…?"

"You just caught me off guard."

"By kissing you?"

He hesitated, considering the excuse she'd just handed him. "Yeah," he muttered, grabbing it.

She didn't believe him. The instant she'd pulled back, his defenses had shot into place like a radar shield.

"It was more than that," she murmured, wondering if it was possible that she'd embarrassed him somehow. But the thought of him being self-conscious about a kiss, of him feeling insecure about anything, seemed too ludicrous to entertain. The man was the epitome of *bold*. When it came to anything about sex, she imagined he was just as bold there, too.

The thought bumped her heart hard against her ribs. "If you're sure you're okay...."

"I am."

"I'm still sorry," she repeated, and offered a small and embarrassed smile of her own.

The faint curve of her mouth drew his glance as he stepped closer. "You don't need to apologize, Lauren." She hadn't done anything he hadn't thought about doing himself. Only what he'd had in mind wasn't nearly so innocent. "I'm sure Jase caught you off guard, too."

"You know he did. I never would have grabbed you like that if I'd thought about what I was doing." She hesitated as her glance slid to the injured side of his neck. Still not looking totally convinced that she hadn't somehow caused him discomfort, she met his eyes once more. "Sam said a guidance system failed. I asked him what happened," she hurried to explain. "He didn't just volunteer it."

Her curiosity didn't surprise him. Even when people didn't ask how he'd come by the injury, they wondered. He knew that. Yet, with Lauren, his first thought wasn't that she was intruding. Or of how he really didn't want to discuss what he'd spend years trying to forget. It was of how quickly she'd vindicated her brother. He liked that about her, her sense of loyalty, of fairness.

"The system was faulty," he confirmed, because that was the official story. The system they'd been testing had actually been geared to jamming systems in other crafts. Unfortunately, radio frequencies had crossed.

"They don't have those in the planes you and Sam fly, do they?"

"There's nothing remotely like it in what we fly. You don't need to worry about Sam."

"I was thinking about both of you," she admitted bluntly, her glance straying back to the wide scar. The quick disquiet in her eyes changed quality, her soft voice growing softer still. "Were you hurt anywhere else?"

Few people knew the extent of his injuries. If he admitted only to what was visible, there were fewer questions, more understated reactions. What was visible wasn't all that bad, anyway. Not compared to what wasn't. But there was something about Lauren's lingering concern and the way she didn't always react the way he figured she would that kept his normal defenses at bay.

"I had a couple of broken bones." Five to be exact.

He inclined his head to the left. "And there's the rest of this."

"How far does it go?"

"Down the side."

The delicate wings of her eyebrows pinched inward. "Of your shoulder?"

"Of my body."

He'd seen pity in people's faces before. He'd seen revulsion. He figured that somewhere along the line, he'd seen everything in between. Especially in the beginning when he'd been living in bandages. But he'd learned to dismiss other people's responses to his injuries as being of no consequence to him. He was trying hard to believe that he wouldn't care about Lauren's reaction, either, when he saw her glance slip down his chest to his thigh.

When she looked up again, he could read nothing in her face that hadn't already been there.

"I burned everywhere my flight suit tore," he explained, because it was easier than waiting for her to ask what had happened. The flames had gotten his shoulder and upper arm, and part of his chest, back and leg. "My gloves and helmet stayed intact."

"How long ago did it happen?" she asked, her eyes steady on his.

"Seven years."

"And it doesn't hurt?"

He couldn't believe how concerned she seemed about that. "Not now."

For a moment, Lauren said nothing else. The thought of a fighter jet exploding into flames was horrifying enough. The thought of him burned and broken, and of what he must have gone through to be standing here now was beyond her comprehension.

Pressing her hand to the odd tightening in her heart, her glance slipped past the hard line of his jaw, the firm set of his mouth. There was absolutely nothing about his manner or bearing that would have led her or anyone else to suspect what he'd endured. Certainly, there was nothing about the way he looked at that moment, so supremely, aggressively male, that invited sympathy. But she ached for him anyway.

She remembered everything he'd said about a man needing solitude to heal, about how a man needed to deal with what life handed him in his own way. She'd had no idea what he had gone through when he'd told her that, but she'd suspected even then that he'd faced much of it alone.

She was almost certain of that now.

In the blue-white light of the stove, Lauren moved to where she'd left a towel on the counter and looped the rectangle of terry cloth over a drawer knob. "Your divorce," she said, not sure why it was so important that she understand what all had driven him to this place. "Did that happen before or after your accident?"

"After," he replied, his faint frown indicating he wasn't at all sure how she'd gone from his accident to his marital status.

"That must be when you bought your cabin."

The fire snapped behind him, the muffled sound blending with the settling groans of the house. Watching her hands slip from the ends of the towel, Zach casually leaned against the counter. She had an intriguing knack for linking points in his life that no one else would have connected. It seemed there were things he didn't have to explain when he talked to her. Things she instinctively understood about why he'd done what he had.

"I didn't do that until a year later." Drawn by her insight, hungrier for the connection she offered than he would willingly admit, he allowed himself to feel the gentleness in her voice, the concern in her eyes. "It was about that long before I finished my initial rehab. I did the rest of it there."

"In a cabin?"

"Not necessarily in it."

He'd spent hours at first walking, then jogging, then running the vast meadows on Gainey Island. He'd climbed the boulders along the rugged beach. He'd lifted weights, chopped wood. He'd done chin-ups from tree limbs. He'd eventually repaired the roof, the floor and the sagging walls of the dilapidated shack he'd called home for over a year, but not until he had just about despaired of ever feeling human again.

He didn't mention that last part. There were things about the year at the cabin and the time he'd spent in hospitals the year before that he didn't care to revisit.

Lauren didn't ask him to. She cut through the heart of those years with the precision of a surgeon's scalpel.

"There had to be other places you could go, Zach. Why did you choose to be so alone?"

"Because it was easiest for everyone."

In the pale light her features clouded. "Is that why you wanted Sam to go? Because it would be *easier* on everyone?"

"I wanted him to go because it's what he wanted. He said he wanted to get away, remember? I just happened to understand that need."

She hadn't understood his rationale the first time they'd discussed it. From the hesitation etched in her lovely face, Zach was sure she didn't get it now, either.

"It's that male thing, isn't it," she concluded, the sudden certainty in her tone removing any trace of query. "That thing that rebels at the idea of you guys letting anyone see you vulnerable."

It seemed she comprehended the theory, even if its application baffled her. He watched her tip her head, her desire to understand so acute he could nearly feel it as she searched his face.

"How did being alone make it easier for you?"

He'd thought she'd do what he figured any other woman would do—what two physical therapists, a burn counselor and one female physician had done—and claim that there was nothing wrong with a man being vulnerable. She could have pointed out that he'd been injured and that no one would have expected him to be brave and stoic and all the other things the men he knew had been raised to be. But she wasn't any other woman. She simply accepted that, for him, what he'd done had been necessary.

"Because I could barely help myself, let alone anyone else," he finally told her, and when she asked what he meant, he found himself telling her other things he'd never talked about, including a few he'd never shared with another living soul.

As he spoke, he kept his voice low, his tone matter-of-fact. Lauren listened silently, drawn by those rich, mellow sounds. She was certain he was downplaying everything he related to her. He spoke of the crash, the endless days of endless pain, the grafting surgeries, all in the same detached way she imagined he might have delivered a debriefing at the end of a test flight.

He'd been in Nevada at the time of the accident, but based out of Virginia. With his family back east, he'd eventually been flown to a burn unit back home, he told her, but except for medical staff, he was alone most of the time. Seeing him as he'd been, in pain, swathed in gel and bandages, and strapped into a bed that looked like a huge gyro so he wouldn't have to lie on his damaged skin, had been too hard on his family. Even in the drugged haze that barely took the edge off his pain, their reactions to him had made him feel worse, so he hadn't wanted them around to witness what made them so uncomfortable.

Once he was out of rehab, he hadn't wanted to be around anyone at all. He'd been too angry, too uncertain about what he could do with his life since all he'd ever wanted to do was fly.

Lauren watched him absentmindedly move his finger along a grout line in the tile counter as his voice trailed off. He'd managed to overcome the anger he felt, she realized, because it wasn't anger that gave him his edge. That edge came from a kind of mental toughness she couldn't begin to comprehend. He'd also obviously beaten down the uncertainty he'd felt about his life and found a way to do what he loved. It was his close relationships, she suspected, that were still suffering.

"What about your family now?" she asked, following the path of his long, elegant hand. "Do you ever see them?"

"We were never what you'd call close. But my folks and my brother call every once in a while. Or I call them."

"And your ex?"

"Nicole left while I was in the hospital in Nevada. I haven't seen or heard from her since."

Lauren glanced across the three feet of shadowed pine flooring separating them. He was still calmly tracing the grout. His tone hadn't changed. Neither had his unremarkable expression.

"She left right after your crash?"

"Not right after. She waited a couple of weeks."

"Two weeks?"

"Maybe it was three. I'm kind of hazy about that first month, and I wasn't in the best shape to argue with her about timing. Not that there was much I could have said," he admitted with an amazingly indifferent shrug. "She couldn't handle the way I looked. The way I was going to look," he expanded, his apathy belied by the way a muscle in his jaw jerked. "Then there was the problem of how what had happened was going to affect her."

His index finger reached the intersection of another line and he started tracing back.

"I don't understand."

"She'd married a jet jockey. I was an officer and part of a program that put us in certain political and social circles in Virginia and D.C. My CO had already told her I'd be getting a medical discharge. That meant the life she knew was over."

"But what about her life with you?"

"What about it?" he asked, his tone utterly indifferent. "I was no longer the man she'd married. As far as she was concerned, whatever we'd had was over, too."

The pool of light from the stove didn't quite reach where they stood, but it threw enough of its cool illumination for her to see easily the betraying nuances etched in Zach's face. His handsome angular features could have been carved of stone as he focused on two intersecting lines. His brow was lowered beneath a few dark strands of hair that fell over his wide intelligent forehead.

His expression could have passed for concentration. It probably would have, to anyone but her. To her, he was wearing a mask, something she suspected he'd always done to hide the feelings he'd locked inside—or, to protect wounds that had never healed.

She knew exactly where those wounds had come from. And she had the uneasy feeling now that his physical scars were nothing compared to the emotional ones his wife had inflicted. If the woman he'd married couldn't handle the thought of him being scarred, it was no wonder his wall had gone up when she'd touched him herself.

With his head down, his right side to her, she couldn't see the injury at all. She didn't even have an impression of how it had felt because the feel of his cheek against her lips, his scent, his very presence had absorbed her senses. But there had been more to his wife's defection than his body's physical imperfections.

The woman had deserted him at the lowest point of his life because all she had cared about was her status as a military officer's wife. She hadn't cared about him, about the man he was inside. The man Lauren knew to be generous and caring and loyal to a fault. Her only concern had been herself.

It was no wonder, Lauren thought, that he'd isolated part of himself, walled up the part that could be hurt. She couldn't imagine a soul on earth who would blame him for not making himself vulnerable.

"For what it's worth," she quietly offered, "that kind of rejection only takes a couple of lifetimes to get over. You obviously have nine lives. Just think of yourself as a cat that's used up one lifetime already."

The remoteness faded from his expression as his head came up. For a moment, he said nothing. He just searched her face until, incredibly, the light of a smile glinted in his eyes.

"I've probably used more than that."

"You've crashed more than once?"

"The other times I bailed. It was just that last time that everything went wrong so fast."

The other *times?* she thought and immediately shook off the image of fireballs that popped into her head.

"I won't pretend to understand what made you want to do what you did for a living," she murmured, truly unable to comprehend why someone would take such risks, "but I honestly can't help admiring whatever it was that got you through the aftermath.

"No," she immediately corrected. Shaking her head, a strand of hair curved against her cheek. "I envy it. Your strength. Your courage." She paused, tracing one of the grout lines, too. "If all that had happened to me, I'd still be at the cabin."

"I'm no one to envy, Lauren."

"You're no one to judge that—"

"And I doubt that you'd still be there," he contended, overriding her protest as he deliberately bumped her finger with his. "You're a survivor."

The playful way he nudged her finger had her glancing up.

"I'll remind you of that the next time you call me stubborn."

"You are stubborn."

"Am not."

"Are, too."

Her mouth curved, her smile easy.

Zach swore he could feel its warmth all the way to his soul.

"You are," he told her, reaching over to nudge back the errant strand of hair. It slid against his finger, soft as satin, cool as silk. "But I won't hold it against you."

Lauren opened her mouth, but whatever she'd intended to say evaporated like a snowflake hitting flame. There was such gentleness in his touch, a tenderness she craved to the very depths of her being. But it was the soul-deep sadness beneath his faint smile that nearly stole her breath. She didn't believe for a moment that he knew it was there. As her head tipped unconsciously toward his hand, she had the feeling he'd cut off a limb before he'd admit it even existed.

"Good," she finally murmured, and felt her breath stall completely when his glance dropped to her mouth.

The look in his eyes shifted, something like need joining a vaguely primitive light as his fingers slipped around the back of her neck. She didn't know if he drew her forward, or if she stepped closer herself. Before she could even begin to wonder, his head lowered, blocking the light, blocking everything but the feel of his hands when he cupped her face and covered her mouth with his.

She had no idea how something that looked so hard could be so soft. His firm lips felt like warm velvet as he brushed them over hers. Once. Twice.

Again.

Each time was the merest breath of touch, almost the tease of a kiss. It was as if he were lingering over something he wanted to sip, to savor, an experience too rare to rush. The caress was unbearably light, incredibly sensual—and sent little shock waves darting along every nerve in her body.

Her fingers fisted in his sweater. Her breathing became faster as their breath mingled. Beneath her hand, she could feel the strong, heavy beat of his heart. Through the back of her pullover, she felt the heat of his palm when it slid down her spine and he slowly drew her hips to his.

A moan came from deep within his chest when their bodies met. Or, maybe, she thought dimly, that aching sound had been her own. It didn't matter. His tongue slipped into her mouth, mating with hers. Gentleness succumbed to demand. In the space of a few erratic heartbeats, he reduced her to putty, and he was free to mold her at will.

She'd craved this. From those few fleeting moments she'd spent in his arms days ago, she'd wanted to be right where she was now. She just hadn't realized how badly she'd longed for it until he was holding her against him, aligning her with the hard angles and planes of his body. She knew he would never admit to need, but need was there. And hunger. She could feel them fighting the re-straints she sensed in him even now.

Heaven help her, she felt that need and hunger inside herself, too.

She had no defenses against this man.

What frightened her most was that she wanted none.

She whispered his name.

To Zach, that single hard syllable sounded like little more than a trembling rush of air as he carried his kiss down the exquisite line of her throat. Wanting to touch all of her, he coaxed her head back, tasting the soft skin beneath the delicate line of her jaw as he pulled the clip from her hair. The soft tresses spilled over his hands like threads of tawny silk before he sought her mouth once more. He pulled her closer, drinking in the honeyed taste of her like a man who'd gone too long without suste-nance.

It had been forever since a woman had kissed him with such abandon, since he'd felt the softness of a woman's body straining against his. He'd felt a jolt of heat at the first touch of his tongue to hers, but he hadn't expected the primal need tearing through him now—a need he held in an iron fist of control, reining it back when everything basic to his being was wanting whatever she would let him take.

He hadn't intended to reach for her. He'd just done it because it had seemed natural and right and at that mo-ment he hadn't felt the threat that usually kept his guard locked so firmly in place.

He had been aware of her since the moment he'd stepped into the warmth of the house. He'd been con-scious of the slender shape of her body beneath the sweater and jeans she wore, the way the soft fabric moved against the fullness of her breasts. He'd been aware of her scent, the chips of turquoise in her blue eyes and the incredible fact that she had actually been concerned about him herself when he'd shown up late. He'd even spent a few moments taunting himself with the memory of how she'd felt in his arms, and wondering for the millionth time how her body would feel moving beneath his.

But until she'd turned her head to his hand, wanting his touch, inviting it, he hadn't honestly thought there was any possibility of crossing the line he'd drawn for himself with this woman.

He let his control slip an inch and tucked his hands beneath the hem of her short sweater. Craving the softness of her, he skimmed up her sides, curved his palm beneath the enticing fullness of her breast—and felt her body go utterly still.

A small, still-functioning part of his brain battled the haze of sensual heat clouding it to remind him that he'd crossed one line. As Lauren eased back and rested her forehead against his chest, she was making it clear she wasn't ready for him to cross another.

For a moment, neither moved. He could feel her trembling beneath his hands, and the hammering of his own heart. They were both breathing as if they'd just run a marathon.

"Hey." He smoothed her hair, the motion as soothing for him as he intended it to be for her. "Are you all right?"

It took a moment, but Lauren nodded, her head moving against his sweater.

"Great," he muttered darkly, still smoothing. "You're not speaking to me."

"Of course I am."

"Good."

She lifted her head, her eyes languid, her mouth damp from his kisses. Even her voice, the faintly breathy sound of it, betrayed his effect on her as she quietly injected a note of reality. "You're bringing my brother back tomorrow."

He had no business wanting to pull her closer when her small hands slipped from his back. And he knew he shouldn't let himself wonder why it mattered that he felt the same disappointment she tried to hide from him. What had happened was just a moment in time.

He felt the disappointment anyway.

"Are you going in the morning, or the afternoon?"

"The schedule is leaning toward afternoon."

She nodded, looking as if she didn't quite know what else to say with him still touching her.

Reluctantly, he let his hands fall from her shoulders. "I should go, Lauren."

She gave him another nod, running her fingers through the hair he'd left so seductively tousled. "You probably should," she agreed, trying to smile, not quite making it. "It's getting late."

As easy as it had been to talk to her before, there didn't seem to be anything else he could think to say, either.

So he said nothing just then. He just let his fingertips graze her cheek before he tipped up her chin and, caving in to the need burning in his belly, settled his mouth over hers once more.

He kissed her thoroughly, deeply, drugging himself with the taste of her. She kissed him back, not with the abandon he'd sensed in her before, but with a sweetness that would have made his heart ache if he'd let himself admit her effect on it.

"See you in the morning," he finally said, and left her at the front door.

She was safe, he reminded himself. He didn't need to worry about getting involved with her, or about anything that had just happened. She wasn't a threat to his hard-won peace. He would bring her brother home tomorrow. Then she would be gone.

At least, that was the plan.

Chapter Nine

"My brother will be back today, but it might be best if you get together with him tomorrow." Lauren smiled at the big Nordic-looking woman holding a blissfully content Jenny. "I won't be here," she explained, because she planned to take the first ferry in the morning, "so I'll ask Sam to call you to work out the details."

Joanne Milford gave an agreeable nod as she bounced the angelic little girl in her lap. The woman was sixty-four, looked fifty and had the vitality of a thirty-year-old. Her short white hair was the same shade of platinum she'd probably been born with, her eyes were a sharp aqua behind silver-framed glasses and her rounded features radiated kindness, a sense of humor and the energy it would take to keep up with two toddlers.

"That's fine with me. I just wish I could place him." Her pleasantly rounded features pleated in consternation. "I know I must have met him at some point. I worked

the toll booth for thirty years and every islander that came
or left from this place had to pay their toll to me at one
time or another.''

''I think he flies most everywhere he needs to go. Even
when he comes home…to Seattle,'' Lauren clarified, ''he
flies in, then just rents a car.''

''That must be why, then.'' Relieved that her memory
wasn't failing her, she shifted the baby in her ample lap.
''I certainly knew Tina, though. What a dear girl,'' she
murmured, gently stroking Jenny's pale curls. ''She was
always so involved in the community.''

A musing look lit her eyes. ''I think she was the same
age as my Emily. Emily's the one with the two boys,''
she reminded Lauren, since she had mentioned all three
of her grown children and their families when Lauren had
first met her. Her easy smile returned, making her rosy
cheeks curve like apples. ''One of them is just a little
older than Jason. But I think I already mentioned that,
too.''

She had told Lauren about her family yesterday when
they had met at the café before Lauren had picked up
Jason. The friendly, spirited woman had also confided
that she had been widowed for three years, that her children had all moved away, and that she very much wanted
to be where she was needed. She'd been retired for a
month, done all the needlepoint she could stand and told
Lauren that if her brother couldn't use her, she was going
to volunteer her time at T. J. Walker's animal shelter.

Lauren hadn't had to ask who T. J. Walker was. She
remembered from her first conversation with Maddy that
T.J. was the woman Maddy had wanted to fix up with
Zach. But Lauren's immediate sense about Joanne had
been that Crystal Walker's daughter was going to have
to look elsewhere for a volunteer.

Lauren had liked Joanne on sight. More important, children seemed to adore her, a fact that had become abundantly clear when half of the kids at the preschool, children and grandchildren of Joanne's many friends, raced up to her when she'd walked over to the school with Lauren to pick up Jason.

The fact that she loved to cook, didn't mind cleaning and was willing to stay at her brother's house made Lauren adore her, too.

All she needed now was for her brother to agree to Joanne staying five nights a week instead of seven and she would have found him a baby-sitter that she wouldn't worry about leaving any of them with.

The thought that at least one thing had gone right that week was interrupted by a heavy knock on the door. It sounded just as the phone rang.

Looking a bit like Mrs. Claus with her white hair and berry-red sweat suit, Joanne rose from the middle of the sofa and expertly slung Jenny onto her hip. "Which do you want me to get?"

"The door. Please."

The thought that it could be Zach caused Lauren's heart to hitch. She hadn't seen him that morning. He'd called first thing, in a hurry and already at the airfield and asked her to take Jason to school herself because the weather wasn't looking good and he wanted to head to Gainey Island first thing.

Even as she reached for the phone, she realized the weight of her concerns had to be short-circuiting her logic. It wouldn't be Zach at the door. If it were, he would be with her brother and Sam wouldn't have knocked.

She would bet her next vacation, however, that it was Andy making the phone ring so impatiently. The manager

of the lingerie department had already called twice about
a shipment that should have been received last week for
a weekend promotion.

Still uneasy with her boss from their conversation two
days ago, Lauren picked up the phone, taking solace in
the fact that she could at least tell him she already had
the vendor running a tracer on the merchandise.

Andy never said a word about the problem in lingerie,
which either meant he didn't know about it, or he already
assumed she was handling it. What he did say, in an
unusually clipped manner, was that he'd just had a meeting with George Hanley, the chief operations officer
she'd missed meeting days ago. Though he didn't mention what the new meeting had been about, he did remind
her, quite unnecessarily, that she was due back in the
office tomorrow. She had said she needed a week, and
the week was up.

"I'll be there, Andy," she promised, scrambling past
the quick regret she felt at the thought of leaving. "My
brother is coming back today. There's a ferry that leaves
here at seven in the morning. I'll be in the office by nine-
thirty. Ten at the latest."

Andy's businesslike tones iced over like water on a
skating rink. "I assumed you'd be here for the depart-
ment-head meeting at eight."

Eight a.m. was impossible. "I'm sorry, Andy. I—"

"You have a meeting with Hanley yourself tomorrow,
Lauren. That's the reason I called. It's set for three
o'clock. I've gone to the wall for you on this promotion,"
he insisted, patience definitely ebbing. "If you want it at
all, you won't miss that one."

"I do. And I won't," she insisted, loath for him to
think she didn't appreciate what he'd done. Guilt merged
with anxiety. "And thank you. I'll be there. I promise."

His tone thawed to just above freezing when he told her she'd better be, and he ended the call a few moments later. But she was still feeling its chill when she hung up the phone and heard the front door close.

"It's the oil man. He went on around back to fill the tank," Joanne announced, when Lauren walked back into the living room. "If you don't have any more questions or have anything else you want to show me," she said, alluding to the quick tour Lauren had given her of the house, "I think I'll get going. That fog's getting a little too thick for me out there." Handing Jenny over, she pulled her raspberry-pink parka from the arm of the chair. "I know lots of folks don't think anything of it, but I never have liked driving in the fog. I'm always afraid I'll hit a deer."

Absently rubbing her niece's back, Lauren shot an uncomfortable glance toward the windows. "It's getting worse?"

It certainly appeared to be. When Lauren walked the woman to the door and looked across the sweep of dormant lawn, the inlet wasn't visible. The other morning, the mist had lain in patches. This morning, when she'd driven Jason into town, the patches had joined to completely obscure the trees at the end of the graveled drive.

"I thought this burned off the later it got in the day."

"Sometimes it does," Joanne replied, closing her silver snaps. "Then, sometimes we go weeks living in the clouds. At least the temperature isn't below freezing," the woman reflected philosophically. "The hoarfrost is gorgeous on the trees, but the roads can get awfully slick. If you're going in to pick up Jason, you might want to start soon. This could be nothing once you get out on the road, or it could be as thick as my clam chowder all the way to the preschool. Watch out for deer," she reminded, ever so helpfully.

Bundled in shades of rose, her white hair fluttering around her pink face, the children's new sitter offered a smile and headed through the damp mist to her little beige sedan.

Fifteen minutes later, having signed for the oil and strapped Jenny and her bunny into the Suburban, Lauren was following the big black truck's red taillights through the mist and onto the narrow highway. Jason probably wasn't going to be happy leaving preschool early, but she'd rather he was unhappy with her than risk not being able to get him.

The good news was that it was daylight, and that the fog wasn't bad at all going into town. She could see banks of it toward the ocean, and hovering low over the trees to the inland side, but along the road itself it was no worse than driving through light smoke. To her surprise, Jason didn't mind leaving his activities, either, though not that many children were there that day and he'd been off coloring alone when she arrived.

The bad news was that on the return trip the fog that had hovered over the trees had sunk to the ground and the filmy gray blanket on the ocean-side had moved in to cover parts of the highway, which made the trip to her brother's house take twice as long as had the trip into town. She also discovered that the reason Jason wasn't unhappy to have left early was because the Xs on the calendar indicated that this was the day his dad was coming home.

The more excited he got about seeing his dad, and the thicker the fog became, the more uneasy Lauren grew.

"There was just no way I could get him. I went up twice trying to find a hole in the fog, but I never even saw Gainey Island. That's where your dad is," Zach explained, pulling his glance from where Lauren stepped back from the door to the sober-eyed Jason. "I almost couldn't see the landing strip here when I came back."

Zach actually hadn't seen it at first. He'd been up for hours and circled so long that his fuel gauge had been tapping empty when he'd finally spotted a thin patch in the fog where his coordinates told him the landing strip on Harbor should be. It had been a long time since he'd cut a landing that close. But he'd known how important it was to bring Sam home, and he hadn't counted on the weather closing in so fast.

"I would have been here sooner, but I had to refuel and do some maintenance on the plane before I left. I tried calling you a couple of times, but the line's been busy."

"I've been on the phone. With the store," she explained. She turned to the window, looking as if she still expected to see her brother appear. "There was no way?"

"None."

Zach pulled off his jacket, his glance straying to where Lauren remained by the coffee table, threading her fingers through her hair. The gesture spoke of concern and frustration. Watching her eyes shy from his, he had the feeling there was a little uncertainty about him in there, too.

He was feeling a little uneasy himself. Remembering how she had responded to him had him feeling as tense as a wolf on the scent of its mate.

His jacket landed on the arm of a chair as he deliberately forced his attention to the more immediate reason for the strain in her pale features. Her nephew. Jason had pulled open the door and, within seconds, his wide grin had dissolved to dejection.

Picking up the television's remote control from the table in front of Lauren, Zach aimed the slender black instrument at the set and punched in a weather channel.

"Come here, Jase. I want you to look at something." The child had been expecting his father all day. Knowing Lauren, she was worrying herself sick about the effect Sam's delay would have on him. "See all this?"

"It doesn't look like anything," the child solemnly replied.

From where Lauren stood by the coffee table, she watched Zach crouch down in front of the television and pull her nephew between his denim-clad thighs. The hard muscles of his shoulders shifted beneath the waffle weave of his charcoal shirt as he traced around the outline of the San Juan Islands superimposed over a huge blanket of cloud.

She'd had a knot in her stomach ever since Andy had called the first time that morning. Within an instant of opening the door a minute ago, the thing seemed to have lodged itself between her lungs. Zach's eyes had met hers, then promptly settled on her mouth. But her pulse had no sooner skipped at the remembered feel of his mouth on hers, than she'd realized he was alone.

All day long, as she'd hurried from one task to the next, changing into her sweats and cleaning the house for her brother in between taking care of her work and the kids, she'd had the nagging thought that Sam might be late getting home. But she'd never once truly considered that he wouldn't return that day at all.

"This is called a fog deck. It's like clouds floating on the ground," she heard Zach tell the somber but attentive child, "and it's making it impossible for planes to take off and land. Even planes with instruments can't use runways because visibility on the ground is too limited and they could hit something. A building. Each other.''

Apprehension as thick and heavy as the mist outside settled over Lauren as she listened. Needing reassurance, she started to ask how long Zach thought it would be before the weather broke. A few hours. Until morning? Even then, how long would it take to get Sam?

The electronic ring of the telephone in the kitchen cut her off cold.

For two rebellious seconds, she debated answering it. But Zach was already talking to Jason about cooling air and the dew point and the phone was sounding more insistent.

Praying there wasn't another problem, she hurried to answer it before the noise could disturb the baby. She'd put the tired little girl down for the night only minutes before Zach had arrived. If Jenny was awakened right after falling asleep, it could take forever to soothe her.

The call wasn't announcing another problem. But it was close enough. It was her mother wanting to know if Sam was back. Beth Edwards also wanted to know why she'd had such trouble getting through.

''The line was busy all three times I called before dinner, dear. Are you having trouble with the phone?''

''I was just on it with the store,'' Lauren explained to her, pacing in the kitchen so she wouldn't disturb the guys in the living room. Andy had called twice more, but she'd lost track of the number of calls from the lingerie manager and the problem vendor. ''And no, Sam isn't back. Zach wasn't able to get him.''

A moment's silence preceded a puzzled, ''Why not?''

''Because we're having a little problem with fog up here.''

"You mean there was nothing he could do to bring him back?"

"Nothing," Lauren confirmed, repeating more or less what Zach had told her. "Everyone around here has been telling me that this happens. Sam told me so himself. That's why I had to find him a live-in."

The silence this time made the line sound as dead as the dodo. Moments later, her mother's voice came through carrying a totally different note of concern.

"We all agree that he needs someone to watch the children until he gets his affairs taken care of there. But you did make it clear to whoever you found that it's not a permanent position, didn't you? And who did you find?" she hurried on, clearly still wedded to the idea that Sam needed to move closer to family.

The deep tones of Zach's voice drifted in from the other room, the sounds capable, comforting. As Lauren paced back toward the kitchen door, she could see Zach still crouched in front of the set with Jason pulled protectively against him.

It was pathetic for a grown woman to envy a three-year-old, but at that moment she truly did. The only time in her life that she'd even glimpsed the sensation of feeling protected was when Zach had hauled her against him to keep her from breaking her neck.

Shamelessly allowing herself to take what comfort she could from his low, honeyed voice, she braced herself for her mom's reaction, told her about Joanne, then admitted that she hadn't mentioned anything to the woman about her brother's future plans.

"I didn't because I don't know for sure what his plans are," she explained, not caring to get into a discussion about what was best for Sam. Not tonight. She'd experienced enough of the community to know that he wouldn't be without support here. She'd also learned enough from Zach to know she couldn't presume to understand what Sam might need as a man. But she simply wasn't up to battling her mom, feeling as edgy as she did just then. "I figure that's something he can take up with her himself."

"That's not being very fair to the woman, do you think?" her mother inquired, sounding as if she hadn't heard a word her daughter had just said. "She needs to know she won't be there very long."

"We don't know that, Mom. We don't know what Sam has decided to do," she repeated, doubting her mother heard her that time, either. Beth Edwards was amazingly hardheaded where the welfare of her children were concerned. Especially when she thought she knew best.

"You're not encouraging him to stay, are you?"

"Mom, he's not back yet. I haven't talked to him about anything." Hoping she didn't sound as exasperated as she was beginning to feel, she took a deep and deliberate breath. "I really should get off the phone now," she continued, still pacing. "Jason's still up, and I want to ask Zach about this weather."

"Zach is there now?"

"He came to tell us why he couldn't get Sam. I haven't even had a chance to ask if he was able to reach him on their radio."

"Ask him now. I'll wait."

Lauren stopped herself mid-pace in front of the stove, pulled a deep breath and dutifully headed into the living room. She couldn't be annoyed with her mother. It was only natural that her mom would want to know how Sam was doing. He was her son. It was her job to worry about him.

Sometime in the last minute, Zach and Jason had abandoned the television. They were now on the sofa looking up cloud formations in the encyclopedia.

Zach obviously thought that if the little boy understood what was going on, he would be less upset about his dad not being home that night.

To him, the approach probably just seemed logical. To Lauren, it made him seem like a remarkably compassionate man who was doing whatever he could to make a disappointment easier for a small child to take. Jason couldn't possibly understand what he was saying about condensation and advection. She barely understood it herself. But there was no way the child could misunderstand how much Zach cared.

Considering Zach's willingness to be there for other people, too, the man's heart had to be huge.

"Sorry to interrupt," she murmured, when he glanced up at the sound of her footsteps, "but Mom's on the phone. We were wondering if you were able to reach Sam today."

"I've talked to him a few times." Leaving Jason with the book, he stepped past the coffee table, a contemplative frown firmly in place as he openly studied her pale features. "The last was about three hours ago when I had to give up on getting him. He said he's fine."

Lauren repeated into the phone what he said as he said it.

"Does he have enough food to stay an extra night?" she asked, repeating her mom's concern.

"He has enough for a month. I keep the place stocked."

"Yes," was all Lauren said, her heart beating a little faster at the intent way he watched her. His glance

touched her taut features, her tight grip on the phone.
"He has plenty.

"Of course," she said, a moment later, "I'll call you
as soon as he tells me he can get him. Sure," she murmured, and handed the phone to Jason.

"It's Grandma, sweetie. She wants to say 'hi.'"

The neck of Jason's space-ship-print pajamas had
slipped off his shoulder. With the heavy book open in
his lap, he pulled the top up and took the phone, holding
it with both hands to his ear.

The child had no sooner said "hi" himself than Zach
curled his fingers around Lauren's arm and edged her a
few steps away.

He'd had the impression of an uneasiness about her
the moment he'd walked in the door. That disquiet had
only increased in the last few minutes. He'd heard it in
her voice as she'd talked to her mom, and in the restless
cadence of her pacing. He could see it now in the strain
shadowing her face.

"Which is it?" he asked her, his voice low as he deliberately lowered his hand. "Jason, your brother, the
weather or your mom? You look like you're ready to start
pacing the walls."

It was such a little thing, but what bothered Lauren
most at that instant was that he had drawn his hand away.
As overwhelmed as she was beginning to feel, she
couldn't think of anything she wanted more than to absorb the solid strength she always sensed in him.

"Mostly the weather," she admitted, hugging herself
since he wasn't offering to do it for her. "I have a meeting tomorrow afternoon. With Sam not back, I can't
make the early ferry." Unless she could get Joanne to
watch the children, she thought wildly, but even as part

of her balked at leaving before her brother returned, Zach pulled the plug on any possible escape.

"The ferries aren't running. I doubt they'll be running by then, either. Unless we get some serious temperature changes and wind shifts, this is going to stick around until at least midafternoon."

"But I promised Andy that I'd be there."

"I'm done," Jason said, holding up the phone.

The panic in her voice was reflected in her eyes. Hating that it was there, not knowing what to do about it, she hid it the only way she could.

Ducking her head so he couldn't see her face, she took the phone and prayed that her mother wouldn't want to chat.

The Fates must have decided she had enough to handle. She got her wish. After reminding her to call if she heard anything, her mother told her she would let her go so she could say goodnight to Zach and get Jason in bed.

If Lauren hadn't been so busy trying to keep the panic at bay, she would also have appreciated that her mother hadn't said anything else about the man helping Jason put the encyclopedia away. The last thing she needed was for her mom to get suspicious about her and the one person Beth was sure would try to talk Sam into staying in Harbor.

It would have eased her mom's mind considerably had she known that Zach was actually going out of his way to not influence her son, but now hadn't been the time for Lauren to explain how she could be so certain of that.

"It's bedtime," Zach announced, coming toward her carrying Jason high in his arms. "Say goodnight to your aunt, sport."

The command was met with surprising compliance. Jason leaned forward, wrapped his arms around her neck and kissed her cheek. Amazed by how accepting he'd been of Zach's explanation, and grateful beyond belief to him for thinking to offer it, she hugged her nephew back, loving the feel of his little arms around her, then headed down the hall behind them to check on Jenny. She'd be fine as long as she kept busy. If she stopped to think about all the ramifications of not being in Seattle on time tomorrow, especially after promising Andy that she'd be there, she was afraid she just might get sick.

She was back in the living room, methodically working her way along the knickknacks with a dust cloth when Zach walked back in a few minutes later. As upset as she was, activity was mandatory. Since she'd done all the laundry, the floors and the bathroom between phone calls, dusting was all that was left.

"Do you want to talk about it?" he asked.

"I don't know what good it would do." Her voice was quiet, her calm tone completely belying how distressed she truly was. "It won't change anything."

"It might make it easier on that duck. You're polishing the brass right off it."

Frowning at the small and very shiny object in her hand, she returned it to its spot in the small collection of metal animals and picked up a palm-size swan.

Zach headed for the fireplace. "I take it that Andy called."

"A number of times."

Too distressed to wonder at his perception, she watched him crouch in front of the dwindling fire and open the screen. The furnace was working now and having been spared the task of keeping the potbellied stove stoked had been one of the brighter spots in her day. But she'd missed the fire in the fireplace that evening, so she'd built one anyway. Something about a flickering fire and the snap of wood lent life and vitality to the place, and the room had seemed cold and lonely without it.

Suspecting that the loneliness she felt actually had little to do with the ambiance of the room, she pulled her glance from Zach's broad back and tackled the swan. Thinking about thwarted dreams would only add to her growing list of anxieties, and she had enough on her mind as it was. Since the moment she'd realized Sam wouldn't be back today, she'd been plagued by the awful feeling that she was about to lose everything she'd worked for. And she had no one but herself to keep it from happening.

A log bumped heavily against the grate. "So what did he want?"

"To tell me about a meeting I have tomorrow," she replied, diligently working on a wing. "It's with one of the men who will decide who gets the new store. I'm supposed to be there by three o'clock." She flipped the bird over, going for its tail. "Then he called to tell me he has to go to the home office in San Francisco in the morning, so I'm in charge of straightening out a problem that started this morning with a missing shipment of lingerie, but that now involves most of an advertised weekend promotion. After spending the day on the phone, the best I can figure out is that when the merchandise came in, it got sent back and it's in transit somewhere. Unfortunately, the person who signed for it is no longer an employee."

Aware of her agitated motions as she spoke, Zach tossed in another log and pulled the screen closed. She was doing the same thing to the swan that she'd done to the duck.

"Do you like your job?" he asked over the snap and

sizzle of greedy flame on fresh pitch. The smell of pine mingled with the lingering scents of disinfectant and lemon oil. She'd been cleaning. Rabidly, from the sparkling look of the place.

"No one I know really loves what they're doing."

"That's not what I asked. And I did. I do," he expanded, rising with a faint creak of his knees to see her trade the swan for one of Jason's toy cars. "I liked flying jets. I liked being a test pilot. I like what I do now."

"It's not polite to brag," she muttered.

She wasn't paying any attention at all to what she was doing, but Zach didn't bother to point that out to her as she ran the white cloth over the bright red plastic. Moving a few feet from where she so diligently worked, he sat down on the thick rolled arm of the sofa, crossed his arms over his chest and waited to see how long it would take her to realize she was dusting a toy.

He lasted ten seconds before his curiosity got the better of him. "If you don't like what you do, how did you wind up doing it?"

"By default," she replied, putting the car back to move on to a framed photo of the kids at the beach. "And it's not that I don't like it. I just don't like that it's all I have."

She had been intent on her task since the moment he'd set foot in the room, so preoccupied she hadn't once paused. She did now. With her hand stalled on the frame, her glance shot to his. Consternation was written clearly on her lovely face.

He didn't doubt for a moment that she hadn't intended to admit what she had. He also had the feeling as she set the photo back in place and quickly started dusting the tops of the encyclopedia that she'd rather he forget that he'd heard it.

After everything she'd pulled out of him, he wasn't about to let her off that easily.

"You don't like that it's all you have," he repeated, mulling over the unexpected admission. "Does the reason it's all you have have anything to do with those plans you mentioned? The ones that didn't work out?"

The dust cloth slowed, her delicate brow pinching as she cautiously glanced toward him.

"You said your life didn't turn out the way you'd expected." He knew all too well how it felt to make do with whatever had been left of a life. "You thought you would have a family by now."

It took no effort at all to recall the way she'd looked the evening he'd pretty much forced her to defend her maternal instincts to him. She had been nearly overwhelmed by children she'd never taken care of before, and stripped completely of the sophisticated polish that somehow suited her as well as the comfortably worn sweats hiding her curves from him now.

At that moment she reminded him very much of the way she had looked that evening. Overwhelmed. And trying desperately to deny it.

He thought about taking the cloth from her and turning her to face him. Not trusting the need he felt to touch her, not wanting to crowd her, he stayed where he was.

"I did think I'd have a family," she quietly admitted. Needing movement, or possibly a sense of purpose, Lauren skimmed the cloth along the long oak shelves to the television centered in them. The set was on, the volume muted. "I thought that by now, I'd have a husband and babies and a home with a yard. I also thought I'd only be working forty hours a week instead of sixty," she confided, "but my life turned into a cliché instead."

She gave a short, disbelieving laugh as she moved past

the television and started on the shelves on the other side. "I didn't even marry a man who could come up with an original way to use me." She shook her head, making her voice light because she wanted to do what Zach had done and downplay how devastating the end of a relationship could be. "Ed and I went together all through high school and got married halfway through college. Only we couldn't afford for us both to be in school so we agreed he would finish, then it would be my turn.

"I helped put him through law school," she continued, scrubbing at something sticky at the edge of a shelf, "then he dumped me after he passed the bar, because by then, he had more in common with one of the female lawyers in the firm where he'd clerked than he did with me." She gave a little shrug. "I was nothing but a clerk in a department store.

"It wasn't that Brenman's wasn't impressive enough," she explained, still scrubbing. "I mean, the store is definitely upscale. It has the right labels, the right sort of customers," she murmured, amazed by how calm she actually sounded. "But it wasn't like I owned the place. Or was even running it. And a clerk definitely wasn't the sort of wife an up-and-coming mover and shaker would need."

She hadn't been the kind of wife her ex had wanted. She hadn't been accomplished enough for him. Hadn't been impressive enough herself.

She didn't have to say another word for Zach to understand that. He knew exactly how used and betrayed she felt. Those feelings were far closer to the surface than she probably even realized. He knew she was trying to deny them, though. He had the feeling she tried to deny a lot about herself. It was a survival technique, one he had no trouble at all recognizing because he was so intimately familiar with it himself.

Her cloth moved silently over the gleaming wood. With her head bent and her hair pulled up in a clip high at the back of her head, he could see the fine pale hairs below her nape, the delicate line of her spine where it disappeared under her soft gray sweatshirt.

Velvet over steel, he thought, only now appreciating how formidable the combination could be. But even steel could break.

Knowing her as he did now, he could see how she would have taken the only skills she'd felt she had and thrown herself into her job, buried herself in it to bury the pain of having her dreams so ruthlessly snatched away. No one knew better than he did just how paralyzing it could be when everything you were working toward suddenly ceased to exist. How stunning it was to discover the life you'd known one second simply… wasn't…the next.

She was still rubbing at the spot, her back to him, when Zach slowly rose from the arm of the sofa. He knew how lost she must have felt. And he knew how lonely she had to feel even now.

Thinking he could cheerfully choke the jerk who'd left her so empty, he walked up beside her. She didn't look up. She didn't say a word. She just kept rubbing.

Reaching past her arm, he stopped her restless motions by laying his hand over hers.

Chapter Ten

Lauren had gone still the moment Zach touched her hand. He stood close. So close she could see the night-time stubble of his beard shadowing the hard line of his jaw when she slowly straightened, and each impossibly long, dark eyelash when she met his quicksilver eyes.

She could feel his heat, breathe the male scent of him. His nearness caused nerves to flutter low in her stomach. With his fingers splayed over hers, she slowly pulled back her hand.

"Talking about your ex isn't helping right now," he murmured, pulling his hand back, too. "You have enough on your mind without me dragging out your old baggage. I'm sorry I brought it up."

One slender shoulder lifted in a self-conscious shrug. "It doesn't matter. It's not that important anymore."

The denial didn't surprise him at all. It was something he'd do himself.

"Of course it's important." Torn between the need to touch her and the lost look in her eyes, he curled his fingers into his palm. "It's why you're so worried about missing your meeting tomorrow.

"I can see now why this promotion matters so much to you," he told her before she could ask what he was talking about. "It's how you'll prove to yourself that you are someone after all."

The flames in the fireplace grew brighter as they curled over the new log, their glow adding a golden hue to the soft pools of light from the brass lamps. The wood snapped, the only sound in the suddenly quiet room.

In that silence, Lauren met Zach's eyes.

She'd never felt as exposed as she did at that moment. He knew that her ex-husband had tossed her out of his life like an outgrown shirt when she'd ceased to be of value to him. He knew she'd been thought of as not good enough, as somehow lacking. He knew her sense of her self and her sense of the future had all been shattered and that she'd struggled desperately ever since to make something out of the pieces.

She was almost afraid to wonder what else he could see as he calmly held her glance. It was as if he were looking straight into her soul—now that he had stripped it bare.

Had he been anyone else, she would have been embarrassed by his insight. What she felt instead was a sense of recognition, and the absolute certainty that Zach understood even better than she did just how long it could take to come back from being so emotionally battered. After all, he'd stripped his soul bare to her, too.

"I didn't know that was what I was doing at first," she admitted. "Trying to prove something to myself, I mean."

"It takes a while to figure it out." He wished he could take away the sadness in her eyes, bring the light back, make her smile. "But you're a quick study. Look how far you've come in just a couple of years."

At the compliment, or maybe the encouragement, a shadow of the smile he'd hoped for curved her mouth. It faded as her arms sneaked around her waist.

"How far I've come might be as far as I get to go. I'm scared to death of jeopardizing what I have. If I blow this, they may never consider me for anything else."

She looked as fragile as glass, hugging herself the way she was. And more vulnerable than he had ever seen her. She needed reassurance, encouragement. He could see that as clearly as he could the twin lines of worry spiking between her eyebrows.

He could have lied and told her she didn't have anything to worry about.

He had more respect for her intelligence than that.

"You know what?"

"What?" she murmured, hopeful.

"There's nothing you can do about anything tonight. And worrying doesn't help. Just take a deep breath and let it all go for now."

He made it sound so easy. Just let it go. Just like that. Lauren tipped her head, not certain which flaw in her personality deprived her of the ability not to be troubled by the people and things that mattered most to her.

"Is that how you get through everything? By just taking one deep breath after another?"

"It's as good a way as any."

Just keep breathing and you can get through anything. There was a wealth of truth in his implied philosophy, but she wasn't feeling all that philosophical at the moment.

"I'm sorry," she said, pushing her fingers through her hair, bumping into the clip. "You've been through more than I can even imagine. And if you can shut your mind off like that, then I envy you that, too. But I'm not that disciplined. And I'm tired. Jason was practically bouncing off the walls waiting for his dad to get home. And Jenny seemed to know the exact moment the phone was going to ring to start fussing for attention or need her diaper changed."

She cut herself off, letting her hand fall. "I'm whining," she muttered. "I hate it when people whine."

She turned away. Looking as if she had no idea what she'd intended to do, she turned right back.

He'd never seen anyone who looked so desperately in need of a pair of arms.

"Lauren?"

She hugged herself again. "What?"

"Come here."

Reaching out, he slipped his hands over her sweatshirt and felt her slender shoulders rise with her indrawn breath.

"It's okay," he murmured, stepping closer, easing her into his arms. This wasn't about the raging need he felt to touch her, to feel her body move against his. This was about doing what he could to make the moment a little easier for her. "You've been worried about your brother, your brother's children and your job ever since you got here. But there really isn't anything you can do about any of it just now."

"I can't help worrying."

"I know," he confided, the scent of her shampoo snagging him, drawing his head down. "And you do a good job of it, too. But try to let go. What can I do to make things better?"

He couldn't see her face, hidden as it was with her head resting against his chest. The tortoise shell clip holding her hair lay just beneath his chin, the golden strands it held shining in the mellow light.

"You're doing it."

She spoke so softly that he barely heard the words. Beneath his hands he could feel the tension in her muscles melting by degrees from her body as she welcomed the support he offered.

All she wanted was for him to hold her.

The realization left him completely disarmed.

His hand drifted upward to settle protectively on the side of her head. It had taken no time at all for him to see that the woman he'd first met had been wearing armor, both in the polished, touch-me-not way she'd dressed and in the defensiveness he'd aroused because of her brother. But the woman he'd come to know was more vulnerable than he would ever have suspected.

He'd thought her dangerous before. She was even more so now. She seemed to need him to be there for her and something about that need made it impossible for him to question the empathy they shared. Somehow, she had managed to work past every defense he'd possessed, tapping into feelings he could have sworn were dead and buried.

"I'll hold you for as long as you want," he finally assured her, and because his head was lowered, his mouth only inches from her temple, he brushed a kiss to the soft skin there. "Just tell me when to stop."

Lauren meant to reply, to say something clever because what she really wanted was for him to hold her forever, and she doubted very much that he would want to hear that. But the truth of that realization—that she didn't want him ever to let her go—effectively canceled any hope of cleverness. As for the panic she might have felt knowing how important he'd become to her, it was totally lost when she felt the warmth of his lips and the gentle brush of his breath feathering her hair.

His big hand cradled the side of her head. His other arm was locked across her back. He held her as if he were protecting her, as if he were using his body and his arms to shield her from the worries she couldn't seem to escape.

She couldn't believe how tender he could be, or how badly she craved what she felt in his arms. Tipping her head back against his chest, his hand still covering her hair, she touched her fingers to his jaw. She'd thought to kiss that hard ridge of bone. But when she looked up, she could see the wide scar above the ribbed edge of his shirt.

Without a thought, she raised on tiptoe and touched her lips to the pale, marbled skin.

Zach went as still as stone.

The instant he did, Lauren's heart gave an uneasy jerk. Lifting her head, she met his guarded eyes.

He looked as if he couldn't believe what she had done. Or, maybe, as if he were waiting for her reaction to what she'd done herself.

She had no idea when she'd fallen in love with him. She just knew she had, that it felt too right to question, and that she hated the thought of what he was bracing himself for at that very moment.

His arms still held her. Encouraged that he hadn't drawn away, she lowered her hand from his jaw and caught her finger under the ribbed necks of his thermal shirt and the white T-shirt beneath it.

He seemed to be holding his breath when she tugged the soft knit aside and placed a kiss on the slick and damaged skin covering his collarbone. Beneath her finger she could feel a hard ridge of flesh. Tugging lower to reveal a darker, mottled patch, she kissed there, too.

He swallowed hard.

"That's enough."

His voice was quiet, and rough with some emotion she couldn't define—until she looked up. She'd seen that hunger in him before. When he'd kissed her. It darkened his eyes to the shade of old pewter, turning the glint in them diamond-bright. But his formidable defenses leashed that need, turning his features taut and tensing every muscle in his long, lean body.

"Why?"

She barely breathed the word. But there was no doubt that he heard it. For a moment, he said nothing. He just stood with his eyes locked on hers while his guard battled the hunger and the hunger turned feral.

His fingers slipped through her hair. She felt them splay possessively at the back of her skull. Then, all she felt was his mouth covering hers and the strength draining from her legs when his tongue plunged into her mouth and he pulled her up hard against his body.

There was no tenderness here. No protectiveness. With the heady taste of him filling her, her senses consumed by his heat, all she sensed in him was a raw, aching need that would have been frightening had she not felt that same need herself. At that moment, she was aware of nothing but him. His body molded to hers. His mouth demanding. His hands shaped her, pressed her hips closer, then skimmed up to slip under her sweatshirt— only to slip back down and press her hips to the bulge straining against the zipper of his jeans.

At the erotic contact, her breath snagged in her lungs. In response, a low groan rumbled from deep in his chest.

But she could already feel him gathering his control, curbing his need as he eased the pressure of his hands and his mouth gentled on hers.

With touches as light as rain, he kissed the corners of her eyes, her temple, then drew her with him as he backed up and sank to the sofa's rounded arm. Keeping his hands on her hips, he pulled her between his legs and trailed those same featherlight kisses along the underside of her throat to the sensitive shell of her ear.

"I know there are a dozen reasons I should let you go." His voice was a low rasp, his breath hot against her skin. "Remind me of what they are."

"I would," she murmured, threading her fingers through the incredible softness of his thick hair. "But I can't think when you're touching me."

Her guileless admission banished any thought he'd had of releasing her. There probably were reasons he should set her back, make himself stop. But when he skimmed his hand beneath her sweatshirt and curved his fingers at the side of her breast, she didn't hesitate the way she had before. Welcoming his touch, she pressed a kiss to the top of his head, cradling it above the fullness beckoning him and he forgot to care about what those reasons might be.

Lifting his lips to her throat, he grazed his thumb over the restraining lace. Her faint moan vibrated against his lips. He heard that kittenish sound again when he opened the catch at the front of her bra and her nipple bloomed beneath his palm.

It wasn't enough to touch her. He needed to taste her, to know the flavors of her skin, to breathe its scent.

Slipping up the hem of her sweatshirt, he trailed a line of moist heat from the low drawstring waist of her loose sweat bottoms to the gentle swell of her breast and closed his mouth over one tight bud.

Lauren felt her knees buckle as something sharp and hot shot straight to her womb. If not for her grip on his shoulders and his arm banded across her bottom, she would have sagged right to the floor. His tongue was hot, his fingers gentle as he suckled and nipped and soothed.

All she could do, all she wanted to do, was hold him closer.

He pushed her sweatshirt higher. "Help me get rid of this."

"The kids," she said, amazed that she'd remembered they were there.

"They're asleep."

"Zach…"

He reached for her hand. "Where are you sleeping?"

"Wait." Her trembling breath came out in a rush. "I don't have anything." She had no protection. "I'm not even on birth control."

There'd been no need for it. She'd come nowhere close to a date in the past two years, much less a relationship.

Her warning froze Zach right where he'd risen in front of her. Pulling a deep breath, he bit back disappointment and touched her cheek, thinking to remind her that there were other ways they could be together. Then, he remembered what he had in his wallet. "I have something," he told her, and could have sworn he saw relief move into her eyes.

Her room was the first off the hall, a frankly feminine space that held an eyelet-covered daybed, an old cabinet sewing machine that held a tulip-shaped lamp and a small floral upholstered chair. Zach left the lamp off and the door partially open so they could listen for the children when he pulled Lauren inside. But the only sounds in the house were from the furnace when it kicked on, the occasional snap from the fireplace in the living room and the soft rustle of clothing when he pulled her sweatshirt over her head and the garment hit the floor.

That was also where the clip from her hair landed, along with the filmy wisp of her bra before he brushed his mouth down her throat to complete the ministrations he'd begun in the other room.

She shivered delicately when his lips closed over her.

Sliding his hand down the long elegant line of her back, he drew her closer. He loved that he could make her tremble.

He loved the way she gripped his shoulders to keep her balance.

He loved the way he eventually left her so breathless her voice was little more than an aching whisper.

"My turn."

He forced himself to ease back as she tugged at the hem of his shirt, to not let hesitation give away how much her reaction to his scars would matter. But before old demons could rise to plague him anyway, Lauren's lips were following the movement of her hands as she gathered fabric, pushing it to the middle of his chest.

In the golden light filtering in from the living room, it was easy enough to see the ridged and scarred flesh covering his left side. Yet, her hands never faltered. She simply slipped them over his shoulders, inviting him to duck his head so she could pull off the shirt and white T-shirt under it.

Thermal knit and cotton landed at her feet. A heartbeat later, her breath came out in a sighed, "Oh," and she touched her fingers to a long keloid bisecting his left pectoral. A thick surgical scar slashed like white ribbon from below his shoulder to under his arm where tightening flesh had been released. She touched there, too. With the fingers of her other hand, she skimmed the darkened grafting sites on the rippling muscles of his stomach and chest and bicep where healthy skin had been removed.

When her eyes moved to his, he thought she would ask what the oblong shapes were.

She didn't say a word. But what she did stole his breath.

With her hands splayed over his chest, she kissed everywhere she had touched, then looped her arms around his neck.

He caught her mouth even as she lifted her head, absorbing the taste and feel of her. He wouldn't think. It was too dangerous. The things he felt were too confusing to contemplate just then anyway. So he emptied his mind, allowed himself only to feel the demands of his body. He couldn't believe how responsive she was to him, how willingly she accepted his touch, gave her own. And, sweet heaven, what he felt when they went to work peeling the rest of each other's clothes away and finally tumbled to the ridiculously narrow bed was incredible.

Skin met heated skin. Hard body to soft. Curves to unyielding angles. Beneath her hands, Lauren felt hard, honed muscle and the warmth of his lean, powerful body as their limbs tangled, their mouths and hands explored, discovered. The textures of his flesh were different, slick in some places, raised ever so slightly in others. There was the roughness of the hair on his legs, and unexpected downiness at the base of his spine. The softness of his hair, the rocklike quality of his broad back. But the contrasts suited him, defined him. They were simply part of who he was and all that mattered to her was that he had let her past the walls he'd raised around himself.

All that mattered to Zach was that he was going to die if he didn't get inside her.

Refusing to let her go, he kept his hand on her shoulder and leaned over the bed to fumble for his pants and the wallet in the back pocket. Leather hit the floor the second he found what he was looking for. With his mouth on hers he rolled the condom over himself and eased back over her soft, supple body.

He was cradled between her thighs when his hands snaked through her hair and he edged himself forward, entering her by degrees. It was all he could do to hold himself back, to keep from burying himself in one long stroke. But he knew he wouldn't last if he didn't take it slow.

She denied him the choice. She arched toward him, whimpering his name, and he knew she wouldn't last, either.

Gritting his teeth against the need, he coaxed her higher, racing after her himself, thinking he'd never get enough of her. Then he felt her shatter, and he wasn't thinking at all.

"It broke?"

The faint confusion he heard in Lauren's voice was mirrored in her expression. He could see it in the dim light filtering from the hallway.

"Yeah. It did." Implications hit like a fist as he stared down at her pale features. Long minutes ago, he'd shifted to his side, drawing her with him to hold her until their breathing quieted and their heart rate calmed. But when he'd slipped off their protection, he'd realized something was wrong.

Bearing his weight on one elbow, he soothed her kiss-swollen mouth with his thumb. "How bad is our timing?"

He prayed it was one of the safer times of the month for her. But he knew even as she ran through her mental calculations that the news wasn't good. The lines between her eyebrows were back.

"It could be better," she replied uneasily. "What happened?"

"I'm not sure. The thing was old. I'd forgotten I even had it, until we needed it."

The condom had been in his wallet for over three years. The only reason it had been there to begin with was because he'd been out with a group of male business associates in Bellingham one evening and one of them had come back to the table with a handful of condoms he'd bought from the machine in the men's room. The guy had been three sheets to the wind, but he'd insisted that they were all going to get lucky that night and dealt the little disks out like cards.

Zach had tucked it away and pretty much forgotten about it. Until half an hour ago.

"Are you all right?" he asked. He could feel her small, soft hand resting on his back, her thumb absently smoothing his skin. She was concerned. He could tell by the way she searched his eyes. But her smile came softly.

"Yes," she told him, because he made her feel very safe just then. "The timing's not good, but it could be worse. And you said worrying doesn't help."

He smiled himself when she quoted him and cuddled closer. He liked the way she sought him, her body touching him everywhere it could. He craved that contact, craved the feel of her.

Brushing his lips over her forehead, he gathered her closer still.

"Hold that thought," he whispered, and though he had no reason to suddenly feel so calm, he closed his eyes, completely at peace.

That peace lasted until the gray light of morning peeked under the curtains in the small bedroom and Zach woke with the feel of Lauren's curvy little body creating all kinds of havoc with his. She still lay curled in his arms, her long legs tangled with his, her small fist curled against his chest. For several very long seconds, his only thoughts were of how incredible she felt against him, cocooned as they were beneath the blankets, and of a very basic and burning need to kiss her awake and slip inside her.

The thought that jerked him to full consciousness seconds later was that he couldn't stay where he was. Her hair spilled like honeyed satin against the pillow. Her beautiful, responsive mouth was softly parted. As tempting as she was, if he didn't get up, he was going to do exactly what his body demanded he do, and he wasn't into playing Russian roulette.

The sound of little feet padding down the hall ended any possibility of further debate.

Slipping from the bed, carefully, so Lauren could get a few more minutes sleep, he pulled on his jeans and undershirt and was pulling his heavier shirt over it when he found Jason on the counter reaching for a box of cereal in the cabinet.

They were sharing that cereal at the table when Lauren walked in a few minutes later.

She'd heard their voices the moment she'd stepped into the hall, the deep one low and reassuring. The child's full of curiosity. Not about why Zach had spent the night, but about why Zach didn't want him to mix orange juice and milk in his glass and when Zach was going to get his daddy.

With them occupied, she'd hurried through the bathroom and thrown on a pair of jeans and a pullover.

It had only taken a couple of minutes to dress.

It had only taken seconds for her to remember everything Zach had helped her forget last night, and for every insecurity she possessed as a woman to knot itself into a little ball in her stomach.

She had her hand on that knot when she stopped by the stove and saw Zach's dark head turn toward her. She had no idea how he would react to any of what had happened last night. She wasn't sure how she was feeling about some of it herself.

"We're having breakfast." His tone seemed as casual as his manner when he rose with the scrape of oak chair legs on pine. Abandoning the two chocolate puffs still floating in his bowl, he crossed to her, his stride completely relaxed. "He said it's his favorite cereal."

"It is," she murmured, and felt a bit of the knot unravel when he reached out and slipped his hand behind her neck.

With his back to the little boy, who was ignoring them, anyway, he lowered his head and kissed her, thoroughly, possessively.

A glint sparked in the smoky depths of his eyes when they met hers a dozen uneven heartbeats later. But there was caution there, too, a sense of disquiet that slipped uneasily over his chiseled features when he scanned her face.

"How long before there's coffee?"

"Less than ten minutes."

"Any chance I could get some before I go?" The disconcerting unease remained as he sifted her hair through his fingers and reluctantly drew away his hand. "Now that you're up, I want to see if I can find a hole in that fog."

He wasn't as unconcerned about what had happened as he was letting on. Lauren was certain of that as she told him she'd have the coffee on in a minute and turned away to fill the glass carafe at the sink. She didn't think it was making love that disturbed him. He wouldn't have kissed her the way he had if he'd regretted taking her to bed. It was what had happened with their protection that bothered him.

It bothered her, too. He'd said that worry didn't help anything. But, like it or not, another item had just been added to her list. There was no time to think about it at the moment, though. Jenny was awake and calling, "Mama," from her crib, and Jason had just spilled his juice.

"You do the diaper," Zach told her, taking the paper towels she automatically reached for. "I'll finish the coffee and cover the spill. And Lauren," he said, catching her arm. His glance moved intimately from her mouth to the furrows between her eyebrows. "It really won't help to worry. About any of it. I'm going to try to get your brother back here in time for you to go."

Chapter Eleven

The fog still hung in heavy patches over the inlet at twelve-thirty, which was half an hour later than the time Lauren would have had to leave her brother's house to catch the ferry that was scheduled to leave at twelve-twenty-five.

She hadn't heard from Zach, either.

As she quietly left Jenny's bedroom after putting the little girl down for her nap, Lauren figured her only option now was to see if by some miracle she could reschedule her appointment with the store's chief operations officer without the man deciding she wasn't management material after all.

Her packed suitcase sat by the door with her black raincoat draped over it. Hoping desperately that Zach would make it back with her brother in time for her to catch the ferry, she had fed the children and changed into her black suit. But hope had grown thin, then vanished completely and now it was too late for her to do anything other than change back into jeans and make her call.

Andy was going to be livid with her for not being at the store at that very moment. It was only a matter of time before she heard from him, too. She'd called his secretary first thing that morning to explain why she wasn't there, and to deal with whatever she could by phone. She'd also called Joanne and explained that tomorrow would be a better day for her to meet with Sam, since her brother wasn't back yet and she wasn't sure when he would be.

It seemed as if everything around her was on hold. Even Jason, who stood like a little sentinel at the living-room window watching for his dad, looked caught in that limbo.

"Do want me to read a book to you, sweetie? Or play a game?"

The child didn't turn around. Nor did he say a word. He just shook his head, his fine hair shining like gold in the filtered daylight, and rubbed his nose on the long sleeve of his blue shirt.

"Do you want to come draw while I make a phone call?"

This time, he didn't respond at all. He didn't even seem to have heard her. Even as she'd spoken, his entire body pulled up sharp, vibrating like a little hunting dog who'd just gone to point.

"He's here! Daddy's here!"

He whirled around, blue eyes wide, more animated than she'd ever seen him as he darted for the door. "He's here!" he repeated and with both hands on the latch, pulled open the door and was running toward Zach's truck before she could get to the threshold herself.

The air was damp and cold, but patches of blue were

visible through the low-hanging mist as she stepped onto the porch and watched Jason launch himself at the big bear of a man bending to scoop him up. With the crack of a slammed door, Zach headed for the back of the big black vehicle and pulled her brother's duffel from the bed of his truck.

Trading anxiety over her job for concern for her brother, she searched his face as he walked toward the porch. It was hard for her to tell if the escape had helped him. A week's worth of thick dark beard obliterated his features, camouflaging the deep creases in his cheeks and the set of his mouth, and making Jason look decidedly skeptical as he ran his little hand over his dad's prickly jaw.

"You look like a lumberjack," she told him.

"Must be the plaid shirt. How's Jenny?" he asked, his eyes still looking tired to her. "Did the kids give you any trouble?"

"Jenny's good. She just went down for her nap. And she's teething, but she does fine with the herbal gel in the refrigerator. She likes it cold," she explained. "And they were no trouble at all." She tipped her head, any difficulties she'd had receding in her preoccupation with him. "How about you? How are you doing?"

For a moment, she thought he was simply going to be her big brother and tell her he was doing just fine. It would have been so typically Sam. So typically stoic male. But as he met the blue eyes so like his own, he seemed to realize how unfair such a response would be. She was asking because she truly cared about him. And because she'd allowed him the escape he'd needed, he owed her more than that.

"I'm…better. I think," he qualified, seeming to welcome the feel of his child as he rubbed his little boy's back. "All I know for sure is that it's really good to be home." He glanced toward the house. "Really good," he repeated with a tight, confirming nod. "That's why I'm not going anywhere else. My home is here. And my work. And the kids have been through enough without taking them away from their home," he expanded, sounding far more certain about what he wanted than he'd claimed. "I don't need anyone trying to talk me into changes I don't want."

Relief at his decision, quick and surprisingly strong, moved into her soft smile. Beyond his shoulder, she saw Zach coming toward them, his long strides athletic, powerful. "I know you're not asking my opinion. But for what it's worth," she murmured, "I think you made the right choice."

For all of you, she thought, and crossed her arms over the nerves in her stomach. She wasn't even totally sure what was knotting them at the moment; the man who approached, openly appraising her sleek French roll and tailored pant suit, the fact that she had probably, irrevocably, loused up her job—or the sudden thought that maybe it didn't have to be so loused up after all.

If Zach had been able to get her brother onto Harbor, she should be able to get off it.

"Tell that to Mom," her brother muttered.

"I think I'll wait until she asks. By the way," she said, her mind suddenly racing as she pulled open the door for the men, "I found you a sitter. She was going to come today, but I didn't know when you'd be back."

"I didn't know when I'd be back, either. I still can't believe we got off of Gainey. That opening couldn't have been there for more than a minute. The fog is still pretty thick in places," he told her, eyeing the raincoat-covered suitcase by the door as he let Jason slide to the floor, "but it's starting to burn off here."

"So it's possible for me to leave, then?"

"Whenever you're ready," Zach said, over the thud of Sam's heavy olive drab duffel bag hitting the floor.

Sam nodded toward her suitcase. "I hear you have to get back for a meeting."

"I do. It's at three o'clock," she told him. Behind her, she found Zach running another glance from her sleek hair to her heels. She had no idea what he was thinking. She could read nothing in his expression or his manner but the easy control that masked whatever was going on inside him. "You can fly me there?"

"That's what I planned to do."

"You did?"

Picking up her raincoat, Zach handed it to her. "I can have you on the ground in Seattle in half an hour. Taking off from here is no problem, and the ceiling is high to the south."

"He'll take you to a municipal airport that's easier for small planes to get in and out of than Sea-Tac. I'll call and have a rental car waiting for you," Sam said, sounding very much as if he and Zach had discussed and decided the best course for her situation. "You should be to your store by two."

Lauren felt awful leaving her brother so soon after his return, but he wasted no time assuring her that she was forgiven and pointing out that she should probably hurry. The need to rush—and the knowledge that she would be able to make her meeting—also tended to mask the worst of her guilt as she tiptoed into Jenny's room to kiss the little girl good-bye, then kissed Jason and explained to her brother where she'd left Joanne's phone number. Sounding frighteningly like her mother, she then told him that she had left a casserole in the fridge for dinner, which he would need to heat at three-fifty for thirty minutes, before her brother gave her a hug and shoved her toward the door.

After hugging Jason again and promising her brother she would call him tonight to check on him and the kids, she grabbed her briefcase and purse and hurried with Zach to his truck.

She couldn't believe how anxious and uneasy she felt when he pulled out of the drive and onto the two-lane road that took her away from her brother and the children. She really hated leaving them. But she was also leaving the imposing, quietly watchful man beside her, and she had no idea how much, or how little, that particular detail mattered to him.

"Sam said he's staying," she confided.

Zach glanced across the wide bench seat to where Lauren was belted in by the door. She looked like a different woman to him with her flawless makeup and her hair sleeked back in its restrained style. Small gold Xs glinted on her ears. The black of her suit and overcoat contrasted starkly with the alabaster and peach of her smooth skin. There was a polished sophistication about her that hinted at reserve. But he knew the look was deceptive. He knew the understanding and warmth beneath the polish. And he knew how very vulnerable she could be.

"He told me."

"You have to be so relieved."

For over three weeks, he'd felt as if he'd been walking around with an iron band wrapped around his chest. Now, knowing there would be no change in the business, no change in his friendship with Sam and his kids, that nothing else about his life was going to be different from what he'd worked so hard to make it, that tightness had vanished and he could finally breathe.

"I am."

"You have a gift for understatement." There was a wealth of understanding in the small smile she gave him before she turned her focus back to the tree-lined road. "Do you think he'll be okay to fly now?"

"I don't know. We didn't talk about it. I imagine part of what was keeping him preoccupied was not knowing if he was staying or going. Now that he's made that decision, that's one thing off his mind."

"Do you think he's any better?"

"I wasn't with him long enough to tell," he replied, conscious of how tightly her fingers were knotted in her lap. "We didn't discuss anything other than getting through the weather and getting you back to Seattle." He lifted one shoulder in a contemplative shrug. "If nothing else, he has a week behind him."

Only time could fill the worst of the void that had been left inside her brother—and the week he'd spent away was a week of that time served.

Lauren knew there had been a time when she would have found a certain cynicism in Zach's response. Knowing him now, she understood that he regarded even that infinitesimal gain as something positive. That kind of response could only come from a man who had once forced himself to find something, anything, redeeming in every twenty-four-hour period he'd survived.

And he'd survived all of that time alone.

At the thought, she curled her fingers more tightly. There was something else she understood as they passed the last couple of minutes of the drive in silence and left his truck parked in front of the gleaming white hangar. Zach had let her past his guard. He'd let her see his scars.

Not just the physical marks on his body, but the deeper, more profound wounds on his soul. She loved him for that. She loved him for all the things he was inside. But whatever bond they shared was far too new and too fragile to withstand any tests. They needed more time themselves. Yet, time was something she didn't have as he led her to the small, six-passenger Cessna he'd left parked on the tarmac.

She'd never flown in a small plane before. With her agitated thoughts on the man moving with quick and easy efficiency to get her where she needed to be, she wasn't sure she noticed much about the experience now, either. Within a minute of Zach completing his checklist, putting on his headset, showing her how to adjust hers and flipping toggles, he was guiding the craft to the impossibly short little runway and they were lifting off through wisps of fog that drifted like pale smoke across the sharply receding land.

She caught a glimpse of emerald-green trees, white-capped gray ocean and a dozen little islands off in the distance. Fog lay like tufts of scattered cotton over those upthrusts of land. Ahead of them, the clouds loomed higher. But mostly what she noticed was the concentration etched in Zach's profile as he glanced from window to instruments, his comfortable grip on the throttle and, through her headset, the rumbling tones of his voice as he radioed approach control at their destination now only ten minutes away.

The same trip would have taken her an hour by ferry and another hour by car.

She also noticed the occasional careful glance he turned toward her, and that he'd yet to say a word about where their relationship might be headed. Not that there was time for conversation. Though he'd told her they could communicate through the mikes and headsets they wore—and which cut out the wind noise rushing around them—his focus was on his conversation with the thin voice giving him the instructions and coordinates that guided them through the clouds hanging over Seattle's airspace.

He had her on the ground and moving toward the only rental car place on site minutes later. Minutes after that, she had tossed her briefcase onto the passenger seat of the small metallic green sedan her brother had reserved for her, feeling as if she'd just stepped through a time warp. Half an hour ago, she'd been on Harbor, surrounded by ocean and pine forest and a fog that had made the place feel vaguely like Brigadoon. Now, she'd stepped out of that mist and was surrounded by an industrial complex, gas stations and a freeway that would have her to her office in only fifteen minutes.

"I don't know how I'll ever be able to repay you," she said, watching Zach slide her suitcase onto the back seat. "But thank you for doing this for me."

Zach closed the door over the drone of another small plane coming in low for a landing. There had been no time to talk on the way over. Now, he wasn't even sure what he wanted to say. "You don't owe me anything. I know the meeting is important."

He knew why it was important, too. And that made what he'd done matter to Lauren even more.

"Thank you, anyway."

She looked the same way she sounded, a little uncertain, uneasy. He felt that way himself, but he didn't want her heading off to her meeting worrying about anything but her job. "You're welcome, anyway," he mimicked, and let himself touch the tips of his fingers to her cheek.

He could swear he saw relief in her eyes just before they drifted closed and she pulled a deep, shuddering breath.

She'd wanted him to touch her. She'd been afraid that he wouldn't.

The realization caught him square in the conscience.

"Hey," he murmured. "Are you all right?"

"Yes. I'm…Yes," she repeated, her eyes as soft as her smile.

"Good," he whispered back and bent his head. "Just focus on your meeting right now. Don't worry about anything else."

His last words vibrated against her mouth as he brushed his lips over hers. Feeling her thready sigh against his cheek, wanting just a little more of her, he drew her closer, kissing her gently despite the quick and more demanding stirrings of his body. He understood his physical need for her easily enough. There was nothing complicated about the male sex drive. It was the possessiveness he felt that he didn't trust—and that had him ruthlessly canceling thoughts of how he'd love to pull the pins from her hair and slip the tailored wool from her slender body.

He eased back, rubbing his moisture from her bottom lip with his thumb, taking away a bit of the blush-tinted lipstick she wore. There was no denying that she'd gotten to him. There was no denying how threatened he felt because of that, either. Knowing he'd never intended for things to go as far as they had, he also had to admit to feeling a sense of responsibility.

The thought that he might have made her pregnant screamed with complications he didn't even want to consider. But he would need to know if she was.

"Let me know how your meeting goes. And let me

know what you want to do about your car. There isn't a
ferry from Harbor to Seattle. But I can send it to Anacortes.''

Which meant she would have to get to Anacortes herself to pick it up. With everything else Lauren had on
her mind, the logistics of how she would accomplish that
completely escaped her.

All she cared about just then, anyway, was that she
would be talking to him again soon. ''I will,'' she told
him, amazed at the relief she felt knowing that. She
glanced at her watch, wincing at how quickly time was
evaporating.

''You'd better go.''

''I know.''

''Now,'' he insisted. Taking her by the shoulders, he
pressed a kiss to her forehead. ''Knock 'em dead,'' he
murmured, and, not sure if he was feeling relief or regret,
turned her toward her car.

The chief operations officer hadn't exactly been lying
at her feet, but when Lauren left her meeting late that
afternoon and sank into the executive chair in her neat
and fashionable office, she was no longer concerned
about being demoted to stock clerk. It had helped enormously that the man had just been through knee surgery
that had put him out of commission for a while, so she'd
had his understanding about unforeseen circumstances
and the time they took to resolve. But he had also sought
her assurance that the company could expect her to be
back on track now.

The corporate shuffling was complete. And the demands on her time were about to increase.

She stared at her day planner, open on the cobalt-blue
blotter in front of her. Andy had been given a bigger

promotion than even he had anticipated and was being moved to the corporate offices in San Francisco next week. Since Andy's promotion was effective immediately, it would be up to her to familiarize his replacement as well as her own with the Seattle store. She had one month to do that—and six weeks to find an apartment in Bellingham. The opening of the new store there was scheduled for the end of May. Because stocking and hiring needed to begin long before, she would start working with the corporate buyers and human resources department in the next couple of weeks.

She had meetings in San Francisco herself next Monday and Tuesday.

On Thursday, she was to meet with the Seattle store's new manager.

Friday was Andy's last day.

She noted it all on her calendar, in pencil in case something changed, which, invariably, it did. She made a note to talk to their secretary about organizing some sort of farewell party for Andy. Another to subscribe immediately to Bellingham's local newspaper.

She didn't know much about the community ninety miles north of Seattle, except that it was closer to her brother and far smaller than where she was accustomed to living. Because of the lower population, the store would be much smaller, too. But that was an advantage as far as she was concerned. What mattered most was that the store was hers.

The sense of accomplishment she felt was enormous. She just wasn't feeling the giddiness she would have anticipated. Feeling slightly overwhelmed by all that needed to be done undoubtedly accounted for part of that. But, as she made another note on her calendar—a small Z next to the numerals of yesterday's date—and counted back to the little witch's hat she always drew next to the date her period started, she knew it wasn't just increased responsibility ruining her high.

It was having dormant dreams awakened.

It was the foolish but undeniable yearning for something she knew would complicate her life beyond belief.

It was knowing she cared deeply about a man who gave easily of everything—except his heart.

"Mr. Nye is on line two, Miss Edwards. And the department manager from women's shoes needs to see you. I think she's ready for her maternity leave. Oh, and when you have a minute," the salt-and-pepper-haired secretary she shared with Andy said as she stood in the open doorway scanning the list in her hand, "Eddie in PR needs to talk to you about where to put the radio personalities. KSEA is announcing from here in the morning and no one knows where to put them."

With a sincere smile, Ruth added her congratulations on her promotion before she turned away. But Lauren scarcely had time to wonder how the woman had come by the knowledge so quickly. By the time she'd taken the call from Andy, whose mood had improved considerably since the last time she'd spoken with him, and dealt with the obviously pregnant manager, a dozen other matters had lined up behind Eddie in PR like planes in a holding pattern over LaGuardia.

She didn't leave the store until nearly midnight. The night guard walked her to her car. She was back by 7:00 a.m. and repeated the pattern all over again. She ate lunch with the woman she was promoting to interim manager in shoes, had dinner at her desk and the only time she took for herself was to call her brother to see what he'd thought of Joanne, since she knew from her two-minute call to him last night that he was to meet with her today.

He'd thought the woman was great, and didn't seem to mind at all that she could only stay there five days a week. But, then, she'd shown up with brownies, which had softened him up from the start.

She'd tried to call Zach, too, to tell him how her meeting had gone because he had asked her to let him know, and because she very much wanted to hear his voice. He more than anyone would understand the sense of accomplishment she felt, and how daunted she was by the opportunity she'd been given. Since the only number she had for him was for E&M's office phone, she left a message asking him to call her and gave him her home and office numbers. She drew the line at leaving her cell phone and pager numbers, too. Something about doing that hinted at desperation and the last thing she wanted was to leave that impression.

They played phone tag for three days before he apparently tired of that particular game and left a message asking her to give him a time when she would be available.

She was calling back, planning to leave a message that she would be home that evening, since she was taking a stack of reports home with her, when he answered the phone himself.

"Hi," she said, shamed by how quickly her heart started to beat when she heard his voice.

"Lauren." He spoke her name flatly, his recognition instant. "You've been busy."

"So have you."

"I guess we have had a little trouble connecting," he acknowledged over the shuffle of papers. "Actually, I'm running late right now. I was supposed to pick up the mail an hour ago.''

"Fog?"

"Flu. Chuck's out with it.''

"I don't want to keep you then,'' she told him, not sure if he sounded distant or simply rushed.

"Hey, before you go,'' he said, before she could decide. "Congratulations on your promotion.'' He paused as the shuffling sound stopped. "I'm glad you got it.''

At the change in his deep voice, the sincerity in it, her fingers tightened on the receiver. "Thanks,'' she murmured, the quick unease she'd felt losing its grip. "I am, too. It's just going to be kind of crazy for a while.''

"When do you move?''

"In about a month. I have to find an apartment first.''

"You're going to need your car.''

She knew that. She just wasn't sure when she would be able to get it. She knew that she missed the children fiercely, though, and that she would find a way to take a weekend off soon so she could see them. She would pick up her car then.

She thought Zach seemed to hesitate for a moment when he realized she would be back for a couple of days. But all he said was to let him know when she was coming and he would fly over for her. It would save her time taking the ferry over.

She told him she would, touched by his willingness to do that for her, and half an hour later, after he'd asked what had happened with Andy and she'd asked how he thought her brother was doing, they hung up with him even further behind schedule and her late for a luncheon.

As much as they had found to share, and as comfortable as their conversation had become, he never mentioned them talking again. All he did before he hung up

was remind her to call when she was ready for the ride
to Harbor.

Two hectic weeks passed before she was finally able
to see her way clear to make that call to the charter office.
When she did, it was her brother who answered the telephone.

"Tomorrow's great," he said, when she told him she
wanted to come for the weekend and that Zach had said
he'd pick her up. "I'll just be working in the basement.
Joanne needs a better place to stay than the sewing room,
so I'm finishing off the downstairs bathroom and closing
in a bedroom down there. I'll put you in the log for
noon."

She told him that would be perfect, thinking that he
sounded good, far better than he had the last couple of
times they'd spoken. He needed to be busy, and she was
glad he had something to do that he could get enthused
about.

He also sounded very much as if he had no idea how
involved she and his friend had become while she'd been
there. All he said about Zach was that he would tell him
she was coming when he got in that afternoon, then he
asked if she could run by a hardware store and pick him
up some plumbing parts that he couldn't get on Harbor.
After she'd written down what he wanted and gained his
assurance that someone at the hardware store would
know what she was looking for, he asked her to meet the
plane on the tarmac when he landed. It would be easier
for Zach than having to leave the plane himself, he explained, since they would just be taking off again.

Chapter Twelve

Lauren stood at the glass doors of the small terminal, watching through the drizzle as the white plane with E&M Charter Service emblazoned on the fuselage taxied to a stop a hundred yards away.

She hated to think how anxious she was to see Zach. And how incredibly nervous. But standing there thinking only compounded the problem, so she headed into the rain with a death grip on her small overnight bag and a fervent prayer that their situation wasn't more complicated than he realized.

Her hurried footsteps echoed the beat of her heart when she saw the passenger door under the wing open. Seconds later, a large hand gripped the bag she held up and she was crawling into the seat beside the man whose lean, carved features held the same caution she felt in the moments before he smiled.

"You're wet."

She smiled back, relieved. "This is Seattle. Everything's wet this time of year." She lowered her hood, raindrops running in rivulets from the shoulders and sleeves of her heavy beige jacket. "Thanks for coming to get me."

His glance slipped over her face with familiar ease, coming to rest briefly on her mouth.

It faltered as his perusal dropped to her lap, then jerked away.

"Anytime." Looking preoccupied, sounding it, he reached past her to check the safety latch after she'd slammed the door. His leather jacket creaked as his shoulder pressed hers, his familiar scent filling her lungs. "It's going to be bumpy," he warned her. "Buckle in tight."

She said she would. At least she thought she did in the moments before his hooded glance briefly caught hers, then he pulled back and handed her a headset. With the quick practiced click of metal, he buckled in himself, adjusted the arm of his microphone and requested permission to depart.

Lauren settled her headset over her ears. The pleasure she felt at seeing Zach was diluted by disquiet as the engine revved and he guided the plane toward the runway. Despite his easy manner, there was a remoteness about him that she couldn't quite define. Having flown with him before, she wanted to believe he was simply focused on what he was doing. It was entirely possible, too, she realized, that she was just feeding off her own apprehension.

She was four days late and trying hard not to worry.

Pulling a deep breath, she caught Zach's careful glance a moment before concentration washed over his features and he became totally occupied with the flight.

Seconds later, she was preoccupied, too. He was right. The ride *was* bumpy, a circumstance that effectively prevented her from thinking about much of anything other than how amazingly calm he looked, how completely she trusted his abilities and how unsettling it could be riding in an airborne roller coaster.

"Are you doing okay?" she heard him ask through the headphones after a stomach-lifting dip.

She tightened her grip on her seat. "Never better," she lied, and felt her heart flip when he gave her an approving smile before he became absorbed again.

With the headwinds, the trip took longer than it had the last time, but they soon broke out of the clouds, and Zach settled them with a bounce on the landing strip paralleling the sea on Harbor. Because he didn't want to mess with tying the plane down on the tarmac in the stiff wind, he parked it near its twin inside the cold and cavernous hangar. Only then, when they were heading across the concrete floor for the office door, was it possible for Lauren to think about anything that didn't have to do with the flight, the plane or the weather.

"You did great up there," Zach told her, taking her bag. "A lot of people lose it when it gets rough like that."

With their footsteps echoing, Lauren pressed her hand to her stomach. "I thought about it a couple of times," she confessed. "But I'm fine. I had a great pilot."

She glanced up at him, looking past the scar visible above the collar of his heavy denim shirt and brown leather jacket. She thought she might see him smile. But his glance had followed her hand, and he wasn't smiling at all.

Conscious of the direction his thoughts might have

taken, not at all anxious to discuss a problem that might
or might not exist, she focused on more concrete concerns. "I'm really looking forward to seeing the kids,"
she confessed. "Sam said Jenny's tooth came in and that
she's doing fine with Joanne. But Jason seems kind of
quiet to him. Do you think he is? Quiet, I mean?"

"Maybe," he replied, leading her past stacks of cargo
to be shipped and a plane that looked ready for salvage
on their way to the azure-blue office door. Parts lay scattered over the concrete floor like pieces of a jigsaw puz-
zle. Across from the plane itself propellers and parts hung
on the white walls above a long, wide workbench. "I've
only seen them a few times myself in the past couple of
weeks. I've been kind of busy here."

She knew he had been. Her brother was working the
office and doing their ground work, but Sam still wasn't
flying. With Chuck out sick, that left Zach to do it all.
"Are you able to keep up?"

"As much as the weather lets me." He reached past
her when they approached the exit, his hand settling on
the knob. Hesitating, he ran a glance over her face, his
features suddenly taut with the same caution that entered
his voice. "What about you?" Eyes the color of the
clouds held hers, searching, guarded. "You look tired,"
he quietly observed. "Is everything…all right?"

She didn't have to ask to know what had him looking
as if he might be mentally holding his breath. There
hadn't been a day that she hadn't thought about what had
happened between them, and about what might have happened because of it. From the way he'd been watching
her, she suspected it had been on his mind about that
long, too.

Her glance dropped to the row of buttons visible between the open sides of his jacket. She could so easily

remember being held against his strong, solid chest. Wishing he would hold her now, aware of how careful he was being not to touch her, she crossed her arms over the funny little void beneath her heart.

"I'm late. But it's probably because of stress," she hurriedly assured him, trying to reassure herself in the process.

His hand slid from the knob. "How late?"

"Just a few days."

"You're not feeling any...ah..."

"Symptoms?" she offered, because he didn't seem quite sure about what he should ask. "No. Nothing." She'd had no symptoms at all. She hadn't felt even the slightest twinge of dizziness or nausea. She'd even managed the turbulence of the flight without any real ill effects.

She would give herself three more days, then she would buy a home pregnancy test. That would make her late by a full week.

"I am tired," she conceded, hugging herself tighter, "but I'm sure that's only because of everything I've had to do lately. Actually, I get tired just thinking about what I have left to do," she said, adding a smile to alleviate the strain threatening between them. "I'm supposed to be moving in a couple of weeks and I haven't even started to pack. I haven't found an apartment yet, either." The smile died. "I haven't even had a chance to look," she emphasized, thinking maybe she did feel a little nauseous after all.

For a moment, Zach said nothing. He simply watched the distress move through her eyes, torn between the need to reach for her and the concern he felt himself at what she'd just said. What he knew about a woman's body was embarrassingly little, beyond how to give or gain pleasure. If she said stress was making her late, then she probably knew what she was talking about. All he knew for certain was that there hadn't been a single day since she'd left that he hadn't thought about her—and that there was something very familiar about the tiny parallel lines digging between her eyebrows.

"So it's just the move and your work that has you worried?"

"I didn't say I was worried."

The look he gave her held enormous patience. "You didn't have to. I know you, Lauren. And I know that somehow you'll tackle whatever's thrown in your path. But, just in case, have you thought about what you'll do if you are pregnant?"

"I'm only a few days late."

"That doesn't answer my question."

"There's no point in discussing something that might not even be a problem."

"Just humor me. Okay?"

She really didn't want to discuss this now. What she wanted was for him to put his arms around her. She *was* tired. Her days had been impossibly long, and her nights had been filled with restless dreams of him.

She'd missed him desperately. She'd missed talking to him, confiding in him, sharing with him. And she'd faced every evening of silence from him wondering if she mattered to him at all.

"I haven't really let myself think about it," she finally admitted, because thinking about carrying his child had only made her want that child more. "The thought of having a baby with everything that's going on right now is just so…enormous," she decided, though even that word didn't seem adequate for all the emotions such an event would encompass. "But I'd continue with the move, I suppose. Or maybe I'd ask to keep my current position so I could stay closer to Mom and my friends.''

Another alternative taunted while Zach somberly considered her, the same alternative that had slipped into her dreams. For the past two years, she'd thought of nothing but work, of proving herself, of making it on her own. But because of this courageous and tenderhearted man, every fantasy she'd ever had of loving a man who loved her back and of having a home and children of her own had been resurrected. She couldn't begin to imagine how they could make their lives work. She just knew she desperately wanted the chance.

''I'm not really sure what my options would be,'' she concluded cautiously, hoping he would offer something for her to latch on to. ''I know we're talking hypotheticals,'' she murmured, ''but what would you suggest?''

A muscle in his jaw jerked as he reached over and tucked a strand of hair behind her ear. The wind outside whistled around the building, sending a cold draft under the door, making her shiver. Lauren barely noticed how her arms tightened. She was far more conscious of the way her heart leapt at his touch, the power in his long, lean body and the speculative way his quicksilver gaze moved over her face.

''If you are pregnant,'' he said, tracing the line of her jaw with his thumb, ''you could give the baby to me.''

For a moment, it felt to Lauren as if every organ in her body had ceased to function. She felt nothing. She just stood in stunned silence while he hesitantly withdrew his hand. But he had no sooner denied her his touch, than the familiar pain of rejection slashed through her heart, bleeding her of the hope that had bloomed only moments before.

Scrambling to keep her hurt from surfacing, she whispered, "Give it to you?"

"I know how much this promotion means to you," he told her, his concern still remarkably evident. "And I know you're in no position to have a child right now. By giving it to me, you wouldn't have to jeopardize what you've worked for."

He sounded so reasonable. So eminently…practical.

"You think I could give up my own child?"

"It wouldn't be just yours."

"I see," she murmured, a numb calm creeping over the hurt, the fatigue. "So you'd have a child of your own without having to bother with a relationship with its mother."

Her conclusion flattened the light in his eyes. "I never made you any promises, Lauren."

"I never asked for any."

"But I won't walk away from a responsibility."

"Responsibility?" she quietly echoed, hating the defense that slipped like a mask over his dark features, hating the defense slipping into her. "Or opportunity?" He wasn't mentioning giving them a chance themselves, about the possibility of raising the child together. He didn't seem to be thinking about where she would fit in at all. "You would make a wonderful father, Zach. You really would. And I know you need a family of your own. But I wouldn't give up my child."

His eyebrows bolted together in a single offended slash. "You think that's why I'd do this? Because I need a family?"

It was entirely possible, she realized, that that was exactly what he was doing. But he clearly couldn't see it himself.

His voice darkened. "If you believe that, then you don't know me at all."

"I do know you," she countered, quieting her tone as his hardened. She refused to let him use that argument. She knew how he guarded his heart. She knew how he held back from any woman who might get close enough to really matter to him. "I know how much you can give a child, Zach. And I know you well enough to realize that the best part of you is still hiding. You might have left Gainey, but you've stuck yourself in a place that's nearly as isolated.

"Do you know what I don't understand?" she asked, because his courage was so great with everything else. "I don't understand how you could risk your neck flying jets, yet be so afraid to risk your heart with anyone over the age of three."

Zach felt the tension creep along his shoulders, tightening the muscles in his neck, his jaw. "I may have risked my neck flying jets," he countered, his voice deceptively calm, "but I also crashed and burned."

Her chin came up, disbelief flashing in her eyes. "Who hasn't?"

Zach bit back an oath. They weren't talking about planes, and they both knew it. But the direction their discussion was headed was a place he didn't want to go. He'd only been thinking of her when he'd said he'd take the child. He knew how overloaded she could get. He knew what she would have to give up if she had a child on her own.

He'd offered the only way he could to help. But he hadn't even considered how he'd get through the infant stage when she'd accused him of being an opportunist.

Feeling attacked, he instinctively countered. "We're talking about what we'll do if you're pregnant," he reminded her tightly. "But just for the record, I'm not the one hiding. This place might be remote, but I'm involved here. I'm living my life. You're the one who's practically killed herself to get a promotion that's demanding even more of you."

"I know that."

"Have you considered how much of a life that would leave you for a child?"

"Hardly any," she conceded, not particularly appreciative of how he wasn't even hearing what she was saying. The muffled slam of a car door penetrated the walls, the sound forcing her voice lower. "But there's no point in talking about any of this now. We don't even know if I am pregnant."

"Let's just hope you're not. Neither one of us needs this."

"No," she concluded flatly. "Neither one of us does." Desperate to keep their discussion from disintegrating further, a faint plea entered her voice. "Let's just let this go until we know something. Okay?"

She was right. They weren't getting anywhere. Zach couldn't deny that any more than he could deny his annoyance at how reasonable she'd sounded.

"Zach? You in there?"

It was Sam. Recognizing his partner's voice an instant before the office door behind them opened, he pulled his glance from Lauren's strained features before he could say anything he'd have to regret.

"Hey, Sis," Sam greeted, looping an arm around her shoulder for a quick squeeze. "Looks like my timing is good. I ran out of plumbing putty so the kids and I were over at Rykers." At his mention of the local hardware store, his glance moved to the man whose clenched jaw threatened serious damage to his back teeth. "I saw the plane come in and thought I'd save you a trip out to the house.''

"Appreciate it,'' Zach muttered.

"You're on your way to Orcas now?''

"Then to Lopez.''

"I'll wait for you in the car,'' Lauren said to her brother.

"Did you get my elbow joints?''

"They're in my bag.''

Zach held it out. Without a word, she took it, skirted the high counter dividing the map-papered office and headed out the door to join the kids in the red Suburban parked outside the window.

The office door had no sooner groaned to a close than Zach plowed his fingers through his hair.

Sam, who rarely saw him agitated, scowled. "Did I miss something?''

"I have no idea how a woman can make a man mad by agreeing with him,'' Zach grumbled, "but your sister has a real knack for it.''

"Lauren? What did she do?''

She hadn't done anything, Zach thought, except give him honest answers about a situation she'd made a point of noting might not even exist. He'd just never encountered a woman who could strike sparks off him the way she could, or who jerked so hard at instincts he didn't even know he possessed. "Nothing. Forget it,'' he muttered.

"Wait a minute.'' Sam's big hand clamped around Zach's arm as he started to pass. His cleanly shaven face pinched in curiosity. "I've never known a woman to get to you,'' he stated flatly. "Is there something going on between you and my sister?''

As private as he could be, as self-protective, Zach

would have liked very much to deny that there was. That's what he would have done, too, had the big man waiting for his response been anyone other than his business partner and his friend.

"Yeah," he muttered, not at all certain about what his friend was going to think. "I'm just not sure what though."

For a moment, Sam didn't say a word. He just stood there balanced between the protective position of big brother and the supportive role of good friend. It wasn't until he'd planted his hands on his hips that the scales tipped.

The glint of a smile lit eyes that hadn't smiled in weeks. "You and Lauren?"

Zach felt his gut tighten. This man was his friend. He'd trusted him to take care of his kids and his sister. But family loyalty came first. If he compromised Lauren, or hurt her in any way, it was entirely possible that Sam would want to string him up in the nearest tree.

"Like I said," he muttered, being as honest as he could without tightening the noose himself, "I really don't know what's going on."

Something suspiciously like sympathy moved over Sam's rugged features in the moments before he clapped his hand to Zach's shoulder. "I don't know if this'll help or not, but that was the way I felt for the first six months I knew Tina."

He had married Tina six months and a week after they'd met. Zach knew that. He also knew that Sam had been crazy in love with his wife. But he wouldn't let himself consider the possibility that he could care that deeply for Lauren. She didn't know him nearly as well as she thought she did. During the time he'd spent in the hospital and on Gainey, he'd buried any longing he'd had for a family of his own. The lesson had been long, hard and painful, but he'd learned he could survive just fine with what he had—and what he had was a home to retreat to when he got tired. He had a plane to rebuild when he got restless. He had his friends and he had his work. He needed nothing else.

With a thin smile for his friend, he turned to the phone to call in a flight plan for his next run. He would wait and see what he and Lauren were dealing with, then take it from there. In the meantime, he would stop by her brother's house before she left tomorrow and tell her he was sorry he'd pushed. He wasn't even sure why he had.

She needed to apologize.

She needed to say good-bye.

She needed to let him know he was off the hook.

The thoughts ran through Lauren's head like a litany as she left her car in the black-topped driveway and approached the cedar-and-glass house overlooking the town of Harbor Cove. Maddy had alluded to Zach's home being something extraordinary, but Lauren hadn't been prepared for the sweeping vistas, or the airy, soaring vaults of the two-story structure.

She wasn't sure why, but she'd envisioned him in something much smaller. And rustic. Like her brother's house. She hadn't expected all the glass, all the openness.

And Zach clearly hadn't expected her.

"What are you doing here?"

As greetings went, his didn't do a thing to make her mission any easier.

He stood in the doorway with the tails of his chambray shirt hanging over tan khakis and his damp sable hair spiking up where he'd toweled it dry. His feet were bare, his jaw was freshly shaved and the curiosity in his eyes was matched only by his caution.

"I'm taking the eleven o'clock ferry to Bellingham, but I wanted to see you first."

Guarded, skeptical, he stepped back, motioning her out of the gray dampness that wasn't fog but wasn't quite rain, either, just the typical Northwest mist that kept everything damp from September through June. "I thought you'd take the twelve-thirty to Anacortes. Are you going over to look for an apartment?"

"As long as I am this far north, it makes sense."

The door closed with a solid thud as she stopped in the wide flagstone entry. Beyond her, pale beige carpet swept across an expansive room dominated by a cinnamon-colored sectional, a tall spike of a rock fireplace and a view that went on forever.

His surroundings were, indeed, impressive. But she was infinitely more aware of Zach's fingers moving deftly down the front of his shirt as he buttoned it, the width of his broad chest and the scent of soap clinging to his skin. She'd obviously caught him fresh from his shower.

He nodded his dark, damp head toward the hallway behind her. "Do you want some coffee?"

"No, thanks. I won't keep you," she said, thinking he sounded a little hesitant. After their little discussion yesterday, she was feeling that way, too. She'd come to a few conclusions last night as she'd lain in the sewing-room bed with a hot pad for her cramps, remembering the last night she'd spent there. Zach had told her himself that when there was nothing she could possibly do to change a situation, the wisest thing to do was let it go. She couldn't change how he had come to feel over the past seven years. She didn't even know how to try. All she could do was bow out as gracefully as possible. And try to keep them from parting badly.

"I just came by to tell you there's nothing to worry about. For either of us. Last night I..." She paused, trying to think of a how a person gracefully said that her period had started. "It probably was just stress," she concluded. "And Sam doesn't know anything," she quickly explained. "About us, I mean. Except that we became...friends. In case you were wondering."

In the gray light pouring through the tall windows beside them, she watched Zach's brow lower as he absorbed what she'd just told him. He had been right when he'd said that neither one of them needed this particular problem. And she had thought for sure he would look relieved. She would have thought she'd feel relief, too. And she did. Sort of.

She just had no idea what thoughts were going through his mind when his expression turned contemplative and his glance narrowed on hers.

His deep voice dropped. "Are you all right?"

She had no idea why his concern made her throat feel so tight. But that concern had always been there, buried beneath irritation at times, but somehow it had always existed.

"I'm fine," she made herself say, telling herself she really would be. In about a dozen years. She never would have believed she could fall so hard and so fast. "It's funny how you can want something that would make a total mess of your life, then actually feel disappointed when you don't get it." She shook her head, managed a faint disbelieving smile. "But I'm sure that'll pass if I just think about how big a mess it really would have been."

Incredulity, or maybe it was skepticism, colored his tone. "You're disappointed?"

"It doesn't make a lot of sense, does it?" She shook her head again, thinking he must surely believe she'd taken leave of her senses. "It would have been hard, but I think we could have worked out something...like the way we eventually worked out how we'd help Sam and take care of Jason and Jenny." They'd knocked heads there, too, at first. "But with your life here and mine clear over in...well," she concluded softly, "it doesn't matter now."

From behind her came the faint gurgle and hiss of a coffeemaker finishing its cycle. "No," he murmured over that strangely domestic sound, "I guess it doesn't."

His agreement tightened the tight band of misery around her chest. She really needed to get this over with and leave. "There's just one more thing. I'm sorry for what I said yesterday. I had no business criticizing how you've chosen to live your life. You've put yours back together a whole lot better than I have mine."

She took a step closer.

"I've learned a lot from you, Zach. And I know that if there's anyone who can help my brother get through what he's dealing with, it's you. Please take care of him." Rising on tiptoe, she brushed a kiss to his smooth hard jaw and gently touched the scar below it. "Take care of yourself, too. Okay?"

Her mouth curved as she stepped back, her smile soft and mercifully easy. "Maybe we'll run into each other again sometime."

He was frowning when she turned to the door and opened the brass latch quickly so he couldn't see that her hand was shaking. He made no attempt to keep her from leaving. He didn't even say good-bye before she slipped out and hurried to where she'd left her car parked at the end of the flagstone walkway.

Zach watched her go from the tall window by the door, his hands jammed on his hips and his frown still firmly in place. He'd been getting ready to go see her, to apologize as he'd decided to do last night and tell her he would do the right thing by her, whatever that turned out to be. His sense of honor, of responsibility, wouldn't allow him to do otherwise.

She'd saved him the trip.

He'd also dodged a bullet.

At the very least, he should have felt relieved.

He had what he'd wanted. Nothing had changed. He'd lost a friend when Tina had died and that loss had left a void in everyone who'd known her. But Sam and the kids were staying. He still had his little buddy in Jason, and his friend and his partner in Sam. The business would go on as they had planned. Lauren wasn't pregnant, so there would be no demands or responsibilities there, and she'd walked out of his life without a fight or a hint of any expectations about a future.

Everything was exactly as he wanted it to be, as he'd been so afraid it wouldn't be from the moment Sam had lost his wife.

He turned from the window, shoving his fingers through his damp hair. He didn't want Lauren to have expectations. He didn't want them himself. As she'd mentioned only minutes ago, just the logistics of a relationship with her were complicated. And the craving he felt for her would eventually succumb if he spent enough hours numbing his mind with calibrations rebuilding the old plane, or running himself into exhaustion along the beach road.

The relief was there, somewhere. It was just going to take him a little time to feel it.

"Here's your ticket for San Francisco, Lauren. I booked your return on the same flight you took last week. That will get you back here in time to meet the real estate agent in Bellingham. And there's a gentleman here to see you. Zach McKendrick. He said he's a friend of your brother's."

Ruth dropped a stack of memos into Lauren's in box and held out the tickets. "Are you available to see him?"

Lauren felt her heart knock against her ribs as she glanced up at the exceptionally efficient middle-aged woman in the boxy teal suit. Taking the tickets from her, she tucked them between the pages of her day planner.

"Yes. Of course," she murmured, wondering how much of her composure had slipped.

"He's a rather attractive man, isn't he? Do you know him well?"

"Well enough," Lauren replied. "Why?"

"I just wondered how he got that awful scar on his neck."

It wasn't just on his neck, Lauren thought vaguely, unable to imagine why he was here, wishing he would disappear. It was so unfair of him to break into one of the few moments in the last ten days that she hadn't been aware of the awful void inside her chest. He hadn't asked for her heart. He hadn't even wanted it. But it felt as if he'd ripped it out, anyway.

Darting a glance toward her open door, she was aware of the ache now. But she needed to be fair. The void wasn't his fault. She'd handed her heart to him herself. "He crashed a jet."

"Oh. My."

"Yes," Lauren agreed, knowing exactly what the woman meant. The man had cheated death. It did sort of give him an aura. "He said he was a friend of my brother's?"

Ruth's salt-and-pepper bob bounced as she turned back. "Isn't he?"

"Yes, but he…never mind," she quickly muttered. She just thought it an odd way for him to identify himself. A rather distant way, considering how close they had been.

Unless, she thought with a sudden concern, he was there because of Sam. "Would you show him in, please?"

The thought that there could be a problem with her brother had Lauren moving around her neat but crowded desk moments after Ruth walked out the door. She hadn't talked to Sam at all since she'd last seen him. With his life settling into a routine of sorts and hers busier than it had ever been, their time was being consumed by the same demands that had caused them to go from one holiday season to the next without seeing each other, and for weeks-long stretches of time when they didn't even touch base by phone.

She had just moved past the two provincial-style visitors' chairs in front of her matching desk when Zach's imposing frame filled her doorway.

He wore a black leather jacket with casual black jeans and a smoke-gray turtleneck that turned his eyes a breathtaking shade of pewter. With his dark hair swept back from his lean, carved features, the longer hair at his nape rakishly covering his collar, she could see why Ruth, who was rarely impressed by anyone, had taken notice of him.

"Is something wrong with Sam?"

At the unexpected question, Zach's brow snapped low. "Sam? He's fine. I just left him an hour ago."

In the bright overhead lights, he watched the faint lines deepen between Lauren's eyebrows. He'd noticed the telltale sign of worry the instant he'd seen her.

His glance shifted over her face, the smooth perfection of her makeup, the sleek coil of her wheat-colored hair. Her dark mocha suit was nipped at the waist, high-collared and skimmed her slender body in a way that made his hands ache to touch her.

Suddenly seeming hesitant, she tipped her head. "You're sure?"

"That I left him? Or that he's okay?"

"That he's all right. I thought you told my secretary you were a friend of my brother because something was wrong."

"Honest, Lauren." He'd never known anyone who wore her concern so openly. "He's fine. So are the kids," he said, because he was sure she was about to ask.

He glanced behind him, into the elegant reception area with its crystal chandelier, marble planters, blue velvet chairs and tables of Brenman's catalogs and fashion magazines.

Wanting privacy, he closed the door with a quiet click and turned back to where Lauren stood in the middle of her equally elegant office. Brenman's obviously took its upscale image seriously. The same cobalt-blue of the reception area carpeted the modestly sized space, covered her chairs and was echoed in the Monet prints on her white walls.

He remembered thinking before that she looked as comfortable in sweats as she did a suit. Seeing her in her own surroundings, he was struck again by the thought—

only she didn't look at all comfortable now as he slowly approached her.

"I mentioned that I was a friend of your brother," he said, leaving a yard of plush carpet between them when he stopped, "because it was the easiest way to identify myself. I'm not sure what I am to you."

With the predictability of sunrise, her arms snaked around her middle. "I thought we were at least... friends."

He had the feeling the word sounded as lame to her as it did to him. "At least?" he echoed.

"I don't understand what you want, Zach."

He didn't imagine she did. A month ago he couldn't have imagined it himself.

A fine tension hummed through his body as he casually looked at his watch. It had been years since he'd experienced that particular feeling. It was the same sensation that had rushed through him every time he'd strapped himself into the cockpit of a test plane. He'd needed to fly like he needed to breathe, but he'd never know quite what would happen up there.

He wasn't sure what was about to happen now, either. He just knew that he needed her more than he'd ever needed that adrenaline high.

"It's almost six. How much longer are you going to be here?"

Beneath his quietly determined expression lurked a hint of unease. Trying to mask her own as well, Lauren shook her head. "I won't be leaving for another couple of hours."

"How about dinner later, then? You have to eat."

"I'm going to dinner with the new manager and her husband." Unease melded with curiosity. "Why do you want to go out?"

"Because I want to be someplace where we won't be interrupted."

A heavy beat slipped into the void. Tightening her arms over it, she watched his glance move over her face. "Why?" she asked, a little defensive, a little puzzled.

For a moment, she didn't think he was going to respond. He just stood with his eyes steady on hers, looking very much the way he had the evening he'd told her of the events that had led him to Harbor. As he studied her, it was almost as if he were weighing how much he should tell her, how much he could trust her to know.

Now, as then, he apparently decided to go for broke.

"Because I miss you, Lauren."

It had been that simple. He'd missed her. Every hour of every day since she'd gone.

The delicate chords of her neck convulsed as she swallowed. "You do?"

"Yeah," he murmured, aware that a bit of her caution had slipped. Encouraged by that, he ventured further. "Actually, it seems I can't get you out of my mind."

He'd really thought he would be able to do that, too. Since everything had returned to the way it had been before he'd met her, it had seemed perfectly logical that everything should be the same after she'd gone. But nothing was the same. The hard-won sense of peace he'd struggled to protect had walked right out the door with her.

"You accused me of hiding," he told her, because that more than anything had preyed on him for days after she'd gone. "I think I denied that."

"You did," Lauren said when he hesitated. He missed her. He'd come to see her simply because he missed her.

"And I tossed the accusation right back at you."

"You did that, too," she replied, wondering how he

thought she was supposed to get over him when he said things like that. When he looked at her as if he really meant what he'd said. She didn't want him raising her hopes. She wanted it all with him or she wanted nothing. He, more than anyone else, should be able to understand that.

"You know what, though?" he asked, jerking at hope anyway as his somber glance held hers. "We were both right. We've both been hiding. But if you think about it, we never hid from each other. We never really even tried."

"No," she said, her voice hushed. "I don't suppose we did."

He ducked his head to see her eyes. "What about you? Do you miss me? Even a little?"

"Zach."

"What?"

"Don't do this."

"Do what?"

"This," she insisted, her eyes suddenly pleading and revealing far more than her pride would have liked. "I know I left like a big girl and made it sound as if it would be great to see you once in a while, but I can't do that. I'm trying to get over you."

She could swear she saw a hint of a smile in his eyes. Or maybe it was relief. "Why?"

"Why?" she repeated incredulous. "Because your life is across a large body of water from where my life is going to be in just a few days—"

"That's logistics."

"And because you don't want what I want," she continued over his interruption.

"You don't know that."

She eyed him as evenly as she could. "I don't want a long-distance affair, Zach."

"I don't, either."

The caution remaining in her eyes slowly changed quality. What he now saw in those luminous blue depths was confusion, uncertainty and a hint of longing that drew him closer.

"I can't stop thinking about what almost happened," he told her, caving in to the need to touch her by skimming his fingers over her soft cheek. "The baby that...wasn't." He could have sworn the dreams of a family of his own were dead. But he'd discovered that they'd only lain dormant—until she had come along and breathed life into them, into him. "The timing would have been terrible now. But the more I think about what you said about being disappointed and the more I think about what we could have together, the more I want it."

Together.

At the word, Lauren pulled a shallow breath. It was the best she could do with the hope swelling in her chest. "The more you want what?"

"You. Us. Do you want that, Lauren?"

More than life itself.

"Do you?"

"Yes." He had to see that she did. "But how could we...? My job is in—"

"I know where your job is," he assured her, letting his hand slip to the side of her neck. The relief he'd been waiting to feel finally washed through him, but it was relief that she was staying in his life, not that she was leaving it. "And we'd work it out. On your days off we can stay on Harbor and you can see your brother and the kids. When you need to be in Bellingham, I'll spend nights with you and fly wherever I need to go from there.''

He made it sound so simple. As simple as falling in love with him had been. He was right. They had never hidden from each other. They had both been burned in the figurative sense, they had both withdrawn to bury the hurt. But they'd somehow recognized the scars on each other's souls and dropped the guard that would have protected their hearts from anyone else.

She'd thought the day she'd left his home that she never would have imagined falling so hard and so fast. She'd never dreamed then that he would actually be there to break her fall.

Her fingers were trembling a little when she touched them to the hard wall of his chest. "So what do we do?"

"We could start by getting married."

The smile in her heart slipped into her eyes. "Married?"

"Sure," he said, sounding offhand, looking dead serious. His glance darkened on her mouth. "I love you, Lauren. I want you to be my wife. When we're ready, maybe in a couple of years," he ventured, his hand drifting to her waist, "I want you pregnant."

His fingers tightened on his last words. Gray eyes glinting, he dipped his head. "I'm really going to enjoy working on that part," he murmured, and covered her mouth with his.

He kissed her deeply, possessively, drawing her close, shaping her to him. She tasted desire in that kiss, and hunger. But mostly, she tasted need, the same sort of longing she felt herself as he urged her closer still.

She was as close as she could get without being inside his sweater when she pulled her head back far enough to see his face.

"So, what do you say?" he asked.

He'd quite effectively altered her breathing. Because of that, her voice was little more than a whisper when she touched the scar on his neck and met his eyes. "I love you, too, Zach."

He smiled, a devastating smile that would have weakened her knees if they hadn't been so weak already. "Is that a yes?"

"It's a yes."

"Good."

"Zach?"

His lips drifted down her throat. "Yeah?"

"How would you feel about going to a business dinner?"

"How long will it last?"

"I promise it won't last long at all."

* * * * *

*Look for Sam's story
from Christine Flynn in 2002.*

Conveniently Yours

SECRETS

A kidnapped baby
A hidden identity
A man with a past

Christine Rimmer's popular *Conveniently Yours*
miniseries returns with three brand-new books,
revolving around the Marsh baby kidnapped over
thirty years ago. Beginning late summer,
from Silhouette Books…

THE MARRIAGE AGREEMENT
(August 2001; Silhouette Special Edition #1412)
The halfbrother's story

THE BRAVO BILLIONAIRE
(September 2001; Silhouette Single Title)
The brother's story

THE MARRIAGE CONSPIRACY
(October 2001; Silhouette Special Edition #1423)
The missing baby's story—
all grown up and quite a man!

You won't want to miss a single one.…
Available wherever Silhouette books are sold.

Silhouette®
Where love comes alive™

Feel like a star with Silhouette.

We will fly you and a guest to New York City for an exciting weekend stay at a glamorous 5-star hotel. Experience a refreshing day at one of New York's trendiest spas and have your photo taken by a professional. Plus, receive $1,000 U.S. spending money!

Flowers…long walks…dinner for two… how does Silhouette Books make romance come alive for you?

Send us a script, with 500 words or less, along with visuals (only drawings, magazine cutouts or photographs or combination thereof). Show us how Silhouette Makes Your Love Come Alive. Be creative and have fun. No purchase necessary. All entries must be clearly marked with your name, address and telephone number. All entries will become property of Silhouette and are not returnable. **Contest closes September 28, 2001.**

Please send your entry to: **Silhouette Makes You a Star!**

In U.S.A.
P.O. Box 9069
Buffalo, NY, 14269-9069

In Canada
P.O. Box 637
Fort Erie, ON, L2A 5X3

Look for contest details on the next page, by visiting www.eHarlequin.com or request a copy by sending a self-addressed envelope to the applicable address above. Contest open to Canadian and U.S. residents who are 18 or over. Void where prohibited.

Silhouette®
Where love comes alive™

Our lucky winner's photo will appear in a Silhouette ad. Join the fun!

SRMYAS1

HARLEQUIN "SILHOUETTE MAKES YOU A STAR!" CONTEST 1308
OFFICIAL RULES
NO PURCHASE NECESSARY TO ENTER

1. To enter, follow directions published in the offer to which you are responding. Contest begins June 1, 2001, and ends on September 28, 2001. Entries must be postmarked by September 28, 2001, and received by October 5, 2001. Enter by hand-printing (or typing) on an 8 ½" x 11" piece of paper your name, address (including zip code), contest number/name and attaching a script containing <u>500 words</u> or less, <u>along with drawings, photographs or magazine cutouts, or combinations thereof</u> (i.e., collage) <u>on no larger than 9" x 12"</u> piece of paper, describing how the <u>Silhouette books make romance come alive for you</u>. Mail via first-class mail to: Harlequin "Silhouette Makes You a Star!" Contest 1308, (in the U.S.) P.O. Box 9069, Buffalo, NY 14269-9069, (in Canada) P.O. Box 637, Fort Erie, Ontario, Canada L2A 5X3. Limit one entry per person, household or organization.

2. Contests will be judged by a panel of members of the Harlequin editorial, marketing and public relations staff. Fifty percent of criteria will be judged against script and fifty percent will be judged against drawing, photographs and/or magazine cutouts. Judging criteria will be based on the following:

   - Sincerity—25%
   - Originality and Creativity—50%
   - Emotionally Compelling—25%

   In the event of a tie, duplicate prizes will be awarded. Decisions of the judges are final.

3. All entries become the property of Torstar Corp. and may be used for future promotional purposes. Entries will not be returned. No responsibility is assumed for lost, late, illegible, incomplete, inaccurate, nondelivered or misdirected mail.

4. Contest open only to residents of the U.S. <u>(except Puerto Rico)</u> and Canada who are 18 years of age or older, and is void wherever prohibited by law; all applicable laws and regulations apply. Any litigation within the Province of Quebec respecting the conduct or organization of a publicity contest may be submitted to the Régie des alcools, des courses et des jeux for a ruling. Any litigation respecting the awarding of a prize may be submitted to the Régie des alcools, des courses et des jeux only for the purpose of helping the parties reach a settlement. Employees and immediate family members of Torstar Corp. and D. L. Blair, Inc., their affiliates, subsidiaries and all other agencies, entities and persons connected with the use, marketing or conduct of this contest are not eligible to enter. Taxes on prizes are the sole responsibility of the winner. Acceptance of any prize offered constitutes permission to use winner's name, photograph or other likeness for the purposes of advertising, trade and promotion on behalf of Torstar Corp., its affiliates and subsidiaries without further compensation to the winner, unless prohibited by law.

5. Winner will be determined no later than November 30, 2001, and will be notified by mail. Winner will be required to sign and return an Affidavit of Eligibility/Release of Liability/Publicity Release form within 15 days after winner notification. Noncompliance within that time period may result in disqualification and an alternative winner may be selected. All travelers must execute a Release of Liability prior to ticketing and must possess required travel documents (e.g., passport, photo ID) where applicable. Trip must be booked by December 31, 2001, and completed within one year of notification. No substitution of prize permitted by winner. Torstar Corp. and D. L. Blair, Inc., their parents, affiliates and subsidiaries are not responsible for errors in printing of contest, entries and/or game pieces. In the event of printing or other errors that may result in unintended prize values or duplication of prizes, all affected game pieces or entries shall be null and void. **Purchase or acceptance of a product offer does not improve your chances of winning.**

6. Prizes: (1) Grand Prize—A 2-night/3-day trip for two (2) to New York City, including round-trip coach air transportation nearest winner's home and hotel accommodations (double occupancy) at The Plaza Hotel, a glamorous afternoon makeover at <u>a trendy New York spa</u>, $1,000 in U.S. spending money and an opportunity to <u>have a professional photo taken and appear in a Silhouette advertisement</u> (approximate retail value: $7,000). (10) Ten Runner-Up Prizes of gift packages (retail value $50 ea.). Prizes consist of only those items listed as part of the prize. Limit one prize per person. Prize is valued in U.S. currency.

7. For the name of the winner (available after December 31, 2001) send a self-addressed, stamped envelope to: Harlequin "Silhouette Makes You a Star!" Contest 1197 Winners, P.O. Box 4200 Blair, NE 68009-4200 or you may access the www.eHarlequin.com Web site through February 28, 2002.

Contest sponsored by Torstar Corp., P.O Box 9042, Buffalo, NY 14269-9042.

SRMYAS2

If you enjoyed what you just read,
then we've got an offer you can't resist!

Take 2 bestselling
love stories FREE!

Plus get a FREE surprise gift!

//////////////////////////////

Clip this page and mail it to Silhouette Reader Service™

IN U.S.A.	**IN CANADA**
3010 Walden Ave.	P.O. Box 609
P.O. Box 1867	Fort Erie, Ontario
Buffalo, N.Y. 14240-1867	L2A 5X3

YES! Please send me 2 free Silhouette Special Edition® novels and my free surprise gift. After receiving them, if I don't wish to receive anymore, I can return the shipping statement marked cancel. If I don't cancel, I will receive 6 brand-new novels every month, before they're available in stores! In the U.S.A., bill me at the bargain price of $3.80 plus 25¢ shipping and handling per book and applicable sales tax, if any*. In Canada, bill me at the bargain price of $4.21 plus 25¢ shipping and handling per book and applicable taxes**. That's the complete price and a savings of at least 10% off the cover prices—what a great deal! I understand that accepting the 2 free books and gift places me under no obligation ever to buy any books. I can always return a shipment and cancel at any time. Even if I never buy another book from Silhouette, the 2 free books and gift are mine to keep forever.

235 SEN DFNN
335 SEN DFNP

Name _____ (PLEASE PRINT)

Address _____ Apt.# _____

City _____ State/Prov. _____ Zip/Postal Code _____

* Terms and prices subject to change without notice. Sales tax applicable in N.Y.
** Canadian residents will be charged applicable provincial taxes and GST.
  All orders subject to approval. Offer limited to one per household and not valid to current Silhouette Special Edition® subscribers.
  ® are registered trademarks of Harlequin Enterprises Limited.

SPED01   ©1998 Harlequin Enterprises Limited

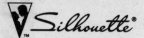

COMING NEXT MONTH

SPECIAL EDITION

SSECNM0901